JESSICA'S DEATH AND SOMETIMES THEY DIE

Personal Crimes, Vol. 3

THE "PERSONAL CRIMES" SERIES

Night Music | *Open and Shut*
It's Her Fault | *The Other Frank*
Jessica's Death | *Sometimes They Die*

JESSICA'S DEATH AND SOMETIMES THEY DIE

Personal Crimes, Vol. 3

TONY GLEESON

WILDSIDE PRESS

To
BOB
reviewer and proselytizer for Jilly, Dan,
Frank and the gang from the beginning.

CONTENTS

JESSICA'S DEATH

ONE

"Mondays stink" is a common sentiment, but for Delino Washington, Mondays *literally* stunk. So, for that matter, did Tuesdays, Wednesdays, Thursdays and Fridays. But Mondays were the worst.

All things considered, Delino didn't really mind his job with the city's Department of Public Works. He took home a decent paycheck and the benefits were good, especially the medical and dental, which meant something for a man with a family. He hadn't experienced a breakdown in some time, due to the recent upgrade of their trucks. Even his fellow sanitation workers were, for the most part, reasonable enough people. Being one of the guys who collect the city's garbage could have been a lot worse.

If only he had a different route.

The neighborhood at five in the morning was lethargic and empty. Traffic, with the exception of his rumbling DPW vehicle, was nonexistent. The dawning light was casting an orange tinge over the quiet emptiness of short, narrow Tustin Street. To Delino, it was neither peaceful nor pretty, just depressing. Large wheeled bins of plastic—green and black—were lined up along the curbs, awaiting the claws of his bright blue truck to reach out like some metal bird of prey, scoop them up one by one and dump their contents into eagerly opening maws.

The locale was known locally as Sheffield, named after the main drag only a block away. The whole neighborhood was festering; that was the perfect word for it, Delino decided as he navigated his truck around parked cars. The garbage actually stunk worse here than in other neighborhoods. On other routes, people were reasonably careful about how they put out their refuse. Here, nobody really cared. They just dumped stuff on the streets. The buildings on this block, owned by absentee slumlords, were neglected and degenerating: peeling paint, broken windows. The people were rotting too. It was a drug neighborhood, deserted by day and dangerous at night, populated almost entirely by people who had given up on the promise of life.

Delino had been born in a bombed-out neighborhood only a couple of degrees better than this one. His father and mother, struggling against the onset of despair, had pulled their family out of it by intelligence, unflagging energy, and a sense of mission. Delino's current family had never needed to experience this kind of thing. They lived in a nice house in a nice part of the city. The kids attended good schools. He did not want his kids to know about places like this. He did not even like driving through them himself. That was the one downside of his job: he wished he had a different route.

He braked the truck next to a large black garbage container and worked the lever that extended the lifting arm towards it. As the arm began to hoist its load, he felt definite resistance from the bin. He had done this long enough to gauge the weight; there was something heavy in this one. Sometimes they dumped stupid junk into the bin, like stolen or broken appliances, even bricks or cinder blocks, only God knew why. The minds of drug addicts, Delino considered. One of these days, he had often thought, he might even find…

He looked out the window at the arm raising the bin. He caught a glimpse of what was sticking out of the top of the black container.

He yanked the lever and brought the arm back down, slapping the bin to the pavement with a loud *slam*. Then he just sat there in the cab for a long time. He was really hoping his eyes had been playing tricks on him.

That *thing* he always feared might happen…had it just happened?

He finally opened the door of the cab and stepped down into the street. He didn't want to look. He was afraid of what he was going to find.

It was exactly what he had dreaded, and just what he worried might someday happen here in this lousy section of town.

* * * *

By seven A.M., tiny Tustin Street contained more people than it ordinarily might have in the space of an entire day. Its one-block stretch had been cordoned off with police vehicles and layers of bright yellow tape proclaiming POLICE LINE DO NOT CROSS in heavy black capital letters. Uniformed officers, jump-suited Scientific Investigation Division technicians, and white-coated medical examiners moved purposefully about, working a well-practiced choreography around one another. The blue sanitation truck remained parked at a nearby curb; its driver, Delino Washington, sat at the same curb, conversing with a standing patrol officer.

One focus of the activity was a large black plastic garbage container which had been overturned, its contents carefully distributed over the nearby pavement. Two investigators were processing the bin and the various detritus on the ground. Nearby on the pavement lay the second focus of attention, partly covered by a heavy white tarpaulin.

It's hard to mistake a human body—in this case a very dead one.

Detectives Jilly Garvey and Dan Lee, who had just arrived, stood over the body, staring down at it. A heavyset man in a white coat had been squatting down beside the body, making notes on a clipboard, and now rose to greet them.

"Well, Detectives, good to see you." He didn't *say* it, he *delivered* it, in the tone of an ironic joke. That was Mickey Kendrick's way, Jilly knew. The veteran ME's droopy bloodhound scowl and deadpan monotone belied a sharp, incisive professional mind. It took a while to get used to Mickey but Jilly was always glad to see him on one of their cases. Very little ever got by him. He prided himself on being quick but thorough and efficient.

"So what have we got here, Mickey?" she asked.

"She took a serious beating. The evidence is consistent with some kind of hard blunt object, and likely fists as well. Broken ribs, skull fracture, broken nose, bruising all over. Some of the bruises seem post-mortem, indicating rage. The attacker didn't stop once she was dead." He nodded his chin toward the container. "Then she got stuffed into that trash bin."

Dan looked pale and solemn. Some things weren't getting any easier, even though he was no longer the rookie detective in the unit. Jilly tried to ignore the uneasiness in her own stomach, feeling the responsibility as the senior partner.

Mickey looked back and forth at them. "I'm through with my examination here, if you'd like to give her a look."

"Thanks, Mickey."

Jilly had already snapped on one of the pairs of disposable plastic gloves she carried in her pocket. She knelt down beside the body, carefully pulling back the tarp to fully expose it, as the ME continued.

"Doesn't seem to be any ID. I'd guess she's in her forties. I'm estimating time of death at around eleven last night. I ought to be able to get to a more extensive examination by tomorrow. You're lucky. No gridlock at the morgue to speak of right now."

"That would be most appreciated," Jilly replied a bit absently as she began to sweep her gaze over the body lying supine on the ground in front of her.

"Besides, looking at what he did to her, I'd think you'd want to make this guy a priority."

Jilly nodded grimly. "If it is a guy."

"Oh, it's a guy. Whoever did this was *very* strong and didn't hold back. He was tall, judging from the directionality of some of the blows. You're looking for a big hulk of a guy. Count on it." Mickey tipped his hat to them and turned away. "She's all yours."

Dan had pulled on his own pair of gloves and had squatted down across the body from Jilly, a notebook in hand. He shook his head. "Thrown away like garbage," he said softly.

"Yep." Jilly looked up at Dan. "You okay, partner?"

"Yeah, this one's just a little raw." He looked around at the street, the buildings. "Pretty crumby neighborhood. Not much left around here."

"The buildings are just being left to rot. A store here and there: pawnshop, liquor store. There's very few families, mostly a lot of homeless squatting in the buildings. I wouldn't be surprised if there are suspicious arsons regularly." Jilly continued her intent scan of the woman's body.

Dan sighed deeply. "Lots of drug traffic around here at night, I'm told."

"She doesn't look like a local," Jilly said. "Not exactly a squatter."

The victim was a small woman, perhaps five foot four. She wore khaki slacks and a pale green button-down shirt. The shirt was expensive and clean, except for blood spatters. She had one camel-colored slip-on canvas shoe; her left foot was bare. There were random blood stains on various parts of all her clothing, as well as what looked and smelled like remnants of trash from the bin she had been stuffed into. Her hair was ash blonde and shoulder-length, now matted, tangled and tinted with blood. Her face was bruised and swollen, especially her cheeks and nose. There were rivulets of dried blood along her nose, cheek and jawline. Jilly reflected that even after many years, she could not become inured to this. She forced herself to tunnel-focus on the dead woman's clothing and began to systematically check the pockets.

"Mickey was right. Doesn't seem to be any kind of ID. Nothing in her pockets at all. No jewelry of any kind: no rings, necklaces, bracelets…" she ran her fingers through the woman's hair to reach the right earlobe, then did the same on the other side of her head. "Her ears are pierced but no earrings. In fact the lobes are torn. Whoever did this may have ripped them right off of her ears. It looks as if it was done after she was already dead."

"Robbery," Dan said, watching Jilly, making notes. Jilly knew from experience that he was quietly making his own observations as he let her work, and his notes would be thorough.

"Certainly looks like it. She's nicely dressed. What was she doing *here*?" Jilly shot a look around them to emphasize her point.

Now she inspected the dead woman's hands. "Manicures. There are what look like defensive wounds. Even with those nice clean, even nails, maybe she still got something from her assailant under them. We can hope."

Dan bent down to peer at the fingers that Jilly gently held up and spread apart. "Cuts, scratches, bruises…but…what are those dark blue stains on her fingers?"

"They look like ink, maybe from a felt-tip pen? Mickey will tell us more." She continued to scrutinize various parts of the body, handling the lifeless body as gently and respectfully as she could—almost tenderly. After this horrible treatment, Jilly somehow felt that she owed that much to the woman. Finally, she arranged the woman carefully, took out her smart phone, and snapped several photos of the victim's face, trying to show as little of the damage as possible and to capture a clear likeness in case they found someone who could solve her identity. There was no way to completely obscure the beating she had taken.

When she was done, Jilly put away her phone and just looked at the body for a long moment. "Whoever this guy was, this was personal. There's a major degree of anger in this attack. He was still beating her after she died."

She wanted to make a silent promise to the woman lying on the ground that she would find whoever had done this and speak for someone who could no longer speak for herself. But she knew from experience that it might be an empty promise, and that made her surprisingly angry this time.

Dan turned to the pile of detritus that had been removed from the can. An SID technician was still meticulously sifting through it, taking photos. "Anything of hers in that stuff, I wonder?" He stood up and took a few steps towards the investigator. The tech looked over his shoulder through goggles at Dan, lowered his camera, and nodded.

"Almost done here, Detective. Doesn't really look like much that could help. Mostly garbage—food scraps, bottles and cans, stuff like that. And of course the inevitable, less savory stuff: a needle, a pipe, condoms…"

"Sometimes I don't envy you your job."

The tech smiled wryly. "We did find her other shoe." He pointed among the banana peels, greasy paper bags, and unidentifiable debris to a slip-on that was an obvious match to the one found on the victim. "Nothing else that seems likely to have come from her."

"No items of jewelry, nothing that might have come from a handbag or a wallet then, nothing that might help us ID her?"

The SID man shook his head.

"Was the body on the top of the bin?"

"Yeah. The driver saw the body in there. He stopped the dump in mid-motion and brought it back down. The can tipped over and she fell out. The victim must have been doubled over and jammed into the container."

"I assume you're checking the other bins along the street as well."

"Of course." He pointed down the street to two jump-suited figures who had upended two other containers and were poring over their contents.

Jilly stood up and joined the conversation. "Is that the driver over there near the truck? He's the one who found her?" The tech nodded.

Jill carefully replaced the tarp over the body. They stripped off their gloves and walked down the street. A husky dark-skinned man in a blue coverall, his hair still full but greying, stood up from his seat at the curb. He had been talking with a female officer; they both turned as Jilly and Dan approached.

The officer smiled. "Well, Detective Lee, fancy meeting you here!" She looked at Jilly, almost as a second thought, and nodded. "And Detective Garvey."

"Officer Kovetsky."

Jilly swore she saw Dan's face redden a little. She remembered the youthful woman patrol officer from other scenes and cases, and clearly she and Dan remembered one another. Kovetsky was considerably more seasoned than she looked; she had worked some of the city's harshest neighborhoods for a few years now.

"This is Delino Washington," Kovetsky said. "He discovered the body this morning."

Jilly turned to him. "Mr. Washington, thank you for waiting. I know this must have been an imposition on your time."

Washington shrugged stoically. "I can't take the truck anyway until your crew is done with it. Or rather the department can't send somebody to come get it from me until they get the okay from you guys. And to tell you the truth, I'm still on the clock."

"So tell us what happened this morning."

"I was running my usual Monday morning route through here. As I hoisted that can over there, I could tell it had something heavy in it. Nothing all that strange about that. You'd be amazed at the crap people throw in those things."

Jilly wondered how much worse it could have been.

"I've done this long enough that I can kind of judge just how much weight is in the container. I figured I'd better check on just what it was, and I sorta peered through the window. As the lifting arm went up, I saw what looked like a *leg* sticking out. It just freaked me out, and I hit the return lever. The can went flying back down to the street with a bang, tipped over as the arm released it, and—well, she came out." He hesitantly jerked a thumb towards the body.

Dan picked up the questioning as he jotted in his notebook. "Did she fall completely out of the container?"

"No…it kinda looked as if she had been wedged in there. The force of the impact jarred her loose but she only came out part way." Washington ran a thick hand over his eyes for a moment. "She was sort of bent in half, stuck in ass-end first. Oh…excuse me, that's disrespectful to the lady. That just sorta came out."

Jilly decided she liked the guy. He seemed a decent sort. "That's okay, Mr. Washington, we understand. What did you do next?"

"I just sat there for a while, you know? It was a shock. Finally I got out of my truck and went over to make sure I had actually seen what I thought. I saw her there, her eyes *staring right up at me*. Damn! I didn't know what to do! Don't know how long I just stood there. I looked around and there was nobody else on the street. Finally I figured out I should call somebody." He pulled a cell phone out of his coverall pocket and held it up. "I called the cops. I mean, you guys. Then I called work. Everybody told me to stay here until they showed up."

"Not a neighborhood you want to stand around in," Dan noted.

"That's for sure," Kovetsky interjected.

Washington nodded. "You got that right. But I didn't exactly have a lot of choice. I decided in any case I would probably be better off standing along this little side street, and it was early enough in the morning that there wasn't much chance of any trouble showing up. Those guys crawl back into their holes to sleep when the sun comes up."

Dan was sweeping his gaze completely around in a circle at the surrounds. "This looks like a war zone here. Where's all the trash coming from in these receptacles?"

"Bars and junk shops around here," Washington said. "Some people actually live here. And, to tell the truth, people bring their trash here from other parts to dump it." He pointed down the street where two decaying mattresses sat atop a pile of unrecognizable plastic and wood items. "I've even found piles of building material dropped here by construction companies. This neighborhood is the city's dumpster."

Not hard to detect the contempt in Washington's voice for the area, or the fact he was highly unsettled. Hard to blame him. Jilly noticed that Dan paused in his writing for a moment at the comment and looked around at the heap of dumped refuse.

Jilly continued. "Did you touch or move the body or any of the contents of the container after that?"

Washington looked a little sheepish. "Well, a little. Like I said, I wasn't really thinking straight. I kinda pulled her out a little bit, just to be sure it wasn't a mannequin or something like that, you know? Those things can be really lifelike. I may have scattered some of the trash out on the street. I don't remember."

"Okay. We're going to have to get your prints so we know which ones are yours."

"Am I going to have to take more time to go down to the station and do that?" Washington asked.

"Maybe not. One of the techs ought to be able to do it right here."

He looked relieved. "Well, then. Sure. Of course."

"And you have no idea who this woman is, right?"

"Hell, no. How would I? Never seen her before."

"You didn't find anything that might help to identify her?"

"Oh, no. No. No." He raised his hands and his eyebrows. "Didn't take nothing. I tell you, I've got nothing to do with this!"

Jilly raised her own hands in placation. "I'm not saying you did, Mr. Washington. We're just hoping to find something to ascertain who she is. At the moment we've got no idea."

"I wish I could help you, Detective. Nobody should die that way." He shook his head sadly. "Treated like another piece of garbage."

"Look who's here," muttered Dan. Jilly looked around to see the van arriving just outside the yellow police tape, emblazoned with the colorful logo of one of the local television stations. One of the directing officers had motioned for it to stop and was walking over to talk to the driver.

"Shit," Jilly muttered. "How did they get word of this so fast?" She had been hoping for at least a little lead time before the news hit. Dan was surprised; she was no choir girl but it was seldom he heard such an epithet from her in public.

Kovetsky turned in the direction of the van. "I can go hold 'em off for a while for you."

"No," sighed Jilly. "We'll go talk to them."

Another aspect of a case like this that she hated, but knew she had to do.

TWO

Lieutenant Hank Castillo sat back in his chair, slightly rocking, his fingertips pressed together against his lips, as he watched the screen of the laptop that Jilly had laid on his desk.

It was a video feed of the afternoon news from a local television station. A carefully-coiffed and serious-looking woman stared into the camera over the top of a huge microphone bearing the numeral 8.

"The identity of the victim has not yet been publicly announced, pending notification of the family of the deceased. Detectives are withholding specific information for the moment but promise that more will be forthcoming shortly. Letitia Nevins, Channel 8 News, reporting from the Sheffield district."

Jilly tapped a key and the video window closed on her screen. She folded up the laptop. She and Dan looked at Castillo and waited.

Castillo sat forward and rested his forearms across his desk. As usual the coat of his three-piece suit was draped over the back of his chair but even in shirtsleeves he bore the air of dapper authority. His graying temples gave him both dignity and world-weariness. He stared alternately at both Dan and Jilly from under his thick eyebrows and scowled through his dense mustache.

"So what do you have?"

"No ID yet. She had no identification of any kind and no jewelry. It appears that she was robbed. There are lots of pawnshops in the neighborhood. We canvassed as many as we could and had the unis do the same, to see if anybody had tried to sell jewelry. No luck so far. We're hoping that SID and the ME will come up with something we can use. For once we might luck out there and get some results reasonably quickly."

"No witnesses, I'm assuming. Not in Sheffield."

"Nobody we can find as yet. We've got unis trying to track down locals. Even on a Sunday night there must have been some traffic around there, buying and selling. Nobody's going to own up to being there, of course."

Castillo stared as if he expected more. There really wasn't much more. Dan finally spoke up, referring to his notes. "The garbage bins are put out by the buildings along that street. There are three buildings on that side of the block, all owned by the same company, whose offices are on the other side of town. The buildings are largely empty. All told, there might be four or five habitable apartments in all of them along with a couple of small storefronts. Not enough to merit big metal garbage hoppers that would be picked up by private haulers that charge a monthly fee. They just put out the plastic bins and let the city pick up every week. We'll be checking with the building management but we don't expect it to be of any help. This is likely a body dump."

Castillo sighed deeply. "Better make this your priority. We need to know who she is. This has the potential for nasty publicity. Upper-class woman, lurid and violent death in a seamy neighborhood. Your gal Letitia will be all over this by tomorrow, maybe even tonight. So will the other channels." He shot them a piercing look. "I don't need to tell you that shit flows downhill here. I'll be getting it from above shortly. And that means you'll be getting it from me."

Jilly nodded gravely. She looked at Dan as Castillo turned his attention back to the papers on his desk. That was his way, the squad personnel had learned, of indicating that the interview was over. They stood without another word. Jilly gathered up her laptop and followed Dan out the door.

The Personal Crimes Unit was unusually quiet this afternoon. Usually by midday the place was bustling with purposeful activity; there was seldom a letup from the onrush of new business being dropped in their laps from their frenetically challenging city. For some reason at this moment, there was a noticeable lack of the accustomed sound and fury. A number of the regulars seemed to be out of the squad room right now.

Years earlier, the unit had officially been called Special Crimes and before that had gone by the prosaic but accurate title Robbery-Homicide. At some point, the Department had decided Personal Crimes bore more solemnity. The unit still dealt with basically the same types of crime, almost entirely felonies: homicides, severe assaults, robberies. Simultaneously, the unit that handled burglaries and similar non-violent crimes, currently housed in a similar squad room one flight up from them, had gained the moniker Property Crimes. The veterans of either unit would likely have remarked that there had been little difference in their function beyond the name changes.

For what it was worth, they could at least hear themselves think right now in the momentary quietude of the space. All they needed was a viable strategy to think about.

They settled on Dan's desk and Jilly pulled up a nearby chair. They wracked their brains for the remainder of the afternoon.

* * * *

Dan had hardly settled into his desk early Tuesday morning before his phone was ringing.

"Detective Lee."

"Hey, Dan. Sandy Kovetsky here."

"Officer Kovetsky. What's up?"

"I've told you before, you can call me Sandy, okay? I think we may have hit some good luck on your Tustin Street murder."

Dan grabbed a pen and pulled one of the ever-present legal pads in front of him at his desk. "Tell me about it!"

"Guy got picked up for holding and dealing last night in a nearby neighborhood. Turns out he had some credit cards and IDs in his possession that weren't his. At any rate, he couldn't convince anyone he was a Jessica."

"The name on the cards was Jessica?"

"Jessica Pidgeon." She spelled the surname. "He had an ATM card, an Amex card, a couple of store cards—even a driver's license. The guy's a noted reprobate around the area. So I made a point to go look at the cards. There are pictures on the license and a couple of the credit cards. Sure looks like it could be our girl."

Dan scribbled the name down. "Can you email over a scan of the photos on the cards?"

"Sure. Give me an addy."

Dan recited his email address. "You've still got him, right?"

"Oh yeah. We're holding him good and tight here at Central Division."

"Jessica Pidgeon. Did he have any other items, like jewelry, anything?"

"Nope. Just the cards. Not even any cash on him. He claimed he found a wallet on the street and took the cards and threw the rest away. He couldn't remember exactly where he dumped them, just a general vicinity of a few blocks. We've got a couple officers looking right now."

"When did he say he 'found' this wallet? Sunday night, Monday?"

"He's not the most compos mentis guy on the block, you know? He told the arresting officers it might have been Sunday night or maybe it was Saturday night, or then again maybe he's had 'em for a while."

"If he really did throw a wallet in the trash Sunday night, it would have gotten picked up in the trash collection Monday. But it's worth the try, you're right. I appreciate that."

"You can come on by at your convenience. Call Finley over here, you know him?"

"Sergeant Finley. I remember him from my beat years. How's he doing these days?"

"Finley's Finley. You can ask him yourself. And I'll let you know if we have any luck on the wallet. I'm going over to check in myself. If you want to come join in dumpster diving, feel free."

The thought didn't appeal to Dan; anyway, he trusted Kovetsky's judgment. "Sounds like you've got it covered. Has anybody made any attempt to contact the woman who owns the cards or the license?"

"We're holding off pending your decision as to whether this is the victim."

"So what *is* this guy's name who had the cards?"

"You're not gonna believe this. Marmaduke."

"What?"

"I'm not kidding. That's his street name, Marmaduke."

"Anybody know his real name?"

"He wasn't carrying any ID of his own. He told them his name is Marmaduke Jones. And it turns out, voilà, he's actually got a record under that name!"

Dan continued to scribble. "Happen to know what kind of record? Violent crimes?"

"Possession, possession with intent to sell, an assault rap. I don't know any of the details. I got a look at the guy. He's a big dumb one. Certainly capable of the kind of assault we're talking about."

"And they picked him up dealing? Where?"

"Maybe five, six blocks from where the victim was found. Marmaduke's apparently a freelancer. There was a disagreement going on between him and a couple of the local establishment boys who were unhappy about his encroaching on their territory. The conversation got intense and involved baseball bats. A few of our guys happened to be in the neighborhood, interrupted them and chased them down. Possibly saved Marmaduke's life, for what that's worth."

"Thanks, Off…uh, Sandy. I appreciate the heads up. We'll get right on this and be over this morning."

"Sad to say, Dan, after I send this over to you, I'm on my way out the door so I'll miss you. If you want me, I'll be up to my neck with the dumpster crew."

"Likely a fool's errand, I'm afraid."

"Maybe so, but it must be done. Talk to you later."

Dan stood up and turned to Jilly's desk. He noted that she was also on the telephone, earnestly absorbed in her own conversation, jotting on a pad. As he approached, she hung up and looked up at Dan. She read his expression and raised her eyebrows in expectation.

"Just heard from Kovetsky. Central Division picked up a guy last night with a pocketful of stolen credit cards and ID. Could belong to our victim."

"And that was Mickey. The autopsy is finished. He's sending me over the results. His original estimate of TOD stands; he's figuring she died around eleven Sunday night. Looks as if she was beaten pretty savagely, with a hard blunt instrument like a cane or a club." Jilly ran a hand through her short red hair, stared into some indeterminate distance, and exhaled deeply. It might have been morning but she looked weary already. She finally looked up again at Dan. "Do we have a name on the cards?"

"Yeah. Jessica Pidgeon. She's sending me over scans." Dan filled her in on the information he had been given by Kovetsky.

"Okay, so we need to trace her down and see what we find, and we need to go over and talk to this perp."

There was a "ding" from Dan's computer. He walked back over to his desk, tapped some keys, and said, "Sandy sent over the scans of the IDs."

"Sandy, is it now," said Jilly as she rose to join him.

"C'mon, don't start, Jilly. She asked me to call her that." He brought up two of the images side by side on his monitor: the driver's license and the photo on the back of the Amex card.

"Uh-huh," she muttered as she stood next to him and peered at the screen. She pulled out her phone and opened up the photos she had taken of the victim. They stared back and forth at the two screens silently for a long time.

"It's her," Jilly said finally.

"Yeah. I agree."

Jilly sighed again. "I guess we start with the address on the license."

"It's Farmington," Dan read, referring to a nice upper-middle class suburb to the north of the city. He sat down and started tapping on his keyboard once again, beginning the search for whatever information they could find on Jessica Pidgeon.

"Someone filed a missing persons on her yesterday. A James Pidgeon, same address." Dan scanned the information. "Her husband. Filed with the Farmington police department."

"I guess that's where we start. Anything else coming up on her?"

"Nothing of consequence."

"Let me get that contact phone number," Jilly said, leaning in. Under the circumstances a telephone call was clearly out of the question; they needed to do this in person. But they had to be able to find the husband. Jilly knew this drill way too well. She would call the husband, tell him simply they were calling in regard to his missing persons' report and ask to meet in person.

Luckily the number belonged to James Pidgeon's cell phone and he answered immediately. He was at work but would meet them at his house within the hour. Jilly expertly fielded his attempts to question her further but there was a certain level of apprehension in this kind of situation that could never be dispelled.

* * * *

Their morning was clearly set out for them: first James Pidgeon, then Marmaduke Jones at Central Division. There was always the hope that a case like this could be cleared up quickly and neatly, to bring some closure to the horrified family of the victim. In this instance, Jilly doubted it. The circumstances were too peculiar.

They checked in with Lieutenant Castillo and brought him up to speed on their recent findings and their plans. He gave them the green light and reiterated that this case took primacy over everything else.

"I know you'll handle the interview with the husband with tact and delicacy," Castillo said pointedly, casting a tight smile at Jilly.

"Yes," Jilly replied with equal wryness. "You do know that, Lieutenant."

Castillo raised his hands in mock surrender. "I have every faith in you, Detectives. Now go and solve this pain in the ass case for me. And keep me updated. There are inquiring minds that want to know."

They took the elevator down to the parking garage. "You want to drive?" Jilly asked.

"I'm good with you driving. While we're on our way over, I'll call Finley and arrange for us to meet the suspect afterward."

"I've noticed you don't seem to want to do much driving lately," Jilly observed.

"You've got a heavier foot than me," Dan said, pulling out his phone and thumbing through his contact numbers. "And we're in a hurry."

* * * *

The Pidgeon residence was one of several large Spanish Colonial style houses, all with red tile roofs, along a winding, sycamore-lined street in the hills north of the city.

"Nice neighborhood," Dan commented as they drove up the hill.

"Certainly is. Comfortable living."

"And our job right now is to make it terribly uncomfortable. I hate this part. That's the house, on the right, 1220 Coventry."

"And you're never going to stop hating it," Jilly muttered as she pulled to the curb in front of the house. "Trust me."

A tall, florid and freckly man with thinning rusty brown hair threw open the door scant seconds after they had pressed the doorbell.

"You're the police?" he said breathlessly. "Here about my wife?" Jilly nodded. They both already had their ID and badges out to show him. He hardly looked.

"Please, come in, come in," he urged, closing the door behind them. "Do you have any information on her? Do you know where she is or what happened?"

"Mr. Pidgeon," began Jilly gently, "let's all go sit down. Are there children in the house at the moment, or anybody else?"

"No, no. They're visiting their grandmother in Pennsylvania. I'm the only one here. What's happened? Is she all right?"

They walked into the living room and Pidgeon anxiously waved to chairs for them to sit.

"Something *has* happened," Jilly began as she took a seat close to Pidgeon, phone in hand. "We're sorry to have to be the ones to tell you."

"To Jessy? Oh no, what? *What?*"

"First of all, we have to find out if it's actually your wife that we're here about. There's no easy way for us to do this. I have to caution you, the photo I'm going to show you could be upsetting. I'm sorry, but this is all we have to go on." She tapped up one of the photos of the victim and slowly handed it to him. "Is this your wife, Jessica?"

He began to nod but then he stopped. He saw the context of the picture. He stared at it blankly for a very long time, saying nothing, not reacting at all.

They waited.

"Oh my God," he finally said hoarsely. "What happened to her? Is she…?"

"Mr. Pidgeon, is this your wife, Jessica?"

He nodded vigorously, pursing his lips, unable to speak. They could see the tears begin to well in his eyes.

"I'm sorry but…you're absolutely positive?"

Continuing to nod silently, he handed back the phone to Jilly.

"I'm very sorry, Mr. Pidgeon."

He suppressed several silent sobs, then found his voice. "What happened?"

"We're still trying to figure that out, sir. She was found on a side street in the city very early Monday morning. She was killed and left there Sunday night." Jilly cautiously provided a few more details. She had done this too many times in the past.

"Where? Where in the city?"

"Tustin Street. It's in the area called Sheffield."

"Sheffield! I've heard of Sheffield, but we don't go through there, not ever. What was Jessy doing there?"

"We don't know yet, sir. We're trying to find out the whole story. I know this is awfully hard but are you up to answering some questions for us now? It could help us a lot."

"No, that's fine. I mean, yes. I mean…yes, I'll try."

"Thank you, Mr. Pidgeon. If this gets to be too much, let us know and we'll stop. When was the last time you saw Jessica?"

"Friday evening. I drove the kids to the airport."

"You didn't see your wife all weekend?"

"No. I had a business trip. I got on a plane myself that night and came back very late Sunday."

"What kind of work do you do?" asked Dan. He was not writing; he was listening, applying a lesson he had learned from Jilly about observing body language and subtle cues.

"Computer tech. I'm in software."

"So you travel a lot. You're away from home often?"

"These days, yes. I helped establish a small startup called JRX. It's about to be bought, so I travel a lot."

"So Jessica was alone here all of last weekend."

"Yes…I'm gone a lot these days. The kids are usually around…well, they're out a lot. Brad is fourteen and Laurie is sixteen and they're both busy kids. There used to be a housekeeper, but she's no longer working here."

"A housekeeper?"

"Yes, but she left our employ last week. She hasn't been here in a week or so."

"Can you tell us about her? Had she worked for you long?"

"Melinda. Melinda Barstow. She worked for us for—oh, about ten or twelve years or so. She also provided child care when the kids were younger. She was here five days a week, sometimes more. She was like a member of the family."

"But she left last week? Did she resign?"

"No. There was some disagreement with my wife. Jessy fired her." Pidgeon shot a look at both of them. "You aren't thinking…no, I couldn't believe Melinda could have done anything to harm Jessica. Never."

Dan now opened his notebook and began to write. It was Jilly's cue to take over. "Do you know where we might contact her?"

"Offhand, no. Jessy kept the information, and it would take me a while to…wait. Melinda called me the other day." He took his own phone out of his pocket and tapped the screen a few times. "Here's the number she called me from."

Jilly opened her own phone and noted the number he was showing her on the screen. "Why did she call you?"

He struggled, haltingly, to reply. "She said that Jessy wouldn't talk to her and she wanted me to help smooth things out between them. She said she'd need a letter of reference from us, that Jessy was refusing and could I help. She called me twice in fact. I told her I'd talk with Jessy. I didn't know what happened. I never got to talk to her about that. I still don't know." He heaved a sigh and his eyes seemed to focus on a far corner of the living room. "I guess I never will. The kids aren't supposed to return until Friday. I'll have to call their grandmother and tell her. Oh my God, this is awful."

"They're with your wife's parents?"

"Her mother, yes. In Pennsylvania."

"What would Jessica do when she was by herself here? Did she ever go anywhere, socialize with friends anyplace particular?"

"She had friends here in the neighborhood. I guess maybe other wives. Sometimes she'd go out to lunch. We belong to a golf and tennis club. She would go there to swim or play tennis or have lunch now and then."

"You weren't with her at the club?"

"I'm too busy to go anymore. She always liked the club thing more than I did anyway. It was her and her friends."

"Was she close to anyone in particular?"

"Dory Snyder, up the street. I remember her. Tamara Marsh, at the club. I don't know who else specifically."

"Other parents, perhaps, from the kids' schools?"

"No. She hadn't had much to do with other parents in some time now."

"Did she go into the city very often?"

"No, not really. She tended to stay in Farmington. I can't think of any reason she would have been down in the city that night. Certainly not in that area."

"I assume she had a car, right?"

"Yes. A gray Audi sedan. Two years old. It's not here. It was gone when I returned from my trip."

"Do you have the information on that, sir? Perhaps the registration, or the title?"

Pidgeon raised his hands, looking disoriented. "I don't know. She might have kept the registration in the car."

"Okay, we can get that from DMV. The car was registered in her name at this address?"

"That's right."

"Did she tend to carry a lot of money with her, anything valuable? Did she wear jewelry?" Jilly thought about the earrings that been ripped from the woman's earlobes.

"Some. I had given her some earrings she liked. She wore a ring that her mother had given her that had sentimental value. Sometimes she wore a gold necklace with a pendant."

"Is there any chance you could describe any of those?"

"They were all gold. She liked real gold. She tended to like dangling earrings, like teardrops or things like that…maybe this big." He indicated with thumb and forefinger. "The ring had a couple of stones set into a plain gold band. I don't know, maybe sapphires? They were blue. The necklace was a plain chain, a circular pendant with a stone. That was blue too." Pidgeon stopped and looked down. They could tell he was beginning to tremble. "I can't understand how someone could do something this horrible to her. Maybe we need to stop now."

"Of course, sir. One last thing, you can't think of anybody who would be capable of doing this to your wife? Anybody at all?"

Pidgeon shook his head and said nothing. When he looked up them, his eyes were red.

Jilly handed him one of her cards, and Dan followed suit. "We'll be in touch, and you can call us at any time, if you think of anything that might help us find whoever did this, or if you just want to talk. And if it might help, we can suggest people who might be able to help you through this."

"Grief counselors," Pidgeon said quietly.

"One of the things I was thinking of, yes. Is there anybody we can contact for you, anything we can do?"

Pidgeon said very quietly, "No. No thank you." He lowered his head and sat mute. Finally he said, "I'm sorry, do you mind…"

"No problem, Mr. Pidgeon, we can show ourselves out. We are very sorry for your loss."

* * * *

"What's your take on Mr. Pidgeon?" Jilly asked as they drove back down the hill past well-trimmed lawns and trees.

"I'm really not sure," Dan said pensively, staring out the window. "I'm not getting a sense that he and his wife were all that close. What about you?"

"The story's kind of strange, I'll give you that. He's gone a lot, the kids are gone, nobody in the house all week. Even the housekeeper's gone."

"He seemed to take it all pretty well, all things considered. That kind of news is a real gut shot. But shock does funny things to people."

"Yes. Yes it does. Sometimes it takes a while to set in."

"We've got to look at him. Something's not right. I just can't put my finger on what."

"Agreed, partner."

"And we'll need to get some more names of the people she hung around with. And talk with the women he mentioned."

"And I really want to talk to that housekeeper," Jilly continued. "The one that Jessica had the argument with. So...off to Central Division. At least we've got some kind of lead, this Marmaduke character."

Dan sighed before answering. "It'd be nice if it turned out to be that easy."

"But? I sense a 'but'..."

"I don't know, Jilly. This guy turns up with all of her credit cards and ID in his pocket. Even if he turns out to be good for this, it leaves so much unanswered."

Jilly nodded. "I see what you're saying."

"If this is just a robbery that went bad...the big question is, what was Jessica Pidgeon from Farmington doing down in Sheffield at night?"

"Let's take this one thing at a time, Dan. We can only answer one question at a time."

"I'll tell you what's on my mind though. Remember how Delino Washington was taking about the neighborhood being a dump site?"

"Sure. He clearly hates that area."

"It makes a lot more sense if she was killed somewhere else and dumped there."

"Could be. There was no car, nothing else connected with her on the scene, just what was on the body itself. Maybe the evidence will tell us more. The detailed autopsy results from the ME should have come through, and maybe SID will have something for us as well."

"I wish we had some of that to go on now before we talked to Marmaduke."

"Everything falling into place in just the right order? Yeah, that happens a lot...in the books and the TV shows. Let's see how this plays out. In any case he's not going anywhere."

* * * *

"So how have you been, Sergeant Finley?" Jilly asked as she signed in at the holding area. "I believe you know my partner, Dan Lee."

Finley, a hefty, ruddy-faced veteran, stretched his mouth into a sardonic smile. "Living the dream, Detective, always fun and games down here. And yourself?" He nodded at Dan. "You lucked out, Lee. You got yourself a great partner."

"Don't I know it," Dan said.

"Aren't we all living the dream, though." Jilly smiled. "So tell me about this guy."

Finley smirked. "A regular brain surgeon, this one. He's kind of a laughing stock in the local 'hoods. Always trying some new scheme that falls through."

"His jacket looks like he's got a tendency toward violence?"

"Yeah, he's done a few violent crimes. He's about as sweet as he is smart."

"You think he's the kind of guy who would do a mugging right on the street?"

"Never got him on that type of thing, but who knows?"

"What was he doing when he got picked up?"

"Peddling product on a boulevard, right in the middle of the Brown Street Skulls territory. Figured he'd just be an entrepreneur and squeeze himself into their market. Standing right out there kitty-corner from one of the Skulls' own guys, flagging down cars that are cruising through. Probably took about three minutes for the Skull to get on his burner and drop that old dime on Marmaduke. A couple of enforcer types pulled up in one of their black SUVs and rolled down a window, and genius Marmaduke asked them what they'd like. They were out of the car with baseball bats like grass out of a goose."

"Batting practice on the freelancer. Very educational. How'd he find himself delivered from their hands and into the gentle loving ones of Central?"

"We happened to have an undercover guy down there setting up a bust. This was going to mess that up good, so he discreetly got on the horn. He caught a nearby squad car that broke up the home run derby. Marmaduke took a few good shots before they all saw the cruiser and turned tail to run. The uniforms were able to run down Marmaduke when he turned down a dead end alley. Hadn't even bothered to scope out his territory before setting up shop."

"And he was still holding. Didn't even have the sense to dump his stash then?"

"Well, he did try, but he didn't start to toss anything until he was actually in the blind alley." Finley shook his head; his smile became more mirthful. He was enjoying the tale. "Dumbest knucklehead you ever met."

"So they caught him holding, and they found the cards and the IDs of the victim on him as well?"

Finley reached into a drawer in the desk and pulled out a plastic bag, handing it to Jilly. "Here you go." He picked up a set of keys on the desk.

"So shall we go meet Prince Charming?"

* * * *

He had been brought to an interview room that was even bleaker and more sterile than the ones in Personal Crimes. Marmaduke Jones was a large man, a baleful six-foot-four lump of dough, with a shaved, notably lopsided head, a squinty left eye, and an aura of dumb malevolence. He sprawled back over his chair, handcuffed to the metal table in front of him, glowering at them through his red-rimmed good eye as they entered the interview room. Neither of the detectives sat down; they stood across the table, looking down at him.

"So, Marmaduke," Jilly began. "Is that really your name?"

"Call me Duke on the street," he mumbled, his stare growing apprehensive, shifting his gaze back and forth at the duo. Curiosity had begun to dawn as to why these two new cops had come to talk to him.

"That's not what we hear. We hear you're Marmaduke. *Mar-ma-duke.* And honestly, without a lot of respect when you're called that." She held up the plastic bag with the cards, by a corner between thumb and forefinger so he could see it. "So what we want to know, Marmaduke, is how you came into the possession of these?"

He shook his head and tried to think for a long moment. "Found a wallet. They were in it."

Dan spoke up now. "And you of course hung on to them so you could go find the rightful owner and return them."

Marmaduke wasn't sure which one of the two to look at, so he kept shifting his good eye back and forth. He shrugged. "Maybe. Somethin' like that." Even he could tell that sounded particularly lame, so he shrugged again. "I hadn't decided, maybe I was gonna try to use 'em, get a few bucks out of 'em. Sometimes they don't cancel 'em right away."

"So this wallet you say you found. Just where was that?"

The big man thought for a long time. "I don't remember. Lyin' on top of a trashcan somewhere."

"Just lying there, on top of a trashcan."

"Yeah. Pretty sure."

"What kind of trashcan, exactly?"

"You know, one of those big plastic ones out on the street?"

"And when was this you found the wallet exactly?"

"He shook his head, looking confused. "Don't remember. The other night."

"It was at night? Or during the day?"

"I think it was night. The other night."

"Last night? Night before last?"

"Sometime on the weekend, I think. Not really sure." He ran his free hand over his face. "I been a little confused the past few days, you know?"

"Using your own product, you mean," Dan said. "Getting high."

Marmaduke just stared at the bag.

"So you found this wallet, full of these cards, just sitting on a garbage bin? What did the wallet look like?"

He waved his free hand around as if trying to catch a word out of the air. "Like…like a book, you know? It was kinda long and it opened up like a book. Had a snap-strap holding it together. Light brown, I think. Yeah, like a yellow brown?"

Jilly broke in. "What was it made of?"

More head shaking and hand waving. "Maybe leather?"

"And what color was the garbage bin?"

He squinted at her. Whether he was trying to actually remember or to make up a believable story, it was obviously not coming very easily. "It was dark. I don't know. Black probably. Most of 'em are black, aren't they?"

"So you found this wallet, and you decided to go through it and take out anything of value? Did you leave anything in it?"

"Don't remember. I think so. I think there were like, pictures."

"Was there money? You took money, didn't you?"

"Don't remember."

"So if we find this wallet, it's going to have pictures and other things still in it, right? But no money. No credit cards."

Dan returned to the questioning. "What did you do with this wallet after you took everything out of it?"

"I tossed it. I don't remember where. Maybe back into the bin where I found it."

Dan bent in closer to Marmaduke. "The woman who owned those cards is dead. But you knew that, didn't you?"

"What?"

"You killed her. You didn't find her wallet on a garbage bin. You robbed her and killed her."

"What? *No!*" The sulking heap of a man suddenly found some energy. His eyes opened wide, his voice raised. "I didn't kill nobody! I've never killed nobody!"

"How do you know?" asked Jilly, folding her arms and glaring down at him. "You say you don't remember much. You were high."

"You took her jewelry too," said Dan. "And you beat her. A big guy like you, beating that little woman until she died. And then you just kept beating her."

"I swear! I didn't rob that lady. I didn't rob any lady! I wouldn't hurt a woman, I wouldn't! I didn't kill nobody! I found that wallet, just like I told you!"

"Then you'd better start remembering better right away."

Jilly softened her tone, rested her hands on the table, and bent closer to the big trembling man. "If you want us to believe you had nothing to do with her death, then you need to give us something to prove your story. You see how this looks? You've got the victim's personal property and you can't account for how you got it? Come on. Tell us where to find something that backs up your story."

"Don't remember. I just don't remember. I didn't kill nobody!"

"If you don't remember," said Jilly, staring him straight in the eye, "just how can you be so sure you didn't kill anybody?"

Marmaduke looked up and met her stare. This time he growled. "I've never killed nobody in my life."

"We saw your jacket. You've got quite a history of violence."

"Somebody messes with me, I stand my ground. Never hurt nobody who didn't have it coming. Never killed no one. And I don't hurt women."

* * * *

The ride back to their own station house was somber. They both sat in their own thoughts for much of the drive. Finally Dan broke the silence.

"He seems pretty good for this."

Jilly sighed heavily. "Maybe."

"I'm hearing a 'but'."

"I keep coming back to why she would have been down in that neighborhood to begin with."

"The guy's got her cards and ID, he's got a history of violence. Fill it in a little bit more and…there are convictions on less than that."

"I don't think so, Dan. It's not enough for a prosecutor. And it's not enough for me. Maybe he did it, but we need to fill in more of the details."

"Back to the body dump, which seems logical. So he robbed her somewhere else and brought her body there. The husband says her car is not at the house. Maybe she was driving somewhere, parking, getting out of her car and he attacked her. Two-year-old Audi sedan. Nice car. Figured her for a rich one?"

Jilly sighed deeply. "We need to find that car."

They descended into a thoughtful silence. Finally Dan pulled out his smart phone, tapped at it for a minute, and then made a clucking noise.

"What?"

"Your pal Letitia must have decided to move on the story. Looks like there's something on the news this afternoon."

"Don't tell me she's got a name."

"Nope, but she tried sandbagging Captain Crowley this morning in front of headquarters when he arrived. The TV station's website has a video here of the conversation." Dan turned up the sound. It was a short clip, but Crowley did a good job of stonewalling the newswoman, continuing his forward motion while feeding her some general statements that actually sounded pretty good: detectives having important leads but not wishing to release specifics pending family notification, that type of thing. Before she could follow up, he was out of microphone range, never hurrying or giving the appearance of concern, but suddenly being swallowed up by a mass of department associates, moving through the door into the station.

"Impressive," Jilly remarked. "The Captain's a smoothie."

"And Letitia's a tough one."

"Tell me about it. I'm sure her competition's breathing down her neck on this. We need to get some public statements out there. At this point it's to our advantage to get Jessica's name out there. We need someone to come forward."

Dan nodded. "At least we've got plenty to potentially work on. With any luck, we'll have the full ME's report…and if we're really lucky, maybe SID will have something for us as well. I'll run her records at Motor Vehicles and get the plate number so we can start putting out inquiries on the whereabouts of the car. Then I'll run Jessica's credit cards and see if anybody's used any of them."

"I'll contact the housekeeper," Jilly said. "And then we should put the word out on the jewelry that the husband described, see if it's turned up in a pawnshop or anywhere else. And maybe your gal-pal Sandy knows some locals who can tell her something more about Marmaduke."

Dan's wince was visible to Jilly even through the corner of her eye as she drove. "My 'gal-pal'? Officer Kovetsky? Come on, Jilly, give me a break."

"I don't know that I've ever seen a Chinese gentleman blush before. It's very sweet, actually."

"She's just being friendly."

"Uh-huh."

"But even if that weren't the case…you've never had a patrol officer flirt with you?"

Jilly smiled brightly. "I think I scare 'em away."

"You scare *me* now and then. But seriously, none of that stuff with Officer Kovetsky or anybody else means anything."

"Just my luck," smiled Jilly, "to get a partner who's fatally attractive."

THREE

It was past lunchtime when they returned to the unit, but neither of them felt hungry as yet. The urgency of the case pressed on them. They both hit their desks and set to their tasks on telephone and computer. Dan entered the victim's name on the Department of Motor Vehicles website and immediately brought up the plate number for a two-year-old Audi A4 sedan registered to Jessica Pidgeon at 1220 Coventry Drive in Farmington. He jotted down the number on a legal pad and posted online alerts on the vehicle. Then he turned his attention to the transparent bag on his desk that held Jessica's cards. He pushed them around in the package so he could read the faces of the cards and picked up his telephone.

Jilly was a blur of multi-tasking. While jotting notes, she turned on her computer and picked up her desk phone. She tried the telephone number she had been given for Melinda Barstow and got an automated voice mail message. She left word to call her back, not leaving any other information. She ran phone number searches for Jessica's friends, Dory Snyder and Tamara Marsh. She found a Dion and Dory Snyder on Coventry Drive in Farmington, which clearly was the right family. She had no luck with a Tamara Marsh or a T Marsh and there were a dozen other Marshes in the general vicinity. Hopefully Dory Snyder would provide her further leads. She called the number and left another voice mail, asking Dory to return her call.

By now she had already brought up her email and discovered that Mickey Kendrick had indeed sent over the results of the autopsy of Jessica Pidgeon. Much of it confirmed the tentative information they had already garnered: time of death was around 11:00 P.M. on Sunday night. Cause of death was blunt force trauma to the head. The skull had been cracked. The victim bore marks and bruises on her body and head consistent with a beating by fists and a rounded hard object, perhaps the end of a stick or a bat, approximately two to three inches in diameter. Three of her ribs and bones in her arms and legs had been broken. Many of the blows had been delivered after death. Further damage had been done to the body postmortem, probably by contorting it to fit it into the refuse bin. There were numerous finger marks on the arms where she had been held tightly. There was no chance of any kind of fingerprint but there was a good indication of the size of the hands of the assailant. The examiner's opinion was that one attacker was responsible.

Jessica's hands and forearms bore defensive bruises, as if she had tried to ward off blows, but there was no skin or other matter under her manicured nails. That was too bad. Jilly had been hoping that somehow the victim had gotten some of her attacker's DNA.

She scrolled to the photographs. They were horrific. Jilly had seen things as bad and much worse, but something about these pictures, the sheer overkill being portrayed, curdled her stomach.

"You miserable son of a bitch," she whispered. "We will get you."

Had Marmaduke Jones done this? He was big enough, strong enough. He was the likeliest of suspects. But they would have to build their case to be sure and to ensure his conviction.

If the motive was robbery pure and simple, why batter her so savagely? Because he was high at the time, deranged?

A recurring theory came back to her again.

"This was personal," she whispered to the picture on the monitor screen. "Wasn't it? He knew you."

"Got a hit on her ATM card," Dan said, interrupting her macabre reverie. "It was used to withdraw four hundred dollars around nine on Sunday night from a bank machine just over the city line from Farmington."

"Four hundred?"

"That's the limit that can be taken out in one day. I spoke to the bank manager and she says there's a camera. We can go over and check it out."

"Anything else of interest on the cards?"

"Not so far. I ran her recent credit history online and there doesn't seem to be any activity since Saturday. I've got a couple more calls to make but it's looking as if nobody's used any of her cards."

"Okay, let me put out some alerts on the jewelry while you make those calls, then let's take a run up to that bank."

"And I wouldn't mind maybe making a quick stop for a bite as well. I'm actually not that hungry but I think we're gonna be running all day. The trail's warming up."

"A lot to be done. Want to split up?"

Dan hesitated. "Naw, I think we're better off staying together for the moment, okay? Give me a holler when you're ready." He turned and headed back to his desk.

Something, Jilly mused, was up with Dan. He usually was the first to suggest they head off in separate directions to cover more territory on a case like this. As soon as they had a spare moment she'd have to explore that with him. She turned back to her keyboard.

As they were leaving, Castillo came out of his office on a clear path to intercept them. Jilly rolled her eyes, hoping it was not noticeable from a distance. The Lou coming to you was never a good thing.

"You two make yourselves available in about two hours. Captain says we're running an impromptu news conference on Jessica Pidgeon."

Jilly nodded. "Good idea."

The corners of Castillo's mouth curled up under his mustache in a slight impersonation of a smile. "And you two will be the stars. Run it by me what you plan to say before it starts." He turned back to his office.

"Oh great," muttered Jilly.

* * * *

The "quick bite" turned into takeout sandwiches that they consumed in the car on the drive to the Scully Boulevard branch office of Continental Interbank, at the north end of the city. The branch manager was ready for them and escorted them to the security office, where they were able to review a printout of Jessica's transaction from Sunday night and the video taken at the ATM that evening. They asked against hope if the bank kept any record of the serial numbers of bills dispensed from the machine, but as expected, the answer was no.

Jessica's account had been accessed at 9:52 P.M. They asked the manager to start the video at 9:50. It was a black and white video of medium-grainy resolution. There was a fairly static view of Scully Boulevard in harsh evening light with some traffic moving sporadically in the background. One or two pedestrians passed the camera without stopping.

"There," said Dan.

A woman came into view from the left side, in a pair of light slacks and a pale tailored shirt. She was looking down at something she held in her left hand. A wallet, a large billfold style, open like a book. She reached into the wallet with her right hand and removed a card. The camera was above the ATM and slightly to the side, so as she approached the machine, it appeared she was looking off to their right and down. A serious, focused expression on her face, she extended her hand with the card and it disappeared out of camera as it slid into the machine.

"That's Jessica," said Jilly.

They scanned the monitor to see if there was a sign of any other person, but nobody else was within view.

"Look," said Dan. "She's looking up at the camera. She knows it's there."

Indeed, for a brief moment, Jessica's eyes stared directly at them, but she did not move her head, only her eyes. Then she looked back down, apparently entering her information into the keys on the ATM. When she was finished, her eyes once again glanced up at the camera without moving the rest of her head. She held the gaze for a beat then looked back down again.

"She's taking the money," Jilly said. "And her ATM card."

Jessica juggled the packet of bills and her card, taking a few seconds to successfully return the card to her wallet but still holding the bills. She stepped away from the machine, turning to their left and walked off camera quickly.

"She didn't take the receipt," Dan noted.

"She looked right at the camera. Twice."

"Maybe I'm reading too much into it. Maybe she was alone, and just being careful. But she seemed edgy and self-conscious. She only moved her eyes, not her head. Her movements were very controlled. You'd think in a strange urban area at night, she'd be looking all around her. Maybe there was somebody else there, who coerced her to take out the money?"

"Certainly possible. If so, they knew to stay to the side, well off camera. And maybe they warned her not to look at them or to give anything away."

"If so, that's a smart gal," said Dan. "She played it cool but shot a couple of looks at the camera. Subtle, but maybe meaningful?"

"That could mean," Jilly said grimly, "that she might have figured she wouldn't have the chance to talk about any of this later. Maybe she had an idea of what was going to happen to her."

* * * *

The media conference was held in the station's small auditorium, which for occasions such as this was officially dubbed the "press room." In a brief consultation beforehand in Castillo's office, Captain Crowley had simply told them to lay out the bare facts and to field whatever questions followed by referring to the ongoing investigation.

It was brief and, to Jilly and Dan's relief, relatively painless. There were representatives of local television news stations and the city's last remaining newspaper. Jilly took the lead and kept to the facts, stressing the victim's name and an appeal for any information that might be of help. She stressed that there were further things that needed to be kept confidential for the moment, and provided a number for possible tips or information. The follow up questions were exactly what she expected: attempts to pry out another factoid or drop of information. She held her ground tactfully but firmly. Finally Crowley called an end to the conference and escorted the detectives and a handful of brass out of the room.

Once out of the auditorium, in a lobby that led to a side exit, Crowley said, "Nice job" to Jilly, nodded to them both, and walked off with his aides.

"Very nice," said Castillo with a tight smile. "You might be doing my job one of these days, Garvey." And then he was gone as well.

Just like that, Dan and Jilly were alone in the empty vestibule. The sudden silence descended on them like a late night snowfall. They stared at each other, momentarily stunned by the suddenness of it all.

"I agree," smiled Dan. "Good job, partner. Maybe you're destined to join the brass."

"Oh, shut up," sighed Jilly. "Come on, let's get back to the real work."

Jilly found a message at her desk that Dory Snyder had returned her call. Some things still worked the old-fashioned way around the unit. She picked up her desk phone and dialed the number that had been left for her.

Jilly glanced at her watch. How had the day flown by that quickly? In a quick conversation, they made arrangements to meet at Snyder's home the next day.

* * * *

Jilly had barely gotten to her desk Wednesday morning and was trying to balance a mug of coffee while moving some papers on her desk when her phone began to ring. She absently picked it up with her free right hand and held it to her ear.

"Detective Garvey."

"Hello," said a softly melodic voice on the other end of the line. "You left a message for me to contact you. This is Melinda Barstow."

Jilly grounded her coffee cup and switched the receiver to her left ear. "Yes, Ms. Barstow, thank you for returning my call."

"I heard about the murder of Mrs. Pidgeon. How horrible. I assume that's what this is in regard to."

"Yes. Yes, it is. We'd very much like to talk to you and see if you can help us."

"Of course. In fact, I received a letter in the mail from her this morning. I think you need to see it."

"A letter, you say?"

"Yes. It's rather strange, and...well, it's easier if I show you."

"Would it be convenient for us to come by and talk to you?"

"Certainly. I'm home all day."

"We can come by right now if that's all right." Jilly took the address from Melinda and hung up. She took a swig of her coffee, stood up, and walked to Dan's desk where he was absorbed in something he had pulled up on his monitor.

"Hey partner. That was the housekeeper! She got something in the mail from Jessica."

"The housekeeper?" Dan asked, momentarily confused. "The mail? The *mail?* As in, post office, snail mail?"

"Does seem strange. In fact she used that very word. Come on, she's waiting."

She dropped the car keys onto Dan's desk. "You get to drive this time."

Dan hesitated. "That's okay. I'm perfectly happy with having you drive." He picked up the keys and handed them back to her as he rose from his chair. "Let's go."

He was several steps ahead of her heading to the stairs before she could say a word. Jilly started to call out to Dan but then stopped and shook her head. Whatever was up with Dan, it would keep.

Melinda Barstow's apartment building was on a well-kept street in a working class neighborhood. There was a short set of stairs leading to a stoop. A handsome dark-skinned man in his thirties sat on the steps, reading a paperback book. He looked up as Jilly and Dan approached from the street.

"Yes, can I help you?" he asked in a soft voice. He was an athletic-looking sort in a sweater and slacks. A pair of heavy horn-rimmed glasses gave an academic touch to his look.

"Is this where Melinda Barstow lives?" Jilly asked.

He eyed them back and forth with suspicion. "And who might you be?"

Jilly had her badge out instantly, staring at him levelly. "We're here to see Melinda."

The man studied the badge for a moment before nodding and pointing back over his shoulder. He returned to his book as they walked past him to the doorway at the top of the stairs.

The door to the Barstow apartment was answered by a young woman, possibly a mature-looking teenager, in a T shirt and jeans. Jilly and Dan showed their badges and identified themselves. Clearly they had been expected. The girl nodded and stepped back to let them into a small but scrupulously-kept living room. She said, "I'll get Mom," and left the room. Dan and Jilly remained standing. They did not have long to wait.

"Detectives, how are you?"

Melinda Barstow carried herself with a palpable sense of dignity: posture erect, head straight, serious expression. She was lean, with dark hair and flawless beige skin, and dressed in a blazer and skirt in earth tones. She met them with a small relaxed smile and clear, intelligent hazel eyes that held their gaze with quiet confidence, extended a hand and introduced herself formally. She invited them to two armchairs and she deposited herself in a third, facing them across a low polished wood coffee table.

"I hope Olivia—my daughter—doesn't need to be here for this," she said. "She has the morning off from school. I asked her to stay in her room while we talk." Now they noticed a definite trace of a Caribbean lilt to her voice.

Jilly nodded. "That's fine."

"That's quite a doorman you've got guarding the entrance," Dan remarked.

Melinda looked momentarily confused, then smiled and laughed lightly. "Oh, that must be Terry. He was out on the stairs, was he? A very nice man, very bright, well informed. He's been a friend of ours for many years. That's something I like about this neighborhood. We watch out for one another. We're mostly immigrants around here, like myself. It's not a bad neighborhood, but there are some things you have to be careful of, you know? Especially a single mother with a daughter. We've got people like Terry who keep an eye out for all of us. He's quite protective. So did he require you to show proper identification in order to pass?"

Jilly smiled. "He did regard us with some suspicion since we were strangers, yes."

"It's our own version of a neighborhood watch. I appreciate the good people who keep us safe." Melinda's bright expression darkened. "I was terribly shocked to hear the news about Mrs. Pidgeon. I worked for her for many years, right up until recently. I left her employ under rather bad circumstances."

"What do you mean, Ms. Barstow?" Jilly asked.

Melinda's brows knitted. She laced her fingers and rested her hands on the table. "We had an argument that came out of nowhere. I still don't understand what happened. But she got terribly mad at me and fired me on the spot. She told me to leave her house immediately and not to come back. That was the last I ever saw her."

"Just when exactly was this?"

"A little over a week ago. Tuesday of last week."

"You say you don't understand why she had gotten so angry with you?"

Melinda shook her head. "It was something she thought I had done. Nothing big, as far as I could tell. She was picky lately about minor things. One time she took exception to the fact I had made the kids hamburgers. She insisted on a lot of rules for their food: very little fat or sugar, no processed white bread, things like that. Lately she had gotten kind of touchy about little things, and this was just another one of those. But she seemed to be already emotional over something that had happened, and she was irrational. She just blew up. It was so unlike her. She blew the issue totally out of proportion. I tried to reason with her, to calm her down, to explain my side of things, but she just exploded at me. She pulled some money out of her wallet and thrust it at me, said that would bring us up to date on my salary, and told me to pick up my things and leave and not to come back. The more I tried to get her to talk, the madder she got. Finally I just agreed and got my things and left. I figured in a day or two she'd come to her senses and call me back and we'd work out whatever the problem was."

She shook her head in a brief reverie. "I worked for her and her family for twelve years and I treated them as I would my own family. I took care of the children as they grew. I was always honest and loyal. I thought she appreciated qualities like that."

"And she never called you back or contacted you?"

"No. I tried to call her after a couple days, left her voice mails, but she never answered and she wouldn't return my calls. Finally I talked to Mr. Pidgeon. I thought maybe he'd have some idea what was wrong. The whole thing came as a total surprise to him." She looked at the detectives with wide, uncomprehending eyes. "It made no sense. It was hurtful to me. And then on top of that, I was really hoping I could get at least a reference from her if I had to go look for a new job. That's over twelve years I'd have to account for. It's not easy right now, the job market. A good employer reference would mean a lot. I don't think I could get work without one. Olivia is starting college in the fall. I need steady employment."

Dan nodded. "We understand, Ms. Barstow."

"I saw on the news yesterday that Ms. Pidgeon had been found murdered. That was terrible, just terrible. Poor woman. That place she was found, it made no sense. It's a dreadful place. And so far from her home. She didn't tend to leave Farmington. Maybe now and then she'd drive to go shopping, but she was generally a homebody. And now this...this confounded me this morning when this came for me in the mail."

There was a manila envelope on the coffee table, which she now picked up. It was covered with stamps and an adhesive label on which an address had been desktop-printed. She opened it and pulled out several sheets of text-filled paper.

"There was this letter," she said, handing it to Jilly, who took it gingerly by a corner with her fingertips. She and Dan bent closer together to read it. It had likely been typed on a computer and then desktop-printed.

Dear Melinda,

Please forgive me for the terrible way in which I treated you. You did not deserve it after all the years of trustworthy service you showed me. All I can say in my own defense is that I have had many serious personal problems of late, and I have just not been myself. I have decided to enroll myself in a recovery program to address these issues. Please find enclosed here, a personal recommendation for your future employment and what I hope is a reasonable amount of severance pay to show my appreciation and help you through until you find new employment, as I know you will.

Fondly and sincerely,

Jessica Carpenter Pidgeon

Only the signature at the end was handwritten, in a dark blue ink that had spread into the fibers of the paper.

Melinda then held up three more sheets. It was a lengthy formal letter of introduction introducing Melinda Barstow and extolling her many virtues as an honest, upright, loyal, and capable woman who had managed the Pidgeon household in multiple ways. Again, everything had been typed on a computer, and was signed at the end by Jessica Carpenter Pidgeon with the same pen as the cover letter.

"And she sent you money as well? A check?"

"No, there were four hundred dollars in cash in the envelope."

"Cash?"

"Yes. In twenties, bound together with a rubber band."

"Was she in the habit of paying you in cash?"

"Yes, she always did. But she never sent it to me. She always handed it to me at the end of the week." Melinda looked back and forth at them suddenly. "I pay my taxes. I declare everything I make. I can't vouch for Ms. Pidgeon, if she reported everything, but I'm on the level. And I'm a legal citizen."

Jilly smiled and raised a hand in a gesture of reconciliation. "Nobody's accusing you of any of that, Ms. Barstow. Just trying to get the facts here."

"She mentions a recovery program," Dan said. "Was she in some kind of rehab? Did she have any kind of problem that you were aware of?"

Melinda shook her head. "You mean like drinking or drugs or anything like that? No, certainly not that I was aware of, and I was around the house a lot. She took a glass of wine now and then or maybe a small cocktail on a special occasion, but no." She stopped and visibly bit her lip tensely, looking down at the table. A long uncomfortable silence fell upon the room.

"Ms. Barstow?" Jill finally said, gently. "I think there's something on your mind. Maybe it will help."

"She had problems with her marriage," Melinda said quietly. "She and Mr. Pidgeon were hardly speaking. He had actually moved out a few weeks before that."

"Moved out?" Jilly and Dan exchanged glances.

"He hadn't been living in the house for a while. He had an apartment somewhere in town, I think."

"So there had been tension between them for some time, then?"

"Oh yes. For months before he moved out, the house was unbearable. I never asked Ms. Pidgeon about it. I figured it wasn't my business. I tried to be supportive in, you know, more subtle ways."

"So Mr. Pidgeon moved out, what, a month or two ago?"

"Let me think. Yes. Six weeks ago, this coming weekend. I remember he loaded up his SUV for a couple of trips. I generally don't work weekends, but I was asked to come on Saturday to help clean up after him."

"Any idea what that might have been about?"

"Not my business, as I said."

Jilly leaned forward with what she hoped was a conspiratorial look. "Sure. But we all pick up on stuff going on at our place of business, don't we? I mean, I sure do. Stuff I'm not supposed to know. If you're smart, you can't help it."

Despite herself, Melinda smiled. "Where the bodies are buried, as they say." She started suddenly and laid a hand across her mouth. "Oh. Forgive me. That sounded...I mean, considering..."

Jilly laid her own hand over Melinda's other hand, the one that had remained on the table. "No no, of course, just an expression. But you understood what I was getting at. My point is that I bet you knew things about that household. You were considerate and discreet, and you acted professionally and responsibly. But you're also clearly a perceptive and intelligent woman, Ms. Barstow. I think you knew a lot about what was going on there."

"I don't want to get anybody in trouble." Melinda said hesitantly. "It's water under the bridge now, all things considered."

Jilly and Dan said nothing. They waited.

"Mr. Pidgeon, well...I think there may have been another woman. A younger lady. Maybe someone he worked with. I got the impression he was going to divorce Ms. Pidgeon. They never talked about it in front of me, but there were little remarks, little references. An indirect barb here and there."

"You thought they were in the process of divorcing?"

"I think so, yes, could be. Ms. Pidgeon—well, she was increasingly on edge the past few weeks. Looked like she didn't sleep well some nights. She might have been drinking a *little* more, an extra glass of wine in her hand now and then, but it's not like I ever saw her tipsy or slurring her words or anything."

"Did she act angry very often?"

"No. More like really quiet and somber. Distracted. Sometimes if I asked her a question, I'd have to repeat myself because she wasn't listening."

"Can I go back to this letter for a minute?" Dan interjected. "You say it wasn't usual for her to mail you things like this?"

"Never. This was the first letter I ever received from her in the actual mail. I'm surprised she knew my address. My phone number, certainly she knew. I mean, she has all my information, and she might well have kept work records going back to my application. But I moved to a different building earlier this year. Of course I gave her the new address, but I got the impression she hadn't paid much attention at the time."

"Is there anything odd about the fact she would type such a personal letter to you instead of hand writing it?"

Melinda thought about that, looking down at the letter. "Well, she does have a computer. Once in a while she'd print out something. But if she needed to leave me a note or anything, it was always hand-written. As I said, she never sent me a formal letter like this before, so I'm not sure."

"Does that definitely look like her signature?"

Melinda pulled the letter back, turned it around so it read right from her viewpoint, and peered at it carefully. She nodded at Dan. "Yes. I'd say so."

"She signed it with her whole name. Jessica Carpenter Pidgeon. I assume Carpenter was her maiden name?"

"Yes."

"Was it her habit to sign her entire name like that?"

Melinda pondered that one thoughtfully. "I honestly don't remember ever seeing her sign anything with her whole name like that. But I could be wrong."

Jilly jumped back in. "The last time you saw her—a week ago last Tuesday?—you said she was noticeably distraught? More than usual?"

"She was dramatically different that morning. Dramatically."

Jilly nodded. "You had been at her house the day before, Monday?"

"Yes. I came Monday through Friday as a rule, usually got there around eight and left around six or seven, depending upon what needed to be done."

"What would you generally do? Was there a routine every day?"

"Pretty much so, yes. There was shopping for food and other necessities, laundry, general cleaning around the house, changing the linens, preparing meals. When their kids were younger, I'd do child care, drop them off at school and pick them up in the afternoon. Laurie, the older one, is midway through high school and Brad is fourteen. They don't require anywhere near as much attention as when they were younger. Brad plays baseball on his school team; now and then I'd still drive him to and from practice."

"So you arrived at the Pidgeon home on Tuesday morning, and something was different with Jessica?"

"Well, she was very touchy all morning, but in a sulky way, do you know? Only speaking to me in a few syllables. Not that that was entirely unusual. She went out to run some errands or meet a friend or something. The real problem started when she returned later that afternoon."

"How do you mean?"

"Laurie had a friend over to study. She was trying to help him. He's a very nice boy, trying to get through school and succeed, but it's as if everything is stacked against him."

"So she was tutoring him?"

"Yes, kind of. Ms. Pidgeon came home and exploded when she realized Laurie had a friend over. She started saying she knew I was 'conspiring' with Laurie, without her—Ms. Pidgeon's—knowledge. She was firing odd questions at me about secret goings-on or something. None of it made any sense."

"When she said 'conspiring' with Laurie—what did she mean exactly? What was she getting at?"

"I'm still not really sure. It sounds as if she had discovered Laurie was doing something she shouldn't have. I tried to ask her what she meant: did she think I was smuggling in drugs to her, for Lord's sake? Or birth control? She kept saying that I knew what she was talking about."

"I can see how that could be very upsetting to you."

"Laurie and her friend came down into the kitchen. Ms. Pidgeon chased the boy out of the house and had a screaming match with Laurie, who first tried to reason with her but lost control herself, yelled a lot and ran out of the room. Then Ms. Pidgeon turned back on me again with more crazy accusations that I didn't quite understand."

"How long did this go on?"

"Not for very long. I realized that she was being irrational and it made no sense for me to even try to talk to her. I confess, I got a little indignant myself. I may have said something to the effect I couldn't talk to her while she was in that kind of state. She must have taken it as disrespect because of how she reacted."

"What did she do?"

"She started to yell some more. Then she stopped. She got really quiet, just simmering and glaring at me. It was kind of scary. Then she just abruptly said something like, 'I think your services are no longer needed here, Melinda. Gather your things and get out.' Something like that. And she shoved a handful of money at me. She just kept telling me to leave in that same quiet, scary voice. I started getting upset myself. Finally I left in kind of a huff. She got to me. It was all so stupid."

Melinda paused and wiped an eye. "And that was the last time I ever saw her or spoke with her."

With self-conscious dignity, Melinda composed herself and looked at them expectantly.

"Ms. Barstow, we're going to need to take this letter with us."

Melinda nodded. "I figured that. If it can be of any help, you're welcome to it."

"I'm afraid we also need the money. We'll give you a receipt. If it was actually sent to you by Jessica, you'll get it back."

Melinda nodded again, this time with a resigned scowl on her face. "I figured that too."

"You could have neglected to tell us about it. You're an honest person. We appreciate that. It might have importance."

Melinda rose from her chair and walked to a breakfront on the other side of the living room and opened a drawer, pulling out a packet of bills with a thick rubber band around them. She brought it back and placed it on the table next to the envelope. Jilly had a clear plastic bag ready to carefully deposit the money.

"Fingerprinting currency is not usually very effective, but we have to give it a shot, along with some other tests the lab can do. We'll certainly fingerprint the letter. We'll need to exclude your own prints. Perhaps you could come to the station and get fingerprinted, unless you already have them on record?"

Melinda began to look more concerned.

"I was fingerprinted when I applied for my work visa here, and when I applied for citizenship."

"Then we'll be able to get them to compare. You'll be in the system, most likely. Where did you come from?"

"The Bahamas, twelve years ago." She set her jaw and glared at Jilly. "I'm a legal citizen. I obey the laws. And I had nothing to do with what happened to Ms. Pidgeon! I didn't do anything! I'm being honest with you!"

Jilly shook her head and waved her hands gently. "You aren't being suspected of anything. But suppose this letter was written by someone other than Ms. Pidgeon. Suppose it has something to do with how she died. We have to be able to eliminate her prints. And yours. That's all."

Melinda did still not look convinced.

Jilly rose from her seat and placed a hand on Melinda's shoulder. "Listen to me, Ms. Barstow. We don't care what your work situation was, or your citizenship status. That's not our job here." She took a breath and fastened a stony, resolute gaze upon her, forcing her to stare back attentively. "You'll have to forgive me for being blunt. Your employer, Jessica Pidgeon, someone you've known for years, a small, slight woman, was brutally assaulted by someone much bigger and stronger than her. The assault continued even after she was killed. Then she was left in a garbage container, like so much refuse. Her last minutes of conscious life were spent experiencing a level of contempt and degradation no human being should ever have to undergo. The person who did this needs to be found and punished and we need your cooperation. That's all we care about. Nothing else matters right now except finding the, the…*monster* who did this."

A tear slowly formed and trickled down Melinda's cheek. She pursed her lips tightly and nodded.

FOUR

"This adds a whole new side to things," Dan said. They were sitting at a table in what was called the station's cafeteria, but which in reality was little more than a self-serve coffee stand, each nursing a cardboard-sleeved cup of hot black coffee. "Considering the husband didn't tell us he wasn't living there anymore."

"And hadn't been for some time," Jilly added. "He didn't feel a need to tell us they were estranged."

"Sounds like we need to go back and have another talk with him. Melinda mentioned he had taken an apartment here in the city. Should be easy enough to track down an address."

"Maybe he'll still be at the house. He had to bring his kids back from the mother-in-law. We need to go to the neighborhood to talk to Jessica's friends anyway. That would make it easier."

The letter and the package of money had been bagged and sent to SID, with hopes of pulling fingerprints. They had agreed to misgivings regarding the letter, the money, and the story. But they had also agreed that Melinda herself seemed a less likely suspect for the murder.

Before sending it off, Jilly had snapped pictures of the manila envelope in which the letter and the money had been mailed. It had been covered with stamps, of the self-sticking variety, that had been stuck down in haphazard fashion—considerably more postage than would have actually been required. The postmark, from a postal station only a few blocks from Jessica's ATM, indicated it had been processed on Monday morning.

They decided that everything pointed to the strong possibility that the envelope had been prepared ahead of time. The money could have been inserted and the package sealed and dropped into a mailbox outside the station sometime on Sunday. A trip to the post office might or might not prove to be helpful—both Jilly and Dan tended to believe not—but they needed to try.

It was a quick trip and as fruitless as they had expected. Nobody at the postal station recalled the parcel nor could they offer any helpful information on how it might have been processed.

It was time to focus on more important objectives, fortunately at two adjacent destinations: another conversation with James Pidgeon and a visit to Dory Snyder up the street. On the drive to Farmington, they discussed the puzzling implications of the mail parcel.

"It could be as simple as Jessica feeling guilty, going to get cash, and sending it off to Melinda," Dan was saying, once again sitting in the passenger side of the car as Jilly drove.

"But you don't think so, and neither do I."

"Too much is too weird. But Jessica definitely withdrew that money."

"It's got to be the same money," agreed Jilly. "I'm hoping there'll be a different set of fingerprints on the letter, the money, the stamps…something to implicate another party."

"Is it possible Jessica did all this, then got robbed and killed after dropping the package in the mail?"

"Maybe. Every scenario I can think of raises questions for me. Why withdraw cash on a Sunday night, and why from *that* bank? I bet that's not her normal branch and that there's one closer to her house. Why would she type a letter of apology that way, and why would she mail it all so far from her home in the dead of night on that Sunday?"

"And then there's the matter of her signature," Dan added. "Using her original and married names."

"That too. Why was she in the city that night to begin with? If she was robbed by Marmaduke or whomever, how did she get to be there?"

"Let's hope Mr. Pidgeon will provide us with some insights," Dan sighed, looking out the window. "Here we are, Coventry Drive."

Jilly pulled up in front of the Pidgeon house. "Dory Snyder lives four houses up the street."

"Might be more efficient to split up, what do you think?"

"Sure. You want to take Dory?"

"I'll walk. I could use the exercise."

The door was answered by a blond girl, presumably Laurie Pidgeon. Jilly identified herself and asked to speak with her father. The girl inspected her badge and ID carefully before stepping back and letting her in.

Smart girl, Jilly thought.

The girl was in the teenage uniform of the day, leggings and a long sweater. She eyed Jilly up and down. The scowl on her face seemed as if it had found a permanent home there.

"You don't look like a detective."

Jilly smiled. "What do you mean?"

"All the woman detectives on TV wear pantsuits. And they have their badges hooked on their belts."

"I hope you're not disappointed, but in real life some of us wear blazers and jeans. And I only display my badge at crime scenes and things like that. You must be Laurie, right? You were in Pennsylvania with your grandmother?"

The girl nodded. "My brother and I just got back this morning."

"I'm very sorry about your mom, Laurie."

"My mom can go to hell," Laurie said sullenly. "She's probably there now."

That took Jilly aback. It was a few short beats before she could gather her wits, but by then Laurie continued, in the same tone of voice, "I'll go get my dad. Have a seat," and pointed to the chairs in the living room before bounding up the nearby staircase. Jilly sat down in the same chair she had taken the day before and found herself lost in thought.

Apparently the relationship between Jessica and her daughter had been rocky of late. Not unusual, she considered. Sixteen was usually a difficult period, for both parent and child. She well remembered being that age, trying to assert herself as an independent person, wanting to be an adult all at once, constantly at loggerheads with her own mother. Add in the traumatic death of Laurie's mom and she could understand that the girl might be confused and prone to inappropriate expression.

Witnessing people dealing with grief was nothing new to Jilly. It was seldom predictable or comfortable.

"Detective, how may I help you?" James entered the room, alone, looking haggard and distracted. Jilly stood up to greet him.

"Mr. Pidgeon, I'm sorry to bother you but I have a few more questions."

"Okay." He sat across from her, looked at her and waited.

"I see your kids have returned. How are they managing through this?"

"Hard to say. Nobody's talking much."

"And how are *you* doing?"

James shrugged. "I think I'm still in shock. At some point it's all going to come crashing down on me, the reality of it. If it was just me it'd be one thing…"

"I understand."

Jilly waited a beat before proceeding.

"Mr. Pidgeon, you said you were out of town on business all last weekend?"

That stopped him short.

"Yes. I was in Portland, from Friday until Monday morning. I was conferring with our prospective buyer, Ubertech. Willy Gauss, the owner, is an old friend and colleague."

"And what airline did you fly back on Monday morning?"

Pidgeon drew a deep breath. "Horizon Air. I got in at about 10. Why…?"

"Would you happen to have kept your ticket?"

"Yes. It's a digital ticket, on my phone."

"I'd like to see it if I may."

Pidgeon sighed deeply and reached in his pocket for his phone. He tapped around on it and handed it to Jilly. She made note of the information and handed the phone back to him.

"This is beginning to sound like I'm a suspect," Pidgeon said cautiously.

"Mr. Pidgeon, you haven't been living here, have you? You've been living in the city for a while now, isn't that right?"

He sank his head very low. Jilly watched him carefully. He finally looked up again, his eyes weary.

"No, I haven't been living here for a while now."

"You and your wife were separated? You were having difficulties?"

"You could say that."

"I find it curious that you didn't mention that to us when we were here yesterday."

"I didn't really think about it, to tell you the truth. You had just told me my wife had…that she had been killed. I'd been worried out of my mind about her since she'd disappeared."

"I need for you to tell me about it now. How long ago did you move out?"

"It was about five or six weeks ago."

"Sounds like something rather serious between you."

"I'd like to say we were working it out, but…no, I don't think we were going to work it out."

Jilly decided to let that hang, see how the silence might move him to elaborate. Finally he spoke. "Jessy was...difficult. I just couldn't deal with her anymore."

"How do you mean?"

"Nothing seemed to make her happy. She was incommunicative—when she wasn't finding fault with everything. Nothing I did was ever good enough. She said I worked too hard, was gone from the house too much. But then when I was home, it was always fault-finding."

James stared across at Jilly. "I guess sometimes marriages just run out of steam. People change too much. I don't know."

Jilly kept waiting. The silence seemed uncomfortable to him. He had to fill it up.

"You have to understand, I still loved her. I always loved her. I don't understand what happened to her. She got so unhappy. Someone once told me that's a good definition of neurotic: being incapable of ever being happy."

"You think Jessica was neurotic? Was she seeing a therapist of any kind?"

"Oh yeah. She went to a couple of them. She gave up on them, didn't think they could help."

"Why do you think she was unhappy?"

"You're asking was it something I did?"

"No, Mr. Pidgeon, I'm just trying to get an idea of Jessica's state of mind, to understand where she may have gone Sunday and why."

"I don't know, Detective. I long since gave up on trying to understand Jessy, what made her tick. I hadn't been paying that much attention to her comings and goings because I wasn't here anymore than I needed to be, to see the kids and such."

Jilly looked up to make sure that neither of the kids were in hearing range.

"I have to ask this. Are you involved with another woman?"

He hesitated, considering his answer. Finally he shrugged in resignation. "It didn't start that way. When I moved out, that wasn't the reason. But, now, yes."

"Did Jessica know, or at least suspect?"

"She *suspected* all sorts of things, most of them groundless. I hadn't gotten around to telling her yet. It wasn't easy to tell her anything any longer."

"Does this woman live with you now?"

"Not exactly. We spend time with each other, but it hasn't gotten to the stage where one of us is willing to give up their own place. You're not going to have to bring her into this, are you?"

"We are going to have to talk to her, yes. I'll need to know her name and some contact information."

He sighed. "Her name's Natasha Hedgefield. She works for me."

Jilly took her notebook out and jotted down the name, address and phone number he provided.

James Pidgeon shook his head with a grimace. "She's still doing it."

"Excuse me?"

"Oh…I'm sorry. It's just that Jessy is still making trouble for me even now." He ran a hand across the top of his forehead. "Forgive me, that was a terrible thing to say. I might not sound like I still loved Jessy but believe me, I did. Nothing in my life was a harder task these days."

"Had your son and daughter been getting along with their mother okay lately? Did they ever confide to you about having problems with her?"

James sighed deeply. "Brad's at that age where he doesn't communicate much. He mostly stays in his room when he's home. That's what he's been doing since he got back this morning. I guess that's how boys process something this awful. Of late he hasn't tended to tell me much anyway. He goes quiet for long periods when he's with me, just brooding."

"And Laurie?"

"Laurie had some feud going on with Jessy over a boyfriend, it seems. Jessy would go on rants about how inappropriate he was for her. "

"Inappropriate. Strange way to put it. Why? Did you ever meet the boy?"

"Sure, once or twice. He's in some trade-technical program at school. I think he wants to be a mechanic or something. Jessy objected that he wasn't going to go to college."

"I assume Laurie plans to do so?"

"I certainly hope so. She's a bright girl. She could have a great future. She's only just finishing her sophomore year in high school; we've talked about it a little."

"And Jessica, I gather, really wanted Laurie to go on to college?"

"Oh my God yes. It was like it was a done deal, no debate."

"So that might have been another bone of contention between them?"

"It was all one big bone. I think Jessy had Laurie's whole life planned out for her. It was as if she lived vicariously through Laurie, searching for the happiness she was missing out on in her own life."

"Whew. That's quite the observation, Mr. Pidgeon. It sounds like you've been thinking about this for a while."

James nodded, slowly, gazing at Jilly with sad eyes. "I've been trying to figure this out for a long time."

"You said she saw a couple of therapists? Recently?"

"The more recent one was maybe a year and a half ago. She first saw a male therapist about three years back but she gave up on him after two visits because she said he didn't understand her. She said only a woman could understand. So I urged her to find a woman. That's why she finally started seeing Claire Orzabal. She saw her regularly for about six months before she gave up on her as well."

Jilly jotted down the name. "What did you think of her?"

"I never met her. I just wrote the checks to her."

"What did Jessica think of her?"

"At first she would come home and say she thought Claire was helping her see things. That's how she put it, see things. She seemed hopeful. She seemed to like going to talk with her. Then after a few weeks all of a sudden her enthusiasm died and she started saying that Claire wasn't what she had thought after all. One day she just didn't make any more appointments and stopped going to see her."

"What was Jessica's state of mind like right after that?"

"She seemed to plunge back into her depression, or whatever it was that was wrong."

"Was Jessica on any kind of medication? Did Dr. Orzabal prescribe anything, perhaps for depression?"

"Not that I know."

"Is there any possibility that Jessica was, well, self-medicating, that there was a drug issue that might have caused her emotional problems?"

"I can't imagine that. Jessy hated to take drugs of any kind. She bought organic foods. It was a task to get her to take something for a headache."

"Where would I find Dr. Orzabal?"

"Her office and practice are in the city. I can probably find her information but I'm sorry, Jessy moved everything around after I left and I'd have to dig through her records."

"I can likely find her easy enough. If not I'll get back to you."

"Do you honestly think Dr. Orzabal can give you any clue into what happened to Jessy?"

"I don't know, Mr. Pidgeon. I have to try. Frankly, Jessica is still a total enigma to me. I've got no idea where the insight is going to come from. I'm going to try everything I can, until the answers come."

"I notice you don't say *if* the answers come. You expect them to come."

"I'm not one to give up." She eyed him levelly. "And in the end I guess I'm an optimist."

James nodded, lapsing into awkward silence before Jilly resumed.

"She made a withdrawal of money from the ATM at the Continental Interbank branch on Scully Boulevard on Sunday night. Is that something out of the ordinary for her?"

"Scully Boulevard? Yes, that's very unusual. I didn't even know there was a branch there. Continental's our bank, but she would have been more likely to use the branch at Farmington Plaza. That's a mall not far from here. A couple of her favorite stores are there. You say she took out money?"

"Yes. Four hundred dollars. There's a video of her making the transaction on Sunday night."

"Why would she do that?"

"I was hoping you could tell me."

"Scully Boulevard, in the city?"

"Yes, sir."

"I can't even think of anything around there that would have been of interest to her. Lately she hated to drive into the city. She wanted to stay here in Farmington. She even avoided driving, as much as possible. As far as I know, she only drove to the club and to the mall. And probably to the market and the kids' schools since she fired Melinda."

"What market did she use?"

"I don't know, I'd guess the Esplanade, near the Plaza. Nice organic food market. Jessy tried to eat healthy. She had a thing about the whole family eating healthy."

Jilly made a quick note. Jessica had to have gone somewhere last weekend. She was willing to grasp at straws.

* * * *

Dan had stepped up to the stuccoed portico and had barely pressed the doorbell when the round-topped door flew open and a small woman with ashen hair and large eye glasses gazed up at him. He had his badge and ID out to show her.

"You must be the detective!" she exclaimed, pulling open the door. "I thought you were going to be a woman! Come in!" She was wearing a smock and had an armful of rocks that looked like pieces of granite. She stepped back to let him in.

"Give me a moment!" she said excitedly. "I've been collecting these rocks for my garden. Let me go put them down!" She scurried out towards the back of the house. Dan looked around uncomfortably. He heard a screen door in the back of the house creak and slam, then a few seconds later it creaked and slammed again. The little woman returned the way she had left, now minus smock or rocks.

"I'm sorry. I spent this morning finding those beautiful rocks up in the hills. They're for my garden."

"Yes, ma'am," Dan replied. "What kind of garden do you have?"

"Why, a rock garden, of course! Come in, please, sit down!" She led him into a high-ceilinged living room sparely decorated in Southwest style: earth tones, numerous terra cotta pots, and a woven wall hanging. They sat on short burnt-orange sofas that faced one another across a low coffee table bearing a few ceramic figurines. She started fingering the turquoise stones of a large chunky necklace she wore.

"I heard about poor Jessica! What a terrible thing!"

The woman had enormous energy, it seemed to Dan. She sat but never stopped fidgeting. When she stopped playing with the necklace, she began to move items around on coffee table. She adjusted her shirt. "That's why you're here, isn't it? I spoke to a young woman earlier…"

"That would be my partner, Jill Garvey. Yes, Ma'am."

"I haven't had the chance to go over to see her family. Those poor children! I'll have to see if I can do anything for them!"

"I understand you were close to Mrs. Pidgeon."

"Well, I don't know if 'close' is the right word. Certainly we knew one another. And we often met for tea or sometimes lunch. At least, we used to."

"You hadn't seen her much recently?"

"Not very recently, I'm afraid. Jessica seemed more comfortable keeping her own counsel of late."

"I don't understand. You mean she just decided not talk to you anymore?"

"Not exactly." Dory hesitated, looking uncomfortable. "It was getting awkward in recent times. She was…aggravated. Frankly, it was hard to talk to her. She was argumentative and testy. Yes, that's a good word for it. Jessica had gotten very testy."

"Do you know why she might have gotten like that?"

"It could have been a number of things. She complained about her children and her family and her life. She said she felt everything was out of control."

"So…you decided to sever connections with her?"

"I just thought I'd give her some time to get things together, become herself again. It was just too hard. Perhaps in a while, things would be back to normal again."

"How long ago did this happen? When did you stop getting together with her?"

"I don't know; it was a few weeks ago. I just stopped calling her and figured if she called me, I'd make some excuses for a while. As it turns out, I didn't need to. After a couple of weeks I realized she wasn't calling me anymore either."

"Did you wonder if there was something specific troubling her? Did you ever ask her?"

"Oh, of course. Many times. She always dismissed my questions and said there was nothing in particular." She looked up earnestly at Dan. "You have to understand something, Mr. Lee. Jessica was my friend. We were close for a long time. She was possibly my best friend in this neighborhood, especially since my husband died a while back."

"I'm sorry," Dan interjected.

"Thank you. He fought a long protracted illness. It was very hard. Jessica was there for me through it and afterward. My point is that I would have done anything to help her if I could. If she would have let me. But she wouldn't let me in. She wouldn't tell me what was the matter."

"Do you think she confided to anybody else? Family, friends?"

"Family?" Dory expelled air through her lips. "Her husband, you mean? I don't think he was there for her very much. She has no other family nearby, at least that I know of. Her mother lives somewhere back east, as I recall. Delaware or Pennsylvania I think."

"Pennsylvania, yes. How about other friends?"

"She didn't seem to have a lot of close friends in the area. She and her husband were cordial enough. There were outdoor barbecues and parties and such. But close friends? Over time she seemed to drop out of the social circuit. There was me and sometimes a couple of friends she met at the club."

"The country club?"

"Yes, I suppose you could call it that. The Cypress Golf and Tennis Club. Jessica liked to play tennis and swim. We'd sometimes meet to play cards or just sit by the pool and have a glass of wine." She smiled a little. "Or two."

"Besides you, who else did she socialize with?"

"Well, Tamara. She and Jessica seemed to have little conspiracies they would laugh about."

"Tamara…?"

"Marsh, I believe is her last name. When we'd play bridge, which wasn't that often, we'd get someone for a fourth. But mostly it was the three of us. I once joked we were the Three Musketeers. Tamara said no, it was more like the Unholy Trinity."

"That's interesting. Tamara sounds like she's a bit of a sharp wit."

"Oh, yes. She likes to say her patron saint is Dorothy Parker."

"So the three of you got along well, and sometimes there'd be a fourth, but nobody regular?"

"No. Nobody ever stuck, you might say."

"Would you know how I could contact Tamara?"

"Tamara lives further up in the hills. Her husband's name is Paul, I think. She mentioned him on occasion. That's all I know. He was always off playing golf. He's a fanatic. But I guess all the husbands are. I don't know anyone who ever just dabbled in golf, do you?"

"Never played it, so I really couldn't say. Mr. Pidgeon never joined the golf games?"

"Oh no. He hasn't set foot in the club in a long time. Only Jessica."

"Do you think Tamara and Jessica were still close in recent weeks, when Jessica became more, well, distracted?"

Dory shrugged. "I don't know. Couldn't tell by me. I'm out of the loop now." She suddenly looked a bit put out.

"So you haven't seen them at the club recently?"

"Oh, I'm not a member. I was always Jessica's guest there. I guess I'm not much of a mixer. Especially since my husband passed."

A furry white cat strolled into the room and leapt into her lap, and she idly stroked it, staring sadly into space. "I'm kind of a loner of late. Just me. And Tabitha here. And my garden."

The ensuing silence grew awkward for Dan. He strained for something to break it. "Your rock garden."

"Yes. I guess I miss having Jessica come to visit. Oh my. And now I'll never see her again."

Dan tried to bring it back in focus. "Do you know of any other friends at all that Jessica might have had? Any other hobbies, activities? Did she go out much, go shopping or horseback riding or anything you can think of?"

"She did things mostly on her own. She liked shopping for clothes but she hated going into the city. She would mostly go to the malls. She liked a couple of the nicer stores out at Farmington Plaza. That was what you'd call her comfort zone."

"What was Jessica's marriage and family life like?"

"I couldn't really tell you. When Dion—that was my husband—was alive, we would socialize with the Pidgeons. But since he died, I can't recall seeing the both of them together. There was only Jessica. I think Mr. Pidgeon was like me, no great desire to mingle."

"She must have talked about it, though. Her marriage, I mean."

Dory's smile was deeply sad. "I don't think she was very happy. She would say strange things about nobody liking her or listening to her. But I honestly don't know if that was her marriage and her family or…"

"Yes? Or…?"

Dory looked as if she were trying to solve a difficult puzzle. "…or if it was just her, if her sense of reality was warping. I really began to think something was wrong with her."

* * * *

The conversation with James Pidgeon continued to be comfortable enough but yielded little insight for Jilly. He seemed willing to talk about everything but to know almost nothing. Apparently he had long since become emotionally removed from his wife, and to only a slightly lesser extent from his children.

"Mr. Pidgeon," Jilly asked, "did Jessica keep any kind of journal? Anything that might give us a clue what she was doing this past weekend?"

"I'd guess not. At least she never did when I was here. She wasn't one to be all that introspective, if you know what I mean."

"Did she write letters to people?"

"You mean, like actual letters? Maybe a thank-you card now and then. Some polite acknowledgment. She was fairly proper about that kind of thing."

"Did she have any kind of stationery to use if she did write a letter? Or would she have just written it up on her computer and printed it out?"

"I'm not sure, Detective. What are you getting at?"

"She sent a letter to Melinda. And she included the letter of recommendation Melinda needed. Everything was typed in a word processing program, printed out on plain paper, and mailed in a plain manila envelope. Would she have done that from her computer here?"

"She wrote a long letter and *mailed* it to Melinda? I don't know. That strikes me as kind of strange."

"Can I see her office or wherever she might have worked from?"

"Probably the bedroom. Follow me."

They rose and he led Jilly up the stairway. At the landing, they walked down a short corridor and James opened a door to a large bedroom. "This used to be ours, but it's been Jessy's room since I left. I couldn't bring myself to sleep in here the past few days. I'm in the guest room down the hall."

Near the bed there was a desk with a small computer and printer. James gestured toward it and said, "Feel free to look. I'm going to go call Jessy's mother. I forgot to let her know the kids arrived safely. I'll only be a moment."

"Of course."

Jilly pulled on a pair of her ever-present latex gloves from her pocket and inspected the desk, carefully leafing through its contents. Each drawer was sparsely filled and neatly arranged. She found two boxes of pastel stationery and small envelopes, but no postage stamps. There were no large manila envelopes, not even a package of plain printing paper. The wide shallow drawer over the kneehole of the desk contained a few pencils and ballpoint pens and a small notepad. Jilly inspected the pad to see if there were any impressions from previous writing on the top sheet, but it seemed to be fresh. She tried out each of the pens on the pad. Two were black and one was red. No blue. No felt tips. The computer and printer were turned off. When she turned them on, there was no password needed to access the screen. A quick perusal yielded no recently-created documents or files of any kind, much less a letter or a recommendation.

It would appear that Jessica had not composed the letter to Melinda on this machine, unless she had then scrupulously removed every trace. Jilly doubted it since the trash file on the screen was full, with items dating back over two weeks.

There were three sheets of standard size paper in the printer, but they were a light buff color, not white like the letter had been.

She sat quietly and took stock. They should get an evidence team up here in any case. There might be some…

She heard slight noises behind her, from the doorway. Not much more than a foot shuffling on the hall carpet.

"Laurie, if that's you, it's okay. You can come in."

The girl slowly entered, looking guilty, sullen and wary.

"I heard you and my father talking down there."

"How long were you listening?"

"A while."

"I'm sorry about what you might have heard. We were hoping to keep this private."

"I'm not a kid." Laurie sat tentatively on the edge of her mother's bed, staring down at her hands in her lap.

"This has to be awful for you. Maybe you shouldn't subject yourself to all this."

"I hate her," Laurie said quietly.

"Your mom? This must just be shock talking."

"No. I hate her. I'm glad she's dead."

"Laurie, I don't think you really mean that. I guess you know how your mother died." The girl nodded. "Nobody should die that way."

"I don't care."

"You're angry right now."

"No kidding. You really are a detective."

"Can I ask you what she did to make you so angry?"

"She tried to run my life. She tried to ruin my life. She just wanted me to be as unhappy as she was. She wanted everybody to be as unhappy as her."

"Why do you think she was so unhappy?"

"I don't know. It's stupid. She's got everything. She could do whatever she wanted, go wherever she pleased, and she never wanted to do anything. She hated us all."

"And what did she do to you in particular?"

"She wouldn't let me grow up. She dictated my life, even what I ate. She ruined everything good that happened to me. If I liked it, it was bad."

"I don't understand when you say she wouldn't let you grow up. I get the impression she was proud of you, of the fact you were a good student and would be going to college…"

"That's what *she* wanted! I don't want to go to college! She suspected me of being a…a…just a really bad person. She thought my friends were evil."

"Evil. That's a heavy word. She disapproved of your friends?"

"She wanted me to hang out with the girls *she* liked at my school. Which is pathetic since she never had anything to do with the schools we go to anymore. She never came around or talked with the parents or the teachers anymore."

"You clearly didn't share your mother's opinion of the girls she did approve of."

Laurie almost spat. "They're a bunch of brown-nosers."

"Brown-nosers?"

"You know. Posers. Suck-ups. Ass kissers. They say all the right things to the adults. They have all the parents fooled that they're sweet, smart and lovable. Actually they're elitist bullies. They act totally different when the parents and teachers aren't around. I hate them. And they hate me. They make life miserable for everybody who doesn't fit into their little clique."

"And the kids you like to hang out with…?"

"My friends are nice people! They're not cool, they're not trendies. They're just good solid people. All she could see was that they were *different*. And a lot of them aren't on the academic track. They're not the *right* people."

"Do you have a boyfriend like that too? Was that an issue?"

"He's not really my boyfriend. He's a friend. A good friend. He's smart and sweet and honest. She hated him. All she could see was that he's not going to college. He wants to work on cars. What's wrong with that? She said he was nasty and a gangbanger. Like she'd even know what a gangbanger was like. She had some other names for him too. She thought he was 'taking advantage' of me and gave me this lecture about what 'that kind of boy' is like. As if she had any idea. Actually the guys she liked at my school are a lot *more* like that. All the socials are like that. They're disrespectful, entitled little fuckers. They treat girls terribly."

"Your boyf…your friend. What's his name?"

"Robbie. That's short for Roberto. Get the picture?"

Jilly sighed. She was getting it all too well.

"Laurie, did all of this have anything to do with Melinda getting fired?"

"Laurie! What are you doing here?" James had returned to the bedroom, still holding a cordless phone in his hand. Laurie jumped to her feet.

"I'm just leaving."

"Wait, Laurie," said Jilly, also rising to her feet. She pulled a business card out of the pocket of her blazer. "Here's my card, with both my numbers on it. Call any time if you'd like to just talk with someone, okay?"

Laurie hesitated but took the card, then turned on her heel and ran out of the room.

"What was all that about?" asked James. "Has she been listening? Did she hear us talking?"

"I think so. How much does she know about how her mother died?"

"I tried to spare her the details. Of course she's going to hear things. I can't totally protect her. But I didn't think she needed to know…"

"I understand. This is coming down on her awfully hard. You're going to have to be very patient with her. She's going to say a lot of things that might shock you, probably deliberately so."

"Yeah. I'm already getting that. When she's not giving me the silent treatment."

"Whether or not she shows it, she needs you very much right now. So does your son. Be there for them. If Laurie feels more comfortable talking to a woman, I'll be glad to sit down and listen. That's why I gave her my card."

She decided, being on her feet already, that it was time to end the visit. She had covered everything that she could for the moment. "Thank you for the time. We'll probably need to do a closer inspection of her things. I'll need you to close off this room. We may need to process some other areas as well. I'll be in touch shortly with more details."

"That's easy. I don't want to be in this house at all. Too many memories. I pretty much stay in the guest room—and the kitchen and living room. The kids stay in their rooms for the most part."

"Mr. Pidgeon, before I leave, one more question."

"Yes?"

"Did your wife ever use her family name, Carpenter?"

James gave Jilly a curious look. "Not really. She went by Jessica Pidgeon ever since we were married. Why?"

"So she wasn't in the habit of signing her name, say, Jessica Carpenter or Jessica Carpenter Pidgeon?"

"No. I never saw her do that."

"But Carpenter was her family name, wasn't it?"

"Yes. Why?"

"That's how she signed the letter she sent to Melinda."

"Maybe on some formal document somewhere she might have done that, if it required her full name, like on our bank accounts or tax forms. But I can't remember ever seeing her use that in a signature."

Jilly's phone buzzed. She excused herself and checked it. A text message from Dan: he was finished; should he meet her at the Pidgeon house? She texted back a quick yes, adding to meet her out front at the car. She turned back to James.

"Thank you for your time, and again I'm sorry I had to bother you. We might be back in touch as questions arise or we get new information. Please contact me or Detective Lee if you think of anything else that might help us."

"Of course. Oh…I got a call this morning. My wife will be available for burial in a day or two. I guess the autopsy is finished."

Jilly nodded. "Yes, it is."

"I can plan the service now. Her mother's flying in tomorrow."

"Are there other relatives?"

"Not really. Her mom's a widow. Jessy had no brothers or sisters, no cousins. Nobody she's been close with in years. She was even kind of sporadic with her mother. That was one reason she decided to send the kids to visit. She actually took them out of school for a week. She hoped it would bring them closer together."

He shook his head. "You're still looking at me, I'd guess."

"Sir? Looking at you?"

"Isn't that the way you express it? I've heard that the spouse is the number one suspect. I find it hard to believe I'd be an exception."

"Mr. Pidgeon, we're looking at everybody and everything right now. We're still trying to establish the facts, exactly what happened."

James shrugged slightly. "I wouldn't blame you. I have to admit, I don't look like the most loving partner in the world right now, do I? I'd probably be suspicious of me too."

"That's a very strange thing to say, sir."

James spread his hands in front of him. "I don't understand it. I loved Jessy. This…horrible *thing*…has happened to her. I still don't feel anything. I'm just numb." He looked with confusion at Jilly. "For a while now I was thinking that she was no longer the woman I knew and loved. Maybe in my heart I had mourned her loss already. I don't know."

Jilly wasn't sure how to reply.

"Detective," he went on. "I'm not capable of doing something like this. I can't even comprehend how someone could have done something like this. Or why."

She said her goodbyes and left him standing there in the living room.

FIVE

By the time Jilly headed down the walkway for the street, Dan was waiting by the car.

"How'd it go with Dory?"

"I don't know that she was all that helpful. She's kind of a ditz. But she mentioned Tamara Marsh at the country club. I recall the husband mentioned her as well. She might be of more help."

Jilly consulted her watch. "We've got time. We should drive over there."

"Sounds good," agreed Dan. "While we're here, why not also take a minute and ask the next door neighbors a question or two. Just in case anybody saw her or spoke with her recently."

"Good idea, partner. Which do you want, right or left?"

They both came up empty. There were neighbors at home on either side of the Pidgeon residence, but nobody in either house had even seen Jessica in several weeks, much less talked with her. It was as if a ghost had been residing there. It became evident to them that it would be futile to take up any more time further up and down the block.

"So much for that," sighed Dan as they returned to the car.

"Back to our plan," Jilly said resignedly. "The country club. And there's the matter of Jessica's therapist, in the city. Maybe she's not too far and it'll be worth taking a spin by."

She held up the car keys. "Okay, come on, it's your turn. You drive, I'll ride and we can trade notes."

Dan stood still. "I'd rather you drove, if it's all the same."

"Okay, look, enough of this. What is going on here, Dan?"

"What do you mean, what's going on?"

She rested her hands on her hips and glared in frustration. "As somebody else just reminded me: I'm a detective, remember? I kind of noticed you haven't wanted to drive in a few days now. You usually like to do the driving or go off on your own. That's what I mean. What is going on, already?"

Dan chewed his lip pensively. Jilly waited, partly annoyed and, despite herself, partly amused.

"This is embarrassing," he finally said.

"What? Come on. *What*?"

He spit it out like one of their perps confessing. "I let my driver's license expire."

It sunk in and then Jilly couldn't help herself. She exploded in laughter. She bent over, right there on the sidewalk, trying to contain herself. Dan looked on, red-faced, as she regained control, straightened up, wiping an eye. She was still smiling.

"You *what?*"

"I...let my driver's license expire. I can't drive. Not legally."

"Are you kidding?"

"We've just been so busy. It got by me. I mean, you can renew your car registration online, but you have to actually go into the Department of Motor Vehicles to renew your driver's license. I just sorta forgot."

"How long ago did it expire?"

"Over the weekend."

There were undoubtedly numerous members of their unit that wouldn't have been discouraged from driving by a mere formality like a lapsed license. She suspected one guy in particular, Detective Morrison by name, had been driving without a license for years now, based on his dubious driving skills. Dan, Jilly reflected, was one of those straight arrows who played it by the book. He would go to extraordinary lengths not to break the law. It was so like his squad rep that it was funny.

Jilly jiggled the car keys, trying to suppress her laughter. "Okay, so I guess I'm driving until you get to the DMV then."

"I made an appointment but the earliest I could get was tomorrow afternoon. I could have just walked in but I could end up waiting in line for hours and hours, and I don't have that kind of time. This case is just taking up so much. As it is, it's going to take me away for too long."

"Dan, I'll cover you. We have to get you back behind the wheel, partner, before you forget how to drive altogether."

She walked around to the driver's side and opened the door. "Now, do me a favor. Get on your phone GPS and navigate us to the Cypress Golf and Tennis Club, will you?"

She was still smiling and Dan was still blushing as they drove away from the curb.

"What's your feeling on the husband?" Dan asked.

Jilly shook her head. "He's a piece of work. Talk about self-absorbed. Pretty much withdrawn from the family. He and Jessica weren't getting along. And there is a girlfriend in the picture."

"Are you liking him for this?"

"Dubious. As I said, he's kind of wrapped up in himself, but he seems genuinely shaken. And he's got a possible alibi from Friday through Monday morning. But we've got to look at him, as he himself put it. I'll check with the company he says he was visiting in Portland, and with the airline. If that pans out, then he wasn't here when she was killed."

"If he was away, any possibility of an arrangement? Maybe he's the link to Marmaduke, a murder for hire?"

Jilly shook her head. "That seems a long shot. Marmaduke doesn't strike me as the kind of guy you'd hire to mow your lawn, much less pull off a clean murder."

"Yeah, but Pidgeon doesn't strike me as the kind of guy who'd have any connections with anybody more professional. Maybe a guy like Marmaduke would be the best he could do."

"Let's see how the rest of the facts fall."

"So we're back to Jessica," mused Dan. "Trying to figure out what she was doing that weekend and why. And then there's that whole business with the money and the letter. There's so much that's strange about that."

"It appears that nobody saw or spoke with her for the entire weekend before she died," Jilly said. "The kids, and let's assume the husband, were gone Friday. She didn't talk with any of her neighbors, not even her friend Dory. She had stopped seeing the therapist and she didn't tend to go out. None of the credit cards we recovered had been used over the weekend. It was like she was a hermit."

"Maybe this Tamara talked with her."

"Let's hope. I'm also thinking we should ask at the stores she frequented at that Farmington Plaza. Maybe she was there and somebody might remember her."

"It's not that far from the club. We can swing by it afterward."

"And Claire Orzabal might be of help. Jessica seems to have been troubled lately. She wasn't opening up to anybody around her."

Dan had his smart phone in hand and was accessing his internet connection. "I'll look her up and give her a call, find out how soon we can see her."

Jilly muttered half to herself, "And I really want to talk to Pidgeon's girlfriend, Natasha."

Dan looked up. "Natasha? Really? Sounds exotic."

"We've got to get some clue to Jessica's state of mind and where she might have gone. I don't think any of this case is going to make any sense until we do."

Dan had found a phone number and dialed it. He had a short conversation and tapped the connection off.

"Dr. Orzabal is right over the city line. She can see us later today, after her last patient. We've got about four hours."

"Let's make the best of it."

* * * *

They lucked out at the country club. The manager was quite cooperative and he said that the Marshes were present. Mr. Marsh was with a golf foursome and Mrs. Marsh could be found on the pool patio. He directed them out to poolside, which only had a few people scattered about, sitting at tables and talking.

They had little problem picking out Tamara Marsh instantly, sitting by herself at a table under a large umbrella. She was a bony, long-haired brunette with oversized sunglasses and a tall cocktail glass in front of her. She pulled down her sunglasses to gaze at them as they approached.

Jilly made the introductions and showed her ID.

"Oh my God," Tamara drawled. Her voice was deep and smoky and it was clear she was not on her first cocktail. "This is about Jessica, isn't it? It has to be about Jessica."

"Yes, I'm afraid so. May we sit down?"

Tamara waved a hand as if it didn't matter to her if they sat or stood.

They pulled out chairs. A waiter in black shirt and pants materialized, seemingly out of thin air, and asked if he could bring them anything. They both shook their heads and he vanished as magically as he had appeared.

"I heard the news only this morning," Tamara said. "It's so terrible. She was killed in a robbery or something like that?"

Her words and demeanor didn't match well. She spoke levelly without emotion, though with a discernible effort to form her words.

"That's what we're trying to figure out. We hoped you might be able to help us. When was the last time you spoke with Jessica?"

"Let's see. It was sometime last week. She came by the club a couple of times. Wednesday. A week ago today."

"And you haven't talked, on the phone perhaps, or had any word from her since last Wednesday?"

"We seldom talked on the phone. Mostly we got together here. Jessica liked to swim and sometimes to play tennis." She regarded Jilly through her dark lenses. "This is so terrible. Poor little Jess."

"What did you talk about the last time you saw her?"

"She was pretty flustered. She was trying to get her kids ready to go visit her mother, somewhere back east. She was f…rustrated."

Pronouncing the word presented some difficulty for her. She picked up her drink and took a long sip. "Now she had to get them ready herself since she had just fired her housekeeper. She said it was like trying to herd wild buffalo lately, her kids all unmanageable and now all this on top of everything else."

"What did she mean by 'everything else'?" Jilly asked.

"They're teenagers. She said they were one hundred percent attitude. I suppose you know her husband had been gone for a while. It was just her and the housekeeper against the world– well, the world according to Jess. And now the housekeeper was out of the picture."

"That would be Melinda Barstow we're talking about?"

Tamara nodded and took another long sip before putting the glass down on the table. She rolled the name out slowly. "Me-lin-da. Uh-huh. I don't know her last name. I was surprised she'd been fired. She was with Jess a long time; she sounded quite capable. Believe me, it's not easy to find a good housekeeper."

"I'm sure it's not. So the firing was rather abrupt?"

"Oh yes. It was the first I heard of any trouble with her."

"So…why did she say she had fired Melinda?"

"It seems she went behind Jess's back. She was conspiring with the daughter."

"Conspiring? Is that what she called it?"

"Her word precisely. Jess was…prone to dramatics." Tamara smiled impenetrably, her eyelids heavy. Jilly shot a look at her partner, who was watching Tamara with a strange expression of his own. "The daughter was running with some crowd she did not approve of. Seems there was a boyfriend, too. They were all putting ideas in her head, according to Jess."

"Ideas. Like what?"

Tamara shrugged. "To be honest, they sounded like pretty normal teenaged kids to me. Normal teenage is plenty scary enough. Do you have any kids, Detective?"

"No. Neither of us does."

"If you ask me, Jess was just scared by the prospect of her kids growing up. Becoming independent. Challenging her. Maybe experimenting with things. I remember my own teenage years. It wasn't *that* long ago."

She smiled more deeply. "Which reminds me. Damn, I wish they'd let us smoke out here!"

"Some specific incident seems to have precipitated the firing. Any idea what it might have been?"

"Jess said she had gone out and came back to find out the housekeeper had brought her daughter home from school." Now Tamara's voice turned dramatic as she warmed to the juicy portion of her tale. "Not only the daughter but also the forbidden boyfriend. They were up in the daughter's room! Apparently Jess had informed the housekeeper that she was going to be gone for a while."

"So she returns home unexpectedly to find Laurie, her daughter, up in her room with the boyfriend."

"And the housekeeper is downstairs in the kitchen, clearly aware of the situation, and acting as if nothing in the world was wrong!"

"Did Jessica find them, well, doing anything?"

Tamara laughed. "That was unclear. Jess was into such a rant by that stage of the story. My impression is, no, they were just sitting on the daughter's bed and talking. But he wasn't supposed to be in the house or anywhere near the daughter. And the housekeeper knew it."

Jilly traded a long look with Dan.

"Jess called it a total betrayal," Tamara continued, her smoky voice lapsing back into a kind of low crackle at the end of the sentence.

Recently, Jilly mused, social commentators had begun to call that a "vocal fry," that popular throaty affect that some seemed to find sensual but many were finding tedious. "She fired the gal on the spot, told her to get out and don't come back. It must have been some scene with the daughter as well. She described it as a screaming match after she chased the boyfriend out of the house."

Dan spoke up. "You seem to think she blew the whole thing out of proportion, though?"

Tamara turned to look at Dan for the first time since they sat down, as if she hadn't been aware of his being there. "He speaks!"

Dan actually flushed a little. Now she addressed them both. "She was doing a lot of that lately. Blowing things out of proportion. For all I know, her story was totally delusional. I was getting worried about her."

"How do you mean?"

"One of the things I've always loved about Jess is that we shared a kind of healthy cynicism, do you know? There were a few of us who hung out poolside here and dished while our husbands did whatever they did, played golf or worked. We loved to deconstruct everything and everybody. It was kind of good naughty fun.

"But lately it wasn't so much fun anymore. Jess had turned a dark corner. She complained all the time. I mean, her complaints were *different*. We weren't co-conspirators anymore. One by one, the rest of the gang dropped out, and I think it was because of her."

"Did Jessica talk about her husband much lately?" Dan asked.

"Just to complain. He was remote and distant, he didn't interact with the kids, he had stopped being close to her, yadda yadda yadda. And they fought about money."

"Money? Anything specific?"

"Her husband had started his own company, some kind of computer thing. She said for all the time he spent away from home, there was not much money to show for it. She began to figure he had a girlfriend, and that was where the time and the money were really going. That must have made for some hellacious arguments."

"Did she have any proof that there was another woman?"

Tamara had picked up her drink once again, and it sloshed as she made a gesture with both hands. "As I said, she was into drama. I don't know where the reality ended and the delusions began. All I know is the proportion of her delusions just kept growing."

* * * *

"You're pretty quiet," Jilly said as they pulled away from the country club's front drive. "What are your thoughts about all this?"

"I'm thinking she had a real bunch of winners in her life. Friends, family. My God."

Jilly nodded grimly. "I see your point."

"We've got time before Dr. Orzabal can see us. Want to spin over to the mall and see if anybody remembers her in the stores she frequented?"

"Sure. It's only about a mile away. She had credit cards to two stores over there. We can split up, show her picture. Maybe we'll get lucky and she did some shopping last weekend."

Almost two hours later, they had *not* gotten lucky.

Dan and Jilly had each taken one of the department stores to which Jessica seemed partial and questioned numerous sales people and managers. In each case two people remembered Jessica by face as a customer (and others quickly recognized her as the recently killed woman in the news) but nobody could remember having seen her in at least a week. She had apparently not been shopping at those stores the weekend she disappeared.

Their mutual disappointment was clear to each of them when they rendezvoused back in the parking lot.

They still had a few minutes so Jilly suggested the Esplanade market nearby. They had the same results: a couple of employees who recognized her, but nobody who recalled seeing her in the past week. Once again they returned to their car discouraged.

"Let's hope for something encouraging or insightful from Claire Orzabal," Jilly sighed as she started up the ignition. "Give me that address again, would you?"

* * * *

Dr. Claire Orzabal was a short, alert-looking woman with cropped dark hair and deep brown eyes behind stylish glasses. She was waiting for them in her reception room and introductions were made. She invited the detectives into her office, where she had already arranged chairs facing a sofa.

"Are you okay with our sitting here instead of around my desk?" she asked, with the slightest trace of an elusive accent. "This just seems more comfortable."

"This is fine, Doctor. Thanks for seeing us on short notice."

"Of course." They sat on the chairs and Orzabal took the sofa. "I was horrified by the news about Jessica. What a terrible thing. Do you know what happened exactly?"

"We were hoping you might help us figure out some of that," said Dan.

Orzabal nodded gravely. "I've considered ethical responsibilities here in terms of patient confidentiality and even sought advice from a couple of my colleagues. There are details I prefer not to divulge if they affect others, but in general, I'm comfortable having this conversation. Jessica is no longer alive, and I also want to see justice done for her."

"Forgive me if I take notes," Dan continued, his notebook already in hand. Orzabal nodded. "How long ago were you seeing her, and for how long?"

"She first started meeting with me a little less than two years ago. We had fairly regular sessions for about six months."

"How often would you meet in that time?"

"We started once a week, then twice a week. For the last couple of months, she had again dropped back to once a week."

Jilly picked up the questioning. "Why was she seeing you, Doctor? What was the problem?"

Orzabal smiled. "That's a complicated question, Detective Garvey. I suppose the easiest way to express it to you is that she was profoundly unhappy. We were trying to get to the root of that."

"She had seen a therapist before you, I understand."

"Yes, a colleague of mine, a very capable man. He in fact referred her to me. She told me she didn't feel comfortable talking with a man, and that she preferred to speak with another woman. That's not unusual."

"Was this…profound unhappiness…something that had just come upon her relatively recently?"

"According to her, yes. She said that she increasingly felt that life had become overwhelming and uncontrollable. She often used that expression— that she felt out of control. She thought people were abandoning her. She felt unloved and unappreciated."

"Were your sessions helping, do you think?"

Orzabal heaved a heavy sigh. "My feeling was that Jessica suffered from severe chronic depression. I felt she needed more. I suggested medication, as well as proceeding with more intensive cognitive therapy."

"Cognitive," interjected Dan, "meaning talking it out, digging up the root causes?"

"An interesting way to put it. Yes, more or less."

"Did she agree to go on the medication?" Jilly asked.

"Not at first. She said she didn't think there was anything 'wrong' with her, that she mostly had to learn how to cope with everybody else, that they were the cause of her problems. That's not an unusual place to begin."

"It sounds as if she resisted the cognitive therapy as well," observed Dan.

"It takes time. She and I got off to a pretty good start. I think she genuinely liked me. More importantly, she began to trust me. Gradually she began to open up in our sessions. That's when we expanded to twice weekly."

"But did she ever agree to medication?" Jilly asked again.

"She finally decided to try something and we began with an antidepressant. After a week she said it made her feel funny and she wanted to stop. We tried a different one, with the same results. You need to take such medication on a protracted basis to begin to see any benefit, but Jessica did not like drugs. She didn't even like taking aspirin or OTC painkillers."

"Do you think you were making any headway?"

"Given more time, we would have. It's a slow process. Medication, in my opinion, would have helped."

"Then she cut back her visits and ultimately stopped coming?"

"Yes. That was her choice. She said she decided that this was not the answer." Orzabal looked deeply saddened.

"Do you think you could have turned her around if she had kept coming?" Dan asked.

"It wouldn't have been me; it would have been she, who might have turned *herself* around. With time, I thought she could have."

"But you definitely think she needed some kind of medication?"

"Detective, clinical depression is a real, almost tangible thing. It can be horribly debilitating, even paralyzing, in a psychological sense. It can spring from physical causes, like a chemical imbalance. I honestly think that was the nature of Jessica's problem. She needed treatment."

"Were you considering hospitalizing her?"

"No. That would have been a last resort. But I honestly believed there was something physically wrong with her. I urged her to visit her regular medical doctor and get a full physical. She would not do that either."

Orzabal stared intently first at Dan and then at Jilly. "If she could have just been more open to the process. At heart she was a lovely woman, well-meaning, wanting to love her family and friends and to be loved by them. But she had hit a major roadblock, you might say. She was incapable of trusting or sharing with them. As she gradually withdrew from what support system she had left, it became a vicious circle: they grew impatient with her own behavior and withdrew from her. She felt terribly isolated. To be so alone, it's very painful on a deep level."

"It must have been hard not only on her but on those around her," Jilly observed.

"Undoubtedly."

"Did you ever have the chance to talk to her friends, her husband, her children?"

"No. I suggested that perhaps it might do some good if her family members also began to see somebody. Not me, but someone else. She said absolutely not, they would never agree to that. Clearly she was the one against it."

Jilly nodded. "Did she ever talk about her husband, perhaps that she suspected him of infidelity?"

"We talked about that, yes. She increasingly believed that. I honestly don't know whether he was unfaithful, but what I stressed to her was to examine her feelings rationally and deal with them realistically. I tried to steer her out of constantly restating a problem and into working out a solution. We got nowhere."

"I understand he was devoting most of his time to work, his startup company."

"What registered with her was that he spent the great majority of his time away from her. For someone who already felt marginalized and insulated, that was particularly difficult."

"What about her children?"

"She often expressed frustration with their unwillingness to communicate with her or to show appreciation to her. The word she used most often was ungrateful." She shrugged. "They're teenagers. A most difficult phase of childhood under the best of circumstances."

"Do you think she was being unrealistic in her assessments of her kids and her husband?"

"I honestly don't know. That was one of the things we were exploring. I'm afraid we weren't getting anywhere yet."

"And the last time you saw her was about a year ago?"

"Yes, actually about fifteen months ago."

Jilly sat back and shook her head. "Doctor, I have to tell you, Jessica is a total mystery to us. We need something, anything, to help us reconstruct the hours and days prior to her death. In the time you saw her, was there ever anything she said or did that might give us some clue as to her actions of the past weekend? Any idea where she might have gone, who she might have seen, what she might have done?"

"My best guess," the therapist replied slowly, looking back and forth at them both, "is that she was likely by herself. In the time I saw her regularly, she was already steadily losing trust in everybody around her. She needed help, Detectives—if not from me, then somebody—and barring that, it would only get worse with time."

* * * *

"So we've got a troubled woman in isolation mode who doesn't seem to have been anywhere or talked to anyone after last Friday," Jilly said, exhaling with exasperation. They were back in the car, pulling out of the parking lot beneath Orzabal's building.

"We've got so many things we need to cover," said Dan. "I feel bad I've made this more difficult that we can't split up."

"Just keep your appointment, partner, and problem solved."

"You know what the DMV is like. Even with an appointment, I might still have to wait."

"At least you can still renew. If you had put it off for 90 days, you would have had to start all over as if you needed a new license."

"Yeah," Dan said. "There's that. I just feel so stupid."

"You're not stupid, Dan. It just got by you."

"Is this what it's like when you get older? Letting stuff get away?"

"You're asking me that because I'm so old?"

"Oh no no *no*. Sorry, Jilly. I'm really off my game today, aren't I?"

"Just keep the appointment tomorrow, will you? And listen, do me a favor, look up another number for us and let's make one more stop before we call it a day?"

"Sure. Who?"

"Natasha Hedgefield. The girl friend."

* * * *

She wasn't surprised to have them show up at her front door. She took one look at their proffered IDs and simply said, "James said you'd be coming. Come on in," and opened the door to her small but airy condo.

Any expectations of James Pidgeon's "other woman" as a femme fatale would have met with utter disappointment. Natasha Hedgefield was a straightforward, no-nonsense type. In an earlier time she would have been considered the "girl next door," of the nerdier variety, with straight shoulder-length brown hair, black-rimmed glasses, and a plain dark pullover and skirt. She seemed genuinely shocked by the death of Jessica Pidgeon and quite willing to speak with the detectives.

Once more today, Jilly and Dan sat in still another parlor asking their questions. Natasha was not chatty; she spoke keenly and precisely, answering their questions directly.

"We understand you work for Mr. Pidgeon, is that correct?" began Jilly.

"Yes, I'm head of software development for JRX. I've been with the company since its inception."

Jilly watched her evenly. "And you and Mr. Pidgeon are currently in a relationship? Outside of the workplace, that is?"

Natasha folded her arms and returned the even stare. "Yes we are."

"How long ago did it begin?"

"We started seeing each other socially maybe four or five months ago. He needed someone to talk to, first during work then we'd have drinks or dinner. That sounds more romantic than it was. Mostly it was takeout at the office while we worked or a quick bite late at night. After a few weeks, we became closer. That was after he moved out of his house into an apartment here in the city."

"So you two did not become intimately involved," Dan said, "until after he had moved out of his house?"

Natasha nodded. "It just sort of happened. He's been having a terrible time at home for a while now. Between that and the stresses of trying to get JRX off the ground, it's been tearing him up. Do you have any idea what it takes to establish a tech startup, even with a large dedicated team, which we do *not* have? We're talking seventy, eighty hours a week. And there was his intolerable family situation on top of that. I just happened to be the one person there for him. And, well…things happened."

"Can we talk about his 'family situation'?" Jilly asked.

"I didn't want to come between him and his wife," Natasha said firmly, still staring at Jilly. "For a long time he seemed to genuinely care about her. He was trying to find some way to make things work. It wasn't until I was convinced that was over that I allowed myself to…well, to become involved with James."

Magnanimous of you, Jilly thought but didn't say. "What exactly was happening?"

"She was just getting stranger and stranger. She began accusing him of all sorts of things. And then there were the kids. They were constantly fighting with him."

"They're teenagers. It's not unusual for them to be difficult."

"Yes, well. I don't know about that. I know nothing about kids and I don't really want to. I just know James found them frustrating. Nobody was getting along in that house. The kids, the wife, James, they were all at odds with one another. What a zoo. He would leave one pressure cooker and go to another."

"We understand she was being treated, possibly for depression."

Natasha pursed her lips. "It didn't sound to me like she was being *treated*. She was just a neurotic, unpleasant bitch."

"You said she was making accusations," interjected Dan. "What kind of accusations?"

"Everything and anything. She didn't think he was bringing home enough money so she decided he must be spending it somewhere else. It was a startup! The money takes time. She never understood that. All she remembered was his salary from when he worked for a big safe tech company. She always complained about the bills and the expenses, but they had a nice house, nice cars, and good schools for the kids. He was paying the bills and keeping everything going. I think she was accustomed to spending a lot on herself and no longer had it. Then she complained he wasn't home enough, that he wasn't spending time with her or the kids. And then she got it in her head that the reason for all that was that James was seeing another woman. Maybe several women. I think it grew into an elaborate fantasy. She had no idea what it took to create a new company, to make it a success. There was no money and there was no time. "

Dan and Jilly silently exchanged knowing looks. "Did you ever meet her?" Jilly asked.

"Once or twice, casually. We never really talked much. Anyway, my point is, she drove him out. Her and those kids."

"And," Jilly said pointedly, "as the cliché goes, right into your arms?"

Natasha's eyes blazed angrily. "Look, I'm trying to help you here.

Whatever happened to her was terrible and I'm sorry for her. But James had nothing to do with this. He cared for her. He tried his best, and in the end he had to get out. Once the company got sold to Ubertech, he would have made a lot of money and could have divorced the bitch and financially taken care of her. He had no reason to do anything to get rid of her because he was already gone. The reason he wound up with me was, yes, because she pushed him away. She was sick."

"Yes," sighed Jilly. "She was."

She was a woman who needed help desperately. And there was none to be had.

* * * *

"You've been quiet," Jilly said to Dan as they drove back to the station.

"We've seen lots worse. Why does this one bother me so much?"

"I know what you mean. Quite a lineup of winners in Jessica's life, wasn't there?"

"The husband's a piece of work," mused Dan. "But I just don't see him as the killer."

"His girlfriend made a good point. He had escaped. With the upcoming buyout he could have paid Jessica off and been free. It made no sense to kill her."

"And especially not in that way. That was a brutal crime of passion and he's pretty passive."

"There was a lot of hate in that," Jilly agreed. "Maybe there's a side to him we haven't seen past that passivity."

"I'm going by what you've taught me, Jilly, to trust my gut. We can't stop considering him but we need to cast a wider net."

"I taught you that? I guess I'm pretty good after all."

"Never for a moment ever doubted that," Dan said, forcing a small smile in spite of himself.

SIX

Sometimes luck just happens. It might be good or bad or it might turn out to be totally different from what it first seems…

* * * *

The two teenagers skulking on the side street in the dark couldn't have felt too lucky. It was a slow night on one of their usual opportunistic swings around the neighborhood.

Generally, four in the morning in the middle of the week was prime time for enterprising thievery. Most residents had long since gone to bed and wouldn't be waking up to get ready for work for some time yet. Auto alarms had for the most part been abandoned here, since they were seen as nothing more than annoyances; nobody ever actually responded to them. It was remarkable how many car doors were left unlocked and windows partly opened. Quick silent swoops usually yielded easy swag to be resold, but tonight there were no open doors or windows.

Refusing to go home empty-handed, they had begun carefully peeking into dark houses and garages and had found a crack in a painted-over alley window on a dilapidated old stucco garage set back off the street, far from the closest street light. It had been easy to push the glass in to make a large enough space for one of them to crawl through. The shards of glass fell almost silently inside, apparently falling onto piles of cloth or newspaper.

"You go in, Littleboy," muttered the taller one, looking furtively back to the street. "You fit better." The smaller kid squeezed through the pane into the shadows of the garage.

"Dark in here," he whispered. "Can't see nothin'."

The tall teen pulled a cheap plastic butane lighter out of the pocket of his hoodie and passed it through the window pane. "Here. See if there's anything you can just hand out." He cast another nervous look out at the street. "Hurry!"

"Give me a second…" came the voice from inside the darkened space. There were several flicking sounds of the flint. Then there was a spark of light.

And then there was a sudden brighter flash.

"Oh shit!" shouted the kid from inside, and instantly his head stuck through the window pane, a panicked expression on his face. Flames flickered behind him. He frantically tried to jam himself back through the window. All of a sudden it felt a quarter of the size it had been when he entered. The bigger guy was already in motion, running back to the street.

"Hey! Don't leave me here, Freddie! Help me!" He struggled to break through the window, cracking more glass panes and splintering wooden strips in the process. It took him a long time, his own panic making it all the harder to extract himself. In his mind a horrific inferno had erupted in the garage, although in reality only a small pile of old newspapers had caught fire. He finally popped himself free, landing on the ground outside the garage. He was bolting down the alley just as the first fire engine had turned down the street, sirens blazing.

Somebody must have called in the alarm almost immediately.

Damn the luck, he thought. Sometimes you'd wait forever for cops or firemen. This would be the time that they'd be right on the scene. How did they get there so *fast?* Everything was just bad luck tonight. He ran as hard as he could, panting and gasping.

Firemen were soon breaking open the garage's shoddy door and were able to extinguish the fire before it could have spread and engulfed the old building. Uniformed police were already arriving on the scene.

One of the unis stopped to talk to one of the firemen in front of the still smoldering garage.

"That's a weird one."

"Yeah. Must have been somebody trying to break in through that window. They touched off a stack of newspapers right underneath it. Good thing we just happened to be a couple blocks away."

The police officer pointed at the car sitting inside the garage, a bit scorched but reasonably unscathed by the fire.

"That's a pretty nice car for this kind of garage, don't you think?"

"I'll tell you," said the fireman, "if I owned a late model Audi like that, I sure as hell wouldn't be keeping it in a garbage can like this."

The officer nodded, pressing a button on her shoulder microphone as she noted the plate number. "There's only one reason I can think of for someone to put a car like that in a building like this."

* * * *

Dan and Jilly both hung up their phones almost simultaneously and looked at one another across the aisle between their desks. Thursday morning was already in full gear.

"You first," said Dan.

"There are no available techs to check Jessica's room and computer for at least another twenty-four hours. But I finally spoke with Wilhelm Gauss of Ubertech in Portland and with the airline. It would seem that James Pidgeon is covered for Sunday and he was on the flight returning here Monday morning."

She looked expectantly at Dan.

"The only good news I've got is that you won't have to do all the driving after I renew my license this afternoon. Everything else was a bust. I was on the phone with several people from Laurie's school before I could finally get hold of a guidance counselor who would even talk to me."

"And?"

"Pure stonewall. She said we'd need the permission of the parents to talk with any of Laurie's friends. Wouldn't give me any contact info. The best I could do was to get her to contact the boyfriend's parents and have them contact us."

"Roberto, you mean?"

"Yep. I'm thinking we're going to have to go down there and be a little more insistent."

Jilly folded her arms in frustration and leaned back, biting her lip. "Any minute now, Castillo's going to be coming out of his office reminding us about the pressure coming down. We have to find something."

"We've still got Marmaduke."

"And he's not good for this until we can establish motive and opportunity. We can't even place Jessica anywhere up until the moment her body was placed in that receptacle. If we can't put them together in a believable manner, any half decent lawyer is going to have an easy time walking him."

It was a technique that Dan had learned from Jilly: go over everything still one more time and hope to see something new. He idly played with his pen as he narrated the scenario again.

"Jessica Pidgeon never leaves her house. She's experiencing severe depression and maybe some paranoia. Maybe she's close to a breakdown. All of a sudden late on a Sunday night, she has a burst of activity. She leaves the house, goes somewhere else where she writes a strange letter on someone else's computer, admits to drug use that nobody else finds believable, signs it in a strange way, drives to an unfamiliar ATM out of her comfort zone, withdraws the maximum amount, puts the money and letter in an envelope that she's already prepared and addressed to Melinda, and drops it into a strange post office box."

"It only makes sense if she was being coerced?" said Jilly. "That she was hoping to subtly tell us something?"

"It's all that makes sense to me at this point."

"I don't see Marmaduke being a part of that."

"No. Maybe the letter, and the robbery and murder, are two separate incidents. Maybe someone convinced her to send the money and left, she went off to do it, and then Marmaduke caught up with her."

"Or maybe Marmaduke has nothing to do with it. Maybe he really did just happen upon her wallet after she was killed."

Dan nodded thoughtfully, still staring at his pen. "We have to keep him in the picture because of the physical evidence, but yeah, it's problematic that he's our guy."

"A lot of maybes," Jilly said. "We need a 'for-sure' of some kind."

Dan's phone began to ring. "Hold on a minute, Jilly." He picked up the receiver. "Detective Lee."

"It's Sandy Kovetsky, Dan. Do you believe in pure dumb luck?"

Dan shot a sideways look at Jilly. "Officer Kovetsky. I'm not sure. Why?"

"I'm about to show you proof it exists. We found your victim's Audi early this morning."

"What? Are you sure?"

"Gray A4, two years old. I ran the plate. Registered to Jessica Pidgeon in Farmington."

"Where? Where was it?" Dan had grabbed a pad and was energetically jotting notes. Jilly, noting his excitement, rose from her desk and joined him.

"Locked up in a moldy old garage on Warwick Street, a neighborhood over from Sheffield. Looks like some kids broke into it and set it on fire. My partner and I were nearby and arrived just after the fire engines. They put out the fire pretty quickly so it didn't have a chance to spread too far. The car got a little singed but it's otherwise okay. The arson investigators are there and SID is on its way now."

"Did you look the car over?"

"Not in detail. There's all kinds of stuff scattered around on the front seat and floor. Some jewelry. What looks like some sort of narcotics, I'd say oxy."

"Whose garage is it?"

"We're not sure yet. There's an adjoining house but it seems deserted. Nobody answered the door and it looks like nobody's been in there in a long time now."

"We'll be right over."

"Sadly, I won't be there. It's been some night. I'm heading home. Good luck."

"What's the address?" He noted it down, said a few more words then told her they were on the way over. Jilly was already hanging over his desk, eager to hear what was happening. Dan told her.

Castillo was just stepping out of his office as they rushed by, almost colliding with him.

"I was about to ask you for an update," the Lieutenant said.

"We got a break, Lou," said Dan, not bothering to stop or even slow down. "They found her car. We're heading there now."

"Fill me in when you get back!" Castillo yelled after them as they headed for the stairwell. He wasn't sure whether they heard him or not.

* * * *

The uniforms on the scene confirmed that the house next to the garage was unoccupied. Somehow the SID and arson investigation teams had each managed to mark out their own turf and stay out of each other's way. Counting Dan and Jilly, there were now nine people in the small garage but they had avoided the potential for chaos and were working in tentative harmony. There seemed a clear demarcation of territories arrived at either tacitly or explicitly; the arson people stayed to their side of the garage while the SID people concentrated on the scorched car and the remainder of the garage.

The head of the SID team was a man named Smithers, whose youthful appearance belied his experience. The detectives knew him well. He had greeted them upon their arrival and apprised them of the situation.

He pointed to the Audi, filling up much of the small garage.

"The car was unlocked, front windows down. The garage door was locked; whoever put the car in here must have had a key. There were no signs of anything being forced."

He indicated the front seat of the car where a jumpsuited tech was snapping photos. "We're almost done and then you can have it. Nothing in the trunk but the jack and the spare in the well. We found a baseball glove in the back seat, but otherwise nothing else there. There are blood stains on the rear seats. Possible signs of a struggle or violence. There was quite a bit of material in the front, scattered around the floor mat on the passenger side. We'll bag it and take it as soon as you've had a chance to look it all over."

"Thanks," said Jilly. She and Dan were already pulling on new pairs of gloves.

Dan picked up the items one by one, carefully looked them over and handed them to Jilly, who handled them just as gingerly. A plain gold necklace with a simple oval pendant holding a single blue stone. A simple gold ring set with three tiny blue stones. Two long golden earrings in a broad teardrop shape. The wire hooks at the end of them were blotched with brownish stains.

"We found what appears to be flesh residue in the earrings," Smithers said, watching them. "We took the samples. We'll also run the dried blood on the hooks."

Jessica's earrings, apparently ripped from her pierced ears...

Dan held up an orange plastic prescription container. He shook it gently. He opened the top and looked inside.

"Oxycodone is my guess. Six tablets. No label." He handed it to her. She peered at the pastel-colored tablets.

Jessica didn't use any drugs. She hated medication in general...

A cheap plastic felt tip pen. Dan pulled off the cap. Navy blue.

Blue ink stains on Jessica's fingers. Her name signed on the letter in dark blue ink.

The baseball glove in the back seat was a fairly new, expensive fielder's model that smelled of oiled leather. BRAD PIDGEON had been neatly inscribed in capitals with marker along the back of one of the fingers.

As the tech had said, there was nothing else in the rear.

Jilly's eyes wandered across the garage. Under normal circumstances it would have been a dark place—there were only two painted-over windows, now broken, along the alley side—but the investigators had set up bright lighting stanchions in the corners. The space was now intensively bright and details stood out to her.

There was a small cluttered workbench in the back corner, covered with tools, car parts and crushed empty beer cans. Similar items littered the ground nearby: cans of oil, more tools, screws and nails, cardboard boxes of different sizes. More beer bottles and cans. Scattered piles of magazines and papers. A small old refrigerator sat underneath the workbench.

The entire garage looked as if it hadn't been occupied or used in some time. There were cobwebs and a coat of dust everywhere.

Not quite everywhere.

She walked to the corner and reached down for the one gleaming item, jammed into the corner debris, that did not seem to be covered in dust or grime. She carefully lifted it up with thumb and forefinger.

"What do you make of this?" she called out. Dan and Smithers both turned to look at her.

It was a bright silver aluminum baseball bat, the kind that high school and middle school teams might use.

Gingerly holding the knob at the end of the handle, she rotated it, making it glint in the bright lights. The darker spots near the top of the barrel were perfectly visible.

"I think we've found our murder weapon," she said.

* * * *

Dan punched off the connection on his cellphone as they headed back to the station.

"The entire block is rental property, all owned by an out-of-state company and maintained by a local property management agency. I'm just getting voicemail at the main office." The impatience was evident in his voice. "We can probably do this just as fast online when we get back."

"We're still a huge step up. She was murdered either in or near her car before she was dumped. And the pen…it wasn't a random robbery. Someone made her sign those letters, and that means they also made her take out the money. This directly involves Melinda."

"Clearly…but some things don't add up if that's true. She doesn't seem capable of that kind of murder. Just on the basis of not being strong enough or vicious enough."

"But she was desperate," Jill pointed out. "She could have gotten someone else to do it for her."

"Or," suggested Dan, "someone took it upon themselves to act on her behalf. Or what they saw as being on her behalf."

"The stuff in the car. Her jewelry. The narcotics. By everybody's account she didn't use any kind of drugs. Her wallet was taken but not her jewelry. Why were those in the car?"

"Hopefully we can get the fingerprinting on those things expedited."

* * * *

Dan seemed to be having a somewhat frustrating telephone conversation with the management firm. Jilly saw him fidgeting at his desk and jotting notes as he spoke. Her own desk phone rang.

"This is Mallory at the front desk. There's a kid here to see you, one of your victim's kids."

Laurie?

"Send her up."

"It's not a her. He's on his way."

She hung up and shouted, "Dan!"

Jilly was waiting when the elevator doors opened.

"You must be Brad, right?"

He was short and looked younger than his age, wearing a hooded sweatshirt, an unruly mop of brown hair, and a nervous expression. He shrugged. "You're the detective?"

"I'm Jill Garvey. Come on in."

She led him down a hall to an interview room, sterile and uninviting but quieter than the bustling squad room. Dan was already seated, waiting.

"Have a seat. This is my partner, Dan Lee. Do you want something, a Coke maybe?"

The boy shook his head, looking apprehensively around the room.

"Hi, Brad," said Dan, trying to manage a smile. "Is it okay if we call you Brad? Do you have a nickname or…?"

"No, that's fine."

"How did you get here? Shouldn't you be at school?"

"School's not important right now. The bus from Farmington is easy. One transfer and I'm a block away from here."

"The bus goes through some kind of sketchy areas. Even in the daytime, isn't it kind of scary?"

"I can take care of myself."

Jilly smiled to herself. Young teens. They're oblivious to the world around them. There was a rock song with the line: immortal for a limited time. After what had happened to his mother, she would have thought he'd be terrified to go out into the dangerous world.

"Why did you come here, Brad? Why didn't you just call us?"

Brad shrugged. "I found your card in my sister's room. I didn't want to go to school today so I decided to come here instead."

"Why?"

The boy stared down at his hands on the table for a long time. "It's not right. It's just not right."

"You mean, what happened to your mom? No. It's not."

"Not just that," he muttered quietly. "Nobody cares what happened."

"We care," said Dan.

"I mean, *they* don't. It's like nothing ever happened. They won't talk about it. They pretend like everything is okay." He looked up at Jilly. He looked as if he was trying not to cry. "Nothing's okay. Nothing."

"Brad, are you willing to talk about it? Is there anything you can tell us that might help us?" said Jilly.

"My mom got really strange lately. Something was wrong. She was scared."

"Scared of what?"

"It's not like there was something to be scared of. She started making things up. She thought we were turning against her. She wouldn't talk *to* us. All she would do was yell *at* us, then she'd go somewhere to be alone and not talk at all, for hours, sometimes."

"I think your mother might have been…well, she might have been sick."

Brad nodded, looking down at the table again. He spoke quietly. They had to lean in to listen. "Two kids in my school killed themselves in the last year. The teachers said they were depressed."

"That's awful. I'm sorry. Did you know them well?"

"One of them, yeah. She was a friend of mine. The other one, not really. They both kept to themselves a lot, didn't talk to people."

Jilly saw the connection, why Brad was bringing this up.

"They spent a lot of time talking to us in the classrooms and in the assemblies afterward. They said things like, we should ask for help if we're unhappy. That we should look for signs in our friends, tell someone."

"Good advice," said Dan.

"But the problem is, if someone's depressed, it's not like they want to ask for help, you know? It seems like they just want to somehow make themselves a real pain in the ass—sorry—to drive their friends further away. I don't think many people would have wanted to help the kids in my school, even if they knew. Not too many kids liked them."

Jilly thought to herself: *my God, this kid has more insight than most adults I know.*

"I think that's what happened with my Mom. She drove everybody away. She didn't see anybody as…someone who could help, you know? Everybody was just…someone trying to make it harder for her."

"So none of you were getting along with her. She was isolating." Jilly was getting tired of that word.

Brad nodded and wiped an eye.

"What happened with Melinda and your mom, Brad? Were you there when they argued?"

He nodded again. "It was after school. My mom was out and Melinda had driven us home. Laurie's friend Robbie came back with her. They had a project they were working on together."

"Robbie is Laurie's boyfriend, right?"

"No, not exactly. They're just good friends. I mean, I don't think they're like boyfriend and girlfriend. Laurie doesn't really have any regular boyfriends. But my Mom thought he was."

"I understand she didn't approve of Robbie hanging out with Laurie."

"No, she hated him. I don't know why. He's a really nice guy. He's really smart in certain ways, like he knows how stuff works and how things are put together, you know? He has trouble in school. He wants to be a mechanic like his dad. But he's got to pass his academics and he doesn't do real well in them. He wanted to quit school and go work in a garage. Laurie was trying to get him to finish school. She was tutoring him. Secretly."

"Why secretly?"

"Because he was ashamed, and because my Mom didn't want her to see him. They had a math test coming up and it was really important and Robbie was worried he wasn't going to pass it, so he had come home with her so she could help him study. Laurie's really good at math. She helps me all the time. But she had to sneak him in while my Mom wasn't home."

"And Melinda knew."

"Yeah. She liked Robbie and was trying to get him to finish school, too. She felt school was really important. She understood what was really going on. So when Laurie asked if Robbie could get a lift home with us, Melinda said sure, even though she knew how Mom felt. She wanted to do the right thing."

"And your mother came home unexpectedly?"

Robbie nodded again, head still down.

"She was in a terrible mood. I'd seen her bad but this was the worst. They—I mean Laurie and Robbie—were in Laurie's room. She, I mean my Mom, went nuts. Started screaming and raving. It was the worst fit she ever threw. She started saying all sorts of totally crazy stuff about what Laurie and Robbie were doing behind her back. She accused them of skipping school and coming back to spend the day in Laurie's room to have sex. She yelled at Robbie and chased him out of the house. Then she turned on Melinda. She called her a conspirator, helping Laurie sneak around behind her back. She worked out this whole crazy plot in her head as she went along, that maybe they hadn't even gone to school that day and Melinda had driven them right back to our house after my Mom had gone out. It was nuts. Melinda was trying to talk sense to her, but my Mom just told her she was fired, to get out right then. She took out a bunch of money and threw it at her."

"Where were you while all this was happening?"

"I was in the living room, texting on my phone, just trying to be somewhere else. I felt awful and stayed quiet. I hunkered down into the cushions. I don't know if she even noticed I was there."

"And Laurie?"

"Laurie went crazy, called my Mom a delusional fucking maniac—I'm sorry, that's what she said—and ran up to her room. She was crying and hollering."

"So your mother ordered Melinda out of the house and told her not to come back?"

"Uh-huh. Melinda tried to reason with my Mom but it was impossible. She got really angry herself, picked up her things and walked out. She drove home and never came back."

"Did you like Melinda?"

Now several tears rolled along Brad's nose and cheeks. He stammered slightly. "She was the last sane one in the house. She was our last friend. Especially for Laurie."

"What about your dad?"

Brad shook his head sharply. "She drove him away a long time ago. He hasn't been there for us in a long time."

The detectives sat in silence for some time.

"What was your mother like after that, Brad?" Dan finally asked.

"It's like she wasn't there. She was like a zombie in one of those movies, the walking dead. She almost never went out, she hardly ever spoke to us. We pretty much got ourselves up and ready for school. She would drive us to school, or me to baseball practice, or Laurie to study groups, but she wouldn't say a word. She was like a robot behind the wheel. I don't know if Laurie and my Mom ever spoke again."

"And then you went to your grandmother's a few days later."

Brad nodded.

And never saw your mother again, Jilly thought to herself.

SEVEN

"You don't need to drive me to the DMV," Dan continued to protest as they crossed the parking lot to the car. "It's not that far. The bus is easy enough."

"Just like Brad said, huh? The bus is easy. This is easier. Come on, get in." Jill hit the remote and the *click* of the car door locks resounded. As they opened the doors, she paused.

"What?" asked Dan, looking at her across the top of the car.

"The bus is easy," she repeated.

"Yeah. And…?"

"Jessica didn't drive to somewhere in the city and get stopped by anybody. Somebody came to her house and made her drive them away."

Dan nodded, digesting that for a few moments. "Okay. Yeah."

"She was saying and doing a lot of regrettable things. There were a lot of people who weren't very happy with her."

"The husband. The daughter. The boyfriend. The housekeeper. And so on."

"The husband was gone, and so were the kids. I don't think it was the boyfriend, or whatever you want to call him."

"Where are you taking this?"

"The pen in the car. Someone had brought those letters, already prepared, and forced Jessica to sign them, to withdraw the money—that was the maximum she could get from her ATM at one time—to be sent to Melinda."

"So…back to Melinda?"

Jilly bit her lip, following her train of thought. "Not Melinda. She's not right for it. Plus…she's got a car. She could have driven over. I think whoever took Jessica came by the bus. I know this is all a jump but I have a feeling."

"And your gut is telling you not Melinda."

"No. Someone who knows Melinda. Someone who cared a *lot* about her getting fired."

"If she's out of work, the daughter doesn't get to go to college," Dan said, picking up the chain of thought. "Or thinks she doesn't. But we saw the daughter. Olivia, right? She's kind of an aesthetic figure. I can't see her committing that kind of violence."

"No. But she could have friends. She *must* have friends."

"So…somebody we haven't encountered yet?"

They got into the car and closed the doors. As Jilly started up the engine she said, "I need to go have another talk with Melinda while you get your paperwork done."

* * * *

Dan only had to stand in the DEPARTMENT OF MOTOR VEHICLES—VISITORS WITH APPOINTMENTS line for twelve minutes, which he figured was doing relatively well. An extremely bored elderly woman gazed blankly at him through smeared bifocals.

"I have an appointment to renew my license," Dan said, holding up his printed form.

"Well, aren't you special, honey," she said in a voice that would cut crystal. She took the form from him, scribbled something upon it, stamped it, and handed it back to him. "Window 16."

He looked in the direction she was pointing and saw another line of six or seven people. She was already rasping out "*Next!*" so he shrugged and moved on.

As he stepped to the back of the line at Window 16, his cell phone rang. He checked the readout: it showed an out-of-town area code, 832.

"This is Detective Lee."

"You're the detective, right?" The voice was unfamiliar: deep, thick-tongued. Perhaps the guy had been drinking a bit.

"This is Detective Lee. Who's this?"

"My name is Tyrone Watney. The rental guy said you wanted to talk with me."

The caller now had all of Dan's attention. For a moment, the line and the DMV did not exist. "You're the lessee of the house and garage on Warwick Street?"

"Lessee means I rent it? That's me. I haven't been there in about four months though."

"What do you mean?"

"I been in the Houston area. Started out as a road trip, you know? Then I had an accident and my car broke down and I was in the hospital for a while…well, story short, I just decided to stay here until my luck changed."

"Hold on. You haven't been here in town in four months?"

"Uh-uh. One thing just led to another. I got a temporary job here, bartending. I owe a few people some money here and, well, they aren't gonna let me leave until I pay them, you know?"

Fascinating life saga, reflected Dan, but please spare me. "But you still rent the house and the garage on Warwick?"

"Well, yeah." He said it as if it were the most obvious thing in the world. "I just send them a money order every month. I got a lease."

Dan ran a hand across his forehead.

"Mr. Watney…is there anybody else who might have access to your home or your garage?"

"As a matter of fact," Tyrone said, "yeah. Got friends who like to work on their cars, change their oil and like that. Maybe drink a few beers and hang out. The police there aren't too friendly with them working on their cars in the street, and they sure don't like 'em drinking in public. Cops get kinda touchy like that. No offense."

Dan sighed. "None taken. Anybody in particular?"

"Well," said Tyrone hesitantly, "there's one guy I lent the keys to before I left. I got a lot of newspapers and stuff in there and he said he'd clean them out for me. Helpful kinda dude. What's this about, anyway? The agent wouldn't tell me nothin'. Am I in any trouble here or something?" Tyrone sounded as if he dreaded to hear the answer to his question.

"No, sir, if you're telling me the truth about being out of town for the past few months…"

"Gospel truth, Detective! I got plenty of people who can vouch for me!"

"Then, no, I can't say that you're in any trouble here, as long as you can tell me the name of this helpful guy you lent your keys to."

Tyrone sounded most happy to do just that.

* * *

As Jilly approached Melinda's building, she saw the same bespectacled young man sitting on the stoop that she had encountered before, again reading a paperback book. He looked up as she reached the steps.

"You're back," he said, looking her in the eye seriously.

"You're Terry, am I right?"

He grinned, a bright smile that seemed to change his whole demeanor. "Well now, how is it you know that?"

"I'm a detective, Terry, remember? Actually, Melinda told me."

His smile faded but did not disappear. He nodded, looking amused. "I'm not sure she's here right now, Detective."

"I'm going to check for myself." Jilly continued to mount the stairs. As she passed him, he looked up at her and said, "Do you honestly think she killed that lady?"

"I don't think anything, Terry. I'm just trying to learn the facts."

"I've known Melinda Barstow for a number of years now. I am proud to be her friend. She is an excellent mother and a wonderful lady. There's nobody with more integrity in this entire city. Why can't you leave her alone?"

Jilly paused at the door to the apartment building. "If she's innocent, she'll help me solve this. She's got nothing to fear. I suggest you stay out of it, unless you've got something to help me?"

Terry shrugged and turned back to his book. Over his shoulder he muttered, "Not a thing. Except I guarantee Melinda hasn't done anything. She's good people."

Melinda's apartment was one flight up from the interior lobby and about halfway down the carpeted corridor. Jilly noticed that the door was slightly ajar as she approached. She stopped and knocked on the door and called out, "Melinda? Ms. Barstow?"

The strains of a classical serenade came from her bag. Her phone ring tone.

"Yeah, hello."

"Jilly, it's Dan."

"Don't tell me you're done already! I'll be over for you in a—"

"No, Jilly. Listen. I just got a call from the guy who leases the house and the garage. He's in Houston. He claims he hasn't been here in several months. He lets his friends use the garage to work on their cars and hang out."

"Great. That's not much help."

Nobody had yet answered the door. Jilly, caught up in the conversation, was momentarily distracted from what little ambient noise there was in the quiet hall. She didn't hear the hushed footsteps coming quickly.

"He says there's one guy who borrowed his keys just before he left town and still has them."

"Okay, does this guy have a name?"

"Yeah. Terry Blaze. He says he's Caribbean of some variety. He lives over near Melinda's street. Wasn't that guy we ran into out front named Terry?"

"Oh damn," said Jilly. Ignoring her phone, she instinctively reached into her bag for her automatic.

All at once she felt the hand on the back of her neck and felt herself being driven forcefully against Melinda's front door.

EIGHT

She never lost consciousness but things got a little confused for a short time. She remembered pitching forward into the apartment and falling onto the floor. She rolled around and began to sit up. She saw her bag and phone several feet away on the floor, and started to go for the bag. A husky arm reached down and pushed her back to the floor.

"Don't move," said Terry, towering over her. Suddenly he looked much bigger than he had seemed before. His hulking figure obscured the doorway as he reached back and slammed the door behind him.

Her bag was on the floor, scant feet away, but she didn't turn her gaze to it. If she could just reach her gun...

"Where's Melinda?" she asked, glaring up at him.

"I honestly don't know. She's not here, though."

"Did you hurt her?"

"*No!*" Terry almost screamed, his eyes widening in disbelief. "Hurt her? Never! I could never hurt Melinda! You really don't get it, do you?"

Jilly slowly brought herself back to a sitting position, staring up at the man who now seemed to be a giant, glaring down at her menacingly. The glasses didn't make him look academic anymore. Somehow they made him more ominous.

"I told you not to move!" he bellowed, his eyes widening. "Why can't you women ever do what you're told!" He started to reach down to push her back, but stopped when Jilly flinched slightly, involuntarily. She silently cursed herself for the moment of weakness, but at least he didn't knock her down again.

"She didn't do what you told her, did she?" Jilly said quietly, locking eyes with the man looming over her. How could she have not noticed how *big* he was? Did he just suddenly become this frightening giant? She pushed back the fear and forced herself to think calmly.

"She? Who are you talking about?"

"You know who I mean," she continued, slowly continuing to raise herself up. No sudden moves. Slow but steady. Keep talking. Keep him involved. "Jessica Pidgeon. She wouldn't do what you wanted, would she?"

"*Fuck* that bitch," Terry growled.

"She got you angry, didn't she? Is that why you killed her?"

She hit the nerve.

"She had no right!" Terry exclaimed. "Ruining people's lives, lying, stealing…"

"What did she steal, Terry?" Slowly moving around, she forced herself not to look directly toward her bag as she calculated the distance and the direct line to it.

"She stole their *lives!*" he yelled.

He was getting angrier by the moment. He had a deep voice but an emotional whine was creeping into it. "Melinda worked for that family for *years*! She took care of them. She did their scut work—things they weren't willing to do for themselves. Isn't that always the case? Smug, selfish rich people, who never want to get their *hands* dirty! Those kids—Melinda was more a parent to them than either of those two ever were! And then that crazy bitch accuses her of that stupid nonsense and fires her, after all those years, won't even give her a *reference…*"

If she wasn't able to reach the bag, she would have to try to defend herself against him. That wasn't the optimum solution. He had a lot of size and weight on her. All she would have going for her was her police training, but that was hardly negligible. She had kept up her self-defense skills. She wouldn't be a scared, slight little woman unable to fight back. At least he didn't have a weapon, as far as she could tell. No baseball bat this time.

"Melinda can't get another job. Nobody's gonna hire her! They'll have to move away from here, from all of us! Olivia won't get to go to college! That girl is so beautiful, so damned intelligent! She's got a *life* ahead of her, better than her mom or me! It's not right to have that taken away from her!"

"So she got you angry, right?" Jilly continued, keeping her voice calm. "You didn't set out to kill her, did you, Terry? You just set out to make things right again. You went to her house to convince her to make it up to Melinda."

Terry just glowered at her, his jaw set. A teary gleam appeared in both of his eyes.

"You went to her house, didn't you? Maybe took a bus? You figured you'd talk to her? You were trying to be a good friend, Terry. You were trying to help them. You *are* a good friend, right?"

"I *am* a good friend! I'm the best friend they've got!"

"So you took the bus there, did you?"

"Of course I did. How else would I get there? I haven't got a car!"

"But she wouldn't listen to you, is that what happened? You argued? Things got out of hand?"

"Arrogant, stuck up bitch!" he hissed, and loudly smacked one of his fists into the palm of his other hand. For a moment Jilly thought he was going to turn on her. The seething transformation of his blind anger was amazing, morphing him into something different, something less rational. "Called Melinda some terrible names. Called *me* some terrible names."

"So what did you do, Terry?"

"I was just going to have her sign the letter, give me some money to put in with it. Tell Melinda she had a drug problem, and that was why she acted the way she did. I wanted to scare her, tell her if she ever told anybody I'd been there, I'd come back and hurt her. But she didn't get scared. She said she'd tell everybody the minute I left. She said she'd call the police."

But Jilly couldn't see that as Terry's actual plan. He couldn't leave Jess there to turn him in. And then there was the Oxycodone. Maybe he decided to drug his victim, even forcibly overdose her.

Right now, though, Jilly needed him to believe that she was buying his story.

"Okay. So you couldn't just leave her there. She wasn't cooperating. She disrespected you. That got you angry. So you decided to, what, have her drive you both somewhere?"

He shook his head, putting the fingers of one hand to his temple, lips moving silently.

For a moment he seemed to be trying to tell himself the story. "I don't remember too many details. She got me madder and madder. I remember I pushed her into her car and told her to drive into the city. It was a Sunday, no banks open but plenty of ATMs. I remember making her tell me the name of her bank and looking for a machine as we drove."

"As you drove…where, Terry? Where did you want her to take you?" She put her weight on one knee and began to raise herself up more.

"I told you to *sit still!*" he suddenly roared. Too quick a move that time. Jilly held up her hands in placation.

"Okay, okay. Just getting more comfortable, okay? The floor's hard! I do want to hear your story. And you want me to hear your story, don't you? Help me understand. So your plan was to have her sign a letter you wrote that made her sound like she had a drug problem, and put in some money for Melinda. Then you were going to, what, take her somewhere? Lock her up maybe?"

"I wasn't going to hurt her!" he wailed. "Yeah, maybe lock her up. I had a place I could keep her for a while. I don't know! I thought I had planned it all really intelligently. But in the end I didn't really think it out all that carefully! I just knew I had to help Melinda and Olivia!"

"I can see that, Terry. You were trying to be a good friend. Things got out of hand."

"Damn straight they did! *Way* out of hand."

"You had drugs with you. You had oxy."

"Yeah. Got it from a friend. Easy to find down here."

"You wanted her to take the oxy, right? Maybe she'd pass out and you'd leave her to be found by someone, they'd assume she was muddled and had a problem, something like that?"

Terry shook his head, wringing his hands in the air in frustration. "I don't know, something like that!"

"You were just trying to make it right," Jilly repeated. The words seemed to have a little effect on him, bringing him down just a little when she said them. "And everything went wrong."

He shook his head, tears trickling down his cheeks. All of a sudden he smacked his fist into his palm again, hard. The *smack* resonated in the small quiet apartment.

Outside somewhere, far away, Jilly swore she could hear a siren. She remembered she hadn't broken off the phone connection with Dan before Terry attacked her. It gave her hope. She hoped Terry didn't detect the siren as well.

Keep him talking.

"You must have gotten awfully angry, Terry. You hurt her terribly. I can't believe you wanted to do that. You're a good guy, right? You look out for women and kids, people smaller and not as strong as you."

"Yes!" he hoarsely whispered, bending lower and looking at her searchingly. "Yes! I am a good man! I care about the folks in the neighborhood! I *help* people! I don't hurt them! But sometimes people can just get me going…"

"She pushed you to your limit, right? Something went too far. What happened?"

"I don't know! I don't remember! I just…went nuts!"

"Where were you? Do you remember how it started?"

"I told her to take out a lot of money from her ATM. I was careful to stay out of any possible camera range. She told me the most she could take out was four hundred. So I told her to take that. Then I had her drive us a little farther, to a bad neighborhood, quiet. No people around at night. I had the letter all set up already. Made her sign it right there, in the car. Told her to take the Oxy. She said no, she would never take it. She didn't seem too scared. Looked me right in the eye, with that arrogant look. It was like she wanted to tick me off. That infuriated me even worse."

"And then what happened?"

"I don't know. I dragged her out of the car, I remember that. Told her she needed to listen to me, do what I said. Somehow she wound up in the back seat. I started hitting her. Kept telling her to do what I said. I was yelling and yelling at her and she wasn't answering and I kept saying *answer me*. Then she was just lying there."

"What about the bat? You hit her with a bat."

Terry's eyes lit up a bit in horrified recall. "Oh my God. Yeah. It was in the car. In the back seat. Must have belonged to one of her kids."

"You don't remember that part, then?"

The sirens were definitely coming closer. He'd hear them soon. She prayed that they were for her.

"All I know is, she was dead. I had to hide her. There were big garbage bins out along the street, the plastic things with the big wheels. Looked like trash pickup the next day. I carried her down the block. Had to work quick before I was seen. I took off her jewelry. She had her wallet with her because I made her bring it. I figured I could dump her stuff around, someone would find it and it'd look like a robbery. Made sense. Druggie woman in a drug neighborhood. Served her right if people thought that of her."

"You threw away the wallet. Someone found it. But why not her jewelry?"

"I was starting to toss stuff, trying to think straight. Didn't want to make it too obvious. Then some people started showing up. Dealers, I guess, like that. Bad sorts, the kind that come packing, you know? Some arguments and stuff started breaking out too. I got worried about being seen, being confronted for being where I shouldn't be. I took the jewelry back to the car with me."

Bad sorts. Very possibly, Jilly thought, Marmaduke, who would shortly find the wallet.

She noted that as he got into trying to tell the story, his agitation subsided somewhat. She tried to keep him going. There was no telling of what he was capable, if that terrifying flash-fire anger was allowed to return. "You hid the car," Jilly said, keeping her voice even. "With everything still in it. You didn't get rid of it."

"I was going to. Wasn't sure what to do. Everything was confused. Figured it'd be safe hidden away for now, while I got my head straight. I couldn't remember…"

Terry suddenly whipped his head around. Jilly figured he had heard the sirens and finally put two and two together. In the moment his attention was away, she steeled herself to spring for the bag. This might be it. She prepared to fight the giant man literally tooth and nail, if necessary.

But the sound that had distracted him was actually the closed front door being tried, followed by the sound of a key in the lock.

"Terry! What are you doing—"

"Melinda!"

She was holding a laundry basket, standing in the doorway, her mouth agape. She caught sight of Jilly on the floor.

"Detective Garvey!" She looked back and forth between them and dropped the basket. Her hand flew to her mouth. She had sized up the situation immediately.

"Melinda…" Terry turned toward her, stretching out a hand to her.

Jilly jumped for her bag. Terry spun around. For a big man he could move awfully fast.

"Terry!" screamed Melinda. "*No!*"

"Time standing still" was a cliché Jilly had often heard, but she would later swear that it actually happened. She hurtled across the floor towards her bag but it was clear that Terry was going to get in front of her and intercept her before she could reach it. It seemed to take forever. She kept repeating the same mantra in her head: she was smaller than him, but she was also a trained police officer. She might go down but she would not go easy.

If she just said it enough, she might totally believe it.

Melinda's scream seemed to halt Terry in mid-air. He froze, unsure whether to continue to go after Jilly or to turn back to Melinda.

Jilly reached the bag, jamming her hand into it for her weapon as she rolled over onto her back.

Terry was still bent towards Jilly but had turned his head back toward Melinda.

"Ms. Pidgeon," Melinda said, her voice breaking. "It was…you?"

"Melinda, listen…"

"You *killed* her?" Melinda yelled. "*You*? You're the one who did *that* to her? Why, Terry? How could you?"

"She was going to ruin your life," Terry said pleadingly. "Those people. They think they're better than us. So comfortable in their lives and so entitled. They have *everything*, and no idea of what it means to have to work for something! They don't care how hard you work…"

"*Those people!*" Melinda shouted indignantly. "I knew and took care of *those people*! Those children did nothing, they're innocent, and now they don't have a mother! You took their *mother* away from them, Terry! Their *mother*!"

"She was going to ruin everything! For you, for Olivia…"

"She was a sick woman, Terry! She wasn't a bad person, she was… mixed up, confused! It would have worked out! I would have worked it out!"

"Melinda, I did it for you! For Olivia!"

Melinda's eyes widened hugely. She stared at him with amazed disbelief, then her face softened into sheer disappointment. "No, Terry," she whispered softly. "You've done nothing for us. Nothing at all."

The fight seemed to go out of him, just like that, and his shoulders drooped. He did not seem to notice that Jilly was now kneeling on one knee four feet behind him, grimly leveling her service automatic in a two-handed grip directly at his back, center mass, as per her police training.

The sirens were very loud now, and they were right outside Melinda's window. The wails died as several police cars screeched to a halt on the pavement, doors flew open, and a tumult of voices and urgent footsteps erupted.

Suddenly the apartment was flooded with uniformed officers, weapons drawn, barking orders. Jilly lowered her weapon and stood back to give them room, lowering her head and taking a deep breath. Amidst the chaotic ruckus, she could still clearly perceive the sound of Melinda Barstow's uncontrolled sobbing. Then she realized she could hear two voices crying. Terry Blaze, already being forcibly handcuffed by two officers, was weeping openly and loudly as well.

NINE

It was only a few minutes later that Dan arrived, and now only he, Jilly and Melinda remained in the apartment. Terry had been taken into custody and the din of the past half hour was now replaced by a heavy stillness. Melinda sat at the edge of one of her armchairs, motionless, hands clasped in her lap, staring down at the ground. She had been that way since the officers had left with Terry.

Jilly and Dan stood across the room, quietly conversing.

"I should have been with you," Dan was repeating for the third time. It seemed to Jilly he was having a difficult time looking her in the eye. "This is my fault. He could have killed you."

"Dan, would you stop saying that? Nothing was your fault. We walk into bad situations all the time, it's part of the job."

"But if I had been with you…"

"If you had been with me, maybe it would have gone down differently, maybe not. But if you hadn't called in the cavalry like that, things could have been very different. Maybe Terry would be dead now."

Or, she thought without voicing, not Terry but someone else.

"As soon as I heard the hubbub on your end of the phone, I was out of there. Got on the horn for backup."

"Got here pretty quick yourself. Hitchhike with a squad car?"

"Uh-huh. Pulled one over on the street, like in a movie."

"So I guess this means you still didn't renew your license."

Dan sighed. "Least of my worries at the moment."

Jilly walked over to Melinda, who did not look up. "How are you doing?" she asked.

"Not well."

"Do you need me to call your daughter or anyone?"

"Olivia is in class right now. She'll be home in a while. No need to let her know anything until then."

"You might have saved my life, or Terry's life, by coming in when you did. You do realize that, don't you? It was going to be him or me."

"I suppose, yes. I still can't believe he did this." She looked up at Jilly with wide, red-rimmed eyes. "I've known Terry for years. I would never have believed him capable of…of what he did."

Jilly said nothing.

Melinda continued. "I got that poor woman killed. I'm the cause of this horrible tragedy to her family."

"No. Absolutely not. You can't let yourself think that way. This was nobody's fault but Terry's. What you said to him before was right. This could have somehow been worked out. Jessica was ill. She needed help. The problem was, nobody was in a position to help her, including you."

"You're very good to tell me these things, Detective. But nothing will keep me from blaming myself for this. At least not for a long time."

Jilly placed her hand on Melinda's shoulder. She knew Melinda was right and there was nothing more she could say.

* * * *

The service for Jessica Pidgeon was small, with only a handful in attendance, including her immediate family and Jilly and Dan. The serious looking young man who stood beside Laurie, they decided, had to be her friend Roberto. She saw Melinda in the back of the church, far from the other mourners. Jilly noted that none of Jessica's friends had showed up, and most interestingly, neither had James's girlfriend Natasha.

It was a melancholy finale to a case that had been unrelentingly depressing.

At the burial site, Jilly and Dan approached the family to offer their condolences. James thanked them for coming and introduced Jessica's mother. Jilly caught sight of Melinda making her way hastily from the gravesite. She had not stopped to talk to anyone.

Shortly thereafter, as they walked back to their cars, Jilly found the opportunity to walk a few steps away with Laurie. "How are you holding up?" she asked the girl. She noted that Laurie had not visibly shed a tear through the service or the burial.

"I'm okay," Laurie said. "All things considered."

"I hope you learn to forgive your mother. She was…"

"Yeah, she was sick. Unhappy. I know. I keep hearing that."

"She needed help but stopped asking for it. She loved you all deeply, even if she couldn't show it."

Laurie looked down at the ground as she walked. "My Dad says he's coming home for good. I think he broke up with his lady friend. She's going to run his company when it's sold, or something like that. Anyway, he says he thinks he's needed more at home."

"He's right."

Laurie made a noise through her lips.

"Give him a chance, Laurie. Maybe he's learned something from all this. Please, will you try to do that?"

Laurie simply shrugged and said no more. They walked until they reached the short line of parked cars waiting to take them away from the cemetery. Jilly made her good-byes and walked the few steps to her own car, where Dan was already waiting. This time, with a half-hearted smile, he got in behind the steering wheel. Jilly dropped herself onto the passenger seat with a deep sigh.

"Terry's arraignment is tomorrow," Dan said as he started up the engine. "Letitia and the rest of the newsies are announcing it all over the place. I wish I could say that's the end of it."

Jilly shook her head. "Me, too, partner."

She sat in thought for a while before continuing. "Terry said that Jessica had everything, that she had no real problems. From his perspective it must have seemed that way. She had a beautiful home in a nice neighborhood, a comfortable life, a family. But none of it could save her from her own demons."

Dan exhaled loudly. "Great support system she had. Didn't seem like anybody close to her wanted to save her."

"I wouldn't be too harsh on them, Dan. She didn't make it particularly easy for any of them. I keep thinking about what Brad told us about how depression pushes people away. That kid's wise beyond his years."

"I was just thinking," mused Dan. "We always talk about how we're the ones who have to speak for the victim."

"Uh-huh."

"It seems Jessica had more people looking out for her *after* her death than she did while she was alive."

"I'm afraid you're right, Dan."

"They're all pretty damaged, aren't they? What do you think is going to become of all of them—the family, Melinda?"

"I have a feeling Melinda and Olivia will leave town and try to start over somewhere else, away from the notoriety of this case. She's a strong lady; she'll make the right choices. James is going to move back in with Brad and Laurie. Better late than never."

She watched the cemetery pass by from the car window and searched for the hope in her heart. "They'll find their way. Not tomorrow but ultimately. It'll take a while but they'll find their way."

"Gotta believe."

"Yeah," Jilly nodded somberly.

That, she reflected, was sometimes all that kept her going. She had to keep believing.

THE END

SOMETIMES THEY DIE

ONE

There are those times when nothing goes right.

It always seems to happen when you're especially in a hurry. And Julie LaRoche was in an *extreme* hurry tonight. Why—*why*—did *crap* like this always happen to him?

His useless excuse for a secretary had left early once again—not that she was much help when she was actually present—but of course his phone never stopped ringing and he had to keep answering, and the calls were all *crap*. His copier jammed up just when he needed copies of a lot of documents. And of course they were all *big* documents, a couple dozen pages each. And several times he dropped the docs and they scattered everywhere and he had to take valuable time to re-collate them. It went on and on and on. It was like a comedy of errors, and not a funny comedy.

The punchline to this unpleasant joke was that he was now running hours late. He had made his third call to the escrow office asking them to stay open for him and this time they had told him he had exactly twenty minutes to get to them before they would lock their doors and head home to families and dinners.

The elevator, of course, was taking forever, even though it was almost seven by now and the building was presumably close to empty. So he slammed open the door to the stairwell, clumsily lumbered down three flights and dashed across the building lobby to the glass double doors leading to the street. He stopped in front of his building, catching his breath in puffs and pants, looking right and left for a taxi. An hour ago there would have been a half dozen of them cruising by here. Now Institution Boulevard was nearly empty, with the barest of traffic.

The sun was setting, casting the street in shadows from the high buildings. While autumn tended to be mild in this city, there was a damp chill in the dark air. Julie didn't even have an overcoat with him; his only thought had been to grab his aging briefcase stuffed with his papers. He shivered slightly in his thin brown suit. When things aren't going right, they aren't going right.

He looked up and down the street. The only other person on the block was waiting inside a plexiglass enclosure at the bus stop on the corner, deep in a conversation on his cell phone.

Julie briefly considered taking the bus, but he had no idea when one would even come along. No cabs were in sight in either direction on Institution. Maybe if he went to the corner of Hunt, he'd have a better chance of flagging one down. He began to walk rapidly in that direction, jamming his briefcase under his arm to have both hands free to pull out his own cell phone and speed-dial the escrow office.

It was a long block, his feet hurt, and he was still trying to catch his breath. When the office answered the phone, he gasped out a few sentences to say he was on his way and they needed to wait for him. They *had* to wait for him—this was important! Apparently the person on the other end of the line did not agree.

Julie sputtered a few pointed epithets and viciously stabbed his finger on the screen to end the call, so hard he almost knocked the phone out of his hand. He bobbled the phone and his briefcase and stumbled slightly before regaining his grip on both.

He almost collided with another pedestrian who had suddenly appeared, approaching from the other direction. He started to mutter an apology and walk around the man, who took a step to the side to block him. Julie halted and looked up at him.

The guy was really big and fairly young. He wore baggy jeans, a denim jacket over a gray hooded sweatshirt and a huge baseball cap pulled down over his ears. Julie hated guys like this. They wore their pants too low—hadn't any of them heard of a belt?—and the way they wore baseball caps, with the brim straight and the size so big it covered their ears like a country bumpkin....

The guy smiled in a way Julie did not like, his dark eyes piercing beneath thick eyebrows.

"Hey, sorry, boss. Can I ask you a question? I'm kinda lost here. Do you know how I get to Hastings Street?"

"Hastings? That's like, way *way* over on the other side of town..." Julie started waving a hand, trying to sidestep the guy and get on his way. He didn't have time to give this moron detailed directions around the city. What was it with people? Couldn't they see when you were in a hurry and something was important? Couldn't he get a GPS, or even a map, for God's sake?

But the guy wasn't moving. It was like he wasn't getting the message. He seemed so *dense*.

The only other person on the block, in the bus stop enclosure, had now pocketed his phone. He anxiously looked up the street and at his watch repeatedly. A bus was finally approaching, from about a block away.

The bus passenger's attention was caught by a sudden flash of motion down the otherwise deserted block. Two men were involved in a familiar urban pedestrian dance, stepping awkwardly one way and the other, as if to disentangle themselves from one another. Suddenly they stopped, and it looked as if one was handing something to the other. Then the onlooker heard two loud, sharp noises, saw one man fall to his knees, saw the other one briefly hold him up and run hands over him, then drop him. The first figure slumped to the ground as if in slow motion, forward onto his face. The second took off into a fast run down the street in the opposite direction.

The spectator to this little drama yanked his phone back out of his pocket and nervously stabbed a number onto the screen. The bus stopped at the corner and pulled away again. He remained in the enclosure, frantically speaking into his phone, all the while looking over at the fallen figure.

* * * *

"Frank, how long has it been since you had a partner?"

Detective Frank Vandegraf was standing in front of the perpetually saturated desk of his Lieutenant, Hank Castillo.

He always marveled at the fact that no matter how covered in paperwork the desk got, it always looked organized and tidy. There had to be six separate stacks of manila folders, loose leaf binders, and sheaves of reports in front of the Lieutenant. Castillo himself was sitting back in his chair, arms folded, staring inscrutably at Frank.

The two struck a contrast: Castillo, graying and distinguished, dapper as usual, in shirt, tie and vest, suitcoat neatly hung on his chair, the picture of corporate police work; and Frank, needing a haircut, in rumpled shirtsleeves and loose tie, hands on his hips, dutifully tolerating his summons to the office and waiting to be able to get back to his own chaotically cluttered desk and his own work.

"I don't know, Lou. A while."

"Well, I appreciate the fact you've made do without one, what with our budgetary problems around here and all. We've been trying to address that issue and slowly partner up our lone wolves as the budget allows us."

"I'm getting along just fine. No complaints."

The truth of the matter was, Frank was very happy to have flown solo ever since his former partner had transferred out of Personal Crimes. It suited his temperament, and he figured it suited the temperament of many of the other detectives in his squad as well. In fact, there was at least one other of his colleagues with whom he could have partnered over the past months, but to put it succinctly, the guy was a human hemorrhoid.

This had worked out better all around. Frank had his own way of doing things and it was just easier to travel unencumbered. As long as he continued to clear his cases at a favorable rate, he figured, nobody would make a fuss over his being without the benefit of a partner.

Castillo nodded, a wry smile playing beneath his salt-and-pepper mustache.

"I've had no complaints about your performance, Detective, but this is just to let you know that we plan to address the situation in the near future and you'll be able to have a partner again soon."

Frank was about to ask "How soon?" but as he struggled to decide the most diplomatic way to pose that question, Castillo's desk phone rang and he grabbed it up. As he spoke tersely, he picked up a pencil that was lying right next to his free hand—the guy was so organized it was scary—and began jotting on a small notepad that was also strategically located nearby.

After a moment he hung up the phone and tore the sheet off the pad, handing it across the desk to Frank.

"We'll finish this conversation later. You're up on this one. Shooting on Institution."

Frank hesitated a moment, not taking the paper. Castillo's eyebrows shot up.

"Is there a problem, Frank?"

"Are you sure you want to give that one to me, Lou? I've got a pile of cases…"

"As I said…you're up. Those cases you're running down are getting stale, if I'm not mistaken?"

Frank sighed. "Yeah, I guess…"

He had been spinning his wheels on several thorny ones with no real relief in sight. Being on evening shift didn't make it any easier to follow up interviews.

"Look at it this way. You'll be off evenings next week. It's always easier to pursue leads in the daytime. Things will run smoother. And we just might have some help for you very shortly."

Castillo pointedly thrust the note closer. "You're up, Detective."

Frank shrugged and took the paper. Castillo turned his attention back to one of the files before him.

The conversation was over.

* * * *

"Officer Pardo, always good to see a familiar face."

"Detective Vandegraf, nice to see you too. Come on through."

Frank stepped under the yellow police barricade tape that had been strung up and down the block. Already the scene was bustling with the usual personnel from the coroner's office and Scientific Investigation Division (SID) as well as several uniformed officers. Powerful arc lighting had been set up that cast a harsh glare and eerie shadows over the entire scene. Two watchful uniformed officers kept an eye on a small throng of curious on-lookers gathered outside the barrier.

Athena Pardo, the young duty officer, pointed to the body lying on the concrete, partially covered with a plastic tarp, where a sad-faced man in a lab coat knelt, solemnly involved in his examination.

"The victim was apparently approached by his assailant, also male, and was shot twice at close range to the chest. He was possibly robbed before the assailant fled on foot in that direction."

Pardo pointed up the street. "We have no witnesses as to his where-abouts after that."

Frank smiled to himself. He could always count on Pardo to be formally professional. She took herself very seriously, but, Frank had long since decided, she was a particularly good cop: thorough, intelligent, and highly motivated.

She then pointed down the street in the opposite direction. "We've got a witness who saw the shooting. His name is Cameron Wardell. He was waiting for a bus when it happened. As far as we can tell, there were no other witnesses."

"Any ID on the victim?"

"Not yet. The assailant must have taken his wallet. According to the witness, he came out of one of the buildings on this side of the block. We've got two officers checking them out to see if anybody's around who might know him."

Frank nodded. "I'm going to talk to the ME. I'll be back."

The medical examiner was Mickey Kendrick, which constituted a good piece of luck. Once you got by Mickey's rather morose sense of humor, he was a blessing. Behind that jowly basset-hound scowl and deadpan monotone was a sharp mind and a keen professional manner. He was thorough, straightforward and, most importantly, expeditious with results.

He looked up at Frank and intoned, "Detective Vandegraf, always a pleasure." Mickey never *spoke*: he delivered lines as if they were dark ironies.

"Evening, Mickey. What can you tell me about our gent, here?"

"Two shots fired at close range to the chest. Probably died almost instantly. No signs of a physical struggle of any kind. There's a mark on the forehead where he must have fallen to the ground, postmortem for all purposes. No other marks or wounds. The shooter got close enough to him to put the two bullets into him, then apparently grabbed his wallet and ran."

"I notice he's still got his watch."

Frank pointed to the left wrist of the supine body on the pavement, the side of the body that was uncovered.

"Likely the perp only took the time to go through his pockets. They're empty."

"So, a straight walkup shooting, you figure."

"Yep. Slugs are still in him. Likely small caliber. I'll be able to tell you more once I get him on a table."

Frank looked around. "Any idea if any shells were recovered?"

"Don't know. Possibly this was a cheap .38 revolver. Been a spate of them lately. Want to take a look?"

Mickey moved back to make room for Frank, who knelt down on one knee, pulling a pair of disposable gloves out of his pocket and snapping them on.

The victim might have been in his late fifties, thinning gray hair, stocky build, in an ill-fitting brown suit more suited for springtime. Brownish blood stains had spread across the front of what had been a white shirt. It was a chilly early autumn evening but the man had no coat. His eyes were wide open in a familiar death stare.

Frank couldn't help but think that they still held the image of whoever had shot him—the last thing he had ever seen. His expression, though, he decided, was noncommittal; perhaps he hadn't had the chance to form an opinion of the attacker.

The witness stood by nervously, hands in the pockets of his orange leather jacket, talking with another uniformed officer not far away. Frank pegged him for late twenties. He kept shaking his bushy blond hair out of his eyes and never stopped moving. The uni seemed to be stoically tolerating the edgy, animated chattering of the young man, nodding politely and impassively.

As Frank approached, he swore he saw a flash of relief in the patrolman's eyes.

"Mr. Wardell, is that right? I'm Detective Vandegraf. I'm told you saw the incident?"

"Yeah, yeah." Wardell nodded rapidly.

He didn't seem as if he was going to stop, like one of those sports bobble head dolls. Frank thought those things were exceedingly annoying and always had to the urge to reach out a hand and stop the head from bobbling. He had that urge at the moment with this guy. He rubbed the back of his neck and stared at the guy until he stopped. Then they just stared at each other.

Finally Frank said, "So, can you tell me what you saw, then?"

"Oh, sure. Sorry. It really flipped me out. I mean, I've never seen anything like that…"

"I understand, sir. So where were you?"

He pointed up the street to the kiosk near the corner. "I was waiting there for the number ten bus. I was looking up the street for the bus and I saw the two of them moving around up the sidewalk. There was nobody else around so it caught my eye…"

"Moving around? How do you mean?"

"They were, like, sidestepping one another on the street. Like the one guy was trying to get around the other. They were right about there."

He pointed to the body on the ground. "Then the one guy kind of grabbed at the other, there were a couple of loud noises, like shots. The one guy, farther away from me, started to drop to the ground and the other guy, with his back to me, kind of leaned into him, like he was trying to grab him or something. Then the first guy was on the ground and the second guy bent over him for a few seconds, then he got up and ran off that way."

Frank looked at the bus enclosure and estimated it was perhaps seventy feet away, maybe six or seven doors down, out of the glare of the crime-scene illumination. A bright halogen-colored light burned inside of the kiosk, illuminating it through the plexiglass windows, which seemed to accent the surrounding darkness of the street all the more. He gave a quick glance up and down the block, noting the relative remoteness of street lighting.

"About what time was this? Was it dark yet?"

"I'd say it was around seven. It was just getting dark."

"So the light hadn't come on yet in the enclosure?"

Wardell shook his head, looking puzzled. "I don't remember. No, I don't think it had."

"Did you remain in the enclosure or did you approach the victim?"

"No, I stayed in there. I got on my phone and called 911. Then I just kind of shook. I guess it took me a while to shake myself out of it."

"Did you happen to see where the victim came from?"

"No, but I'm thinking he must have come out of one of these buildings on the block. I was looking up the street now and then for the bus and I don't remember seeing anyone walking up the street."

"You said the attacker's back was to you. Did you get a look at him at all?"

"No, not really. He was a big guy. Hooded sweatshirt. No, wait…he might have had a jacket over the sweatshirt. His pants might have been baggy. All I remember is his clothes were dark."

"Was he wearing a hat or could you see his hair?"

Wardell took a deep breath and stared at the ground, trying to remember. "I can't be sure but I think his hair was dark. I'm just not positive though."

"And you didn't see his face, is that right?"

"No. It all happened so fast. I wasn't paying attention. I mean, you don't pay attention, you know? Just people on the street. Then something happens and you don't think to…"

"I understand, Mr. Wardell. But sometimes your mind can surprise you. Some little detail will stick out that you didn't expect. That's why I ask a lot of questions, just in case something like that pops up. Did the guy move in any way unusual?"

"Move?"

"Did he, maybe, have a limp? When he took off running, did he seem athletic, or was he kinda heavy on his feet?"

"I don't remember a limp or anything unusual. He just started running."

"Was he fast?"

Wardell thought. "Yes. Yes, I'd have to say he was pretty fast. He kind of took off like a deer, in fact."

"Good. See, little things like that might be a big help to me, you never know. So he was likely fairly young then, do you think?"

Wardell nodded vigorously, his eyes lighting up. "Yeah! Yeah, now that you mention it! He did run like a younger guy would. He moved pretty fast for a big guy!"

Frank's continuing questions of the witness didn't seem to glean any new information. He could not identify any features of the attacker other than he was a big younger man in a dark jacket and baggy pants, just maybe with dark hair.

That was it. Frank gave him his card in case he remembered anything else that might be of import, and took Wardell's own contact information. He noted that the address he was given was on the other side of town from the scene of the crime.

"Just curious, are you in this neighborhood often, sir?"

"Not really. I'm taking courses so I take the bus back and forth."

"Courses?"

"Yeah, I'm studying internet tech. HTML, website development and search engines and so on. So I take the bus." He shook his head and almost shuddered. "Great luck that I happened to be here tonight, huh? I hope I never have to see something like that ever again."

Frank nodded. There were many days he found himself wishing the same thing. "Okay, thank you, sir, you can go. Thanks for your help. I'll be in touch if I have any further questions."

Wardell looked up the street. "And there's actually another bus coming. Thanks, Detective."

Frank waved to the officer to let the witness through the taped-off area and he jogged off for the bus kiosk.

Frank looked up and down Institution Boulevard, frowning. There were too many cases like this, probably a crime of opportunity by a predator lying in wait on a quiet street after hours. The odds were with the perpetrator: a quick swoop and mugging, few or no witnesses, return to their own neighborhood, likely far away. Robberies like this happened regularly. They often involved pointless violence, maybe simply to gratify an attacker's brutal streak, or just because they knew they could get away with it.

And sometimes, the victims died. Senseless deaths, the kind that especially infuriated Frank.

He had a feeling that the slugs would provide the only viable clue and that they had come from an untraceable illicit weapon. He hoped he was wrong on both counts. He turned to look for somebody from SID to consult before they left.

Officer Pardo was approaching with a distraught-looking young woman in tow, the duo looking spectral under the intense arc lights. She waved at Frank as they weaved around the techs and unis on the pavement, careful to give a wide berth to the actual body.

"Detective, this woman says she knew the victim."

The woman nodded, eyes open wide in alarm, lips pursed tightly. One of Frank's colleagues had once remarked on that familiar look: it was as if they had buttoned themselves up so tightly, the only place for the fear to escape was through the eyes. She looked as if she might explode at any moment.

Pardo gently put her hand on the young woman's shoulder. "This is Detective Vandegraf. Can you please tell him what you told the officer over there?"

"Oh my God, it's Mr. LaRoche," she stammered, running her fingers across her face.

"Do you know his full name, miss?" Frank asked.

"Julius. Julius LaRoche. He's a lawyer. His office is next to where I work."

Now Frank had his notebook out and began to jot rapidly.

"Which building?"

She pointed to a nearby doorway, a façade with a pair of glass doors topped with a glass panel with the number 1313 painted onto it.

"We're on the third floor. He's in 312. Was. Oh my God."

"And you're in the office next door?"

She kept nodding frantically. Now she was wiping a tear from one eye. "Y-yes. 314. Quality Imports."

"And…I'm sorry, what is your name?…"

"Lucy McGinty."

"Ms. McGinty, do you know anything about him? Is he married, does he have any next of kin, how we might get in touch with them?"

"No…I'm sorry. I have no idea. I just knew him to say hello to in the hall."

"Do you think there'd be anybody still up in Mr. LaRoche's office now?"

"I…I don't know. He's got a partner and I think they have an assistant, but it's not a big office. It didn't look like anybody was still there."

Frank looked at Pardo, who nodded. "We'll go check it out." She turned back to Lucy McGinty. "Is there anybody else in your office who might also be able to tell us anything about Mr. LaRoche?"

She shook her head. "No. I was the last one there tonight."

"Okay. Stay here with Detective Vandegraf. I'll be back in a few minutes."

Frank watched her hustle off towards the brick building. Quite a cop, he thought.

Frank turned back to Lucy. "I'm sorry, I know this is hard, but can you tell me anything about Mr. LaRoche that might help me understand what might have happened to him tonight?"

"I don't know. I don't know him that well. I mean, *didn't*. I would see him in the hallway to say hello. He wasn't *unfriendly*, exactly; he just wasn't very friendly. He always seemed in a hurry, kind of distracted."

"What's the name of the law firm?"

"Jellicoe and LaRoche. Mr. Jellicoe is an older man. He looks like he could be in his sixties. I don't know his first name. I think it's just the two of them. I've seen different people coming in and out of there for short periods, probably clerical help. I think they have a big turnover of help."

"Did you see Mr. LaRoche tonight? I mean, earlier tonight?"

"No. We've been crunched the past couple of days with documentation and I've been working day and night. I hadn't seen him in several days. He's usually out of his office. I mean, *was*…"

There was not much more that she could tell him and she didn't seem to show any signs of calming down soon. Frank was relieved to see Pardo returning. He hoped she could shepherd the overwrought Ms. McGinty back to her office.

Pardo was shaking her head. "Nobody in the office. In fact I think she's the only one left on the entire floor."

That information inspired a new wave of panic through Ms. McGinty. "I'm the only one up there? I can't go back there! What if they came back…?"

Pardo nodded reassuringly, as much to Frank as to McGinty. "I'll accompany you back up and wait while you get your things together. Do you have a car I can escort you to?"

"Oh yes, thank you so much."

Pardo smiled at Frank as they turned to the building, an unusual departure from her usual earnestness. "Hey, by the way, I passed the Detective's Exam a couple of weeks ago. You might not be seeing me on the street all that much longer."

"Seriously? I'm impressed! We'll be sorry to be losing you out here, let me tell you, but some detective department is going to be very lucky."

"Well, thank you. They'll probably stick me in Property or the like. I'm told there are going to be openings. I'll take whatever they give me."

"I hear Personal Crimes might have an opening."

"That would be great, but you know how that usually works. There's a waiting list for your unit. They'll promote someone with tenure from another department."

"No doubt breaking down doors to get to work with me. Well, good luck, Officer."

Pardo guided a shaking McGinty back through the throngs once again.

That got him thinking again: he really hoped he wasn't going to get saddled with a partner soon. Maybe he was getting too set in his ways. The joke around the unit was that he was a dinosaur.

Pardo was right: Personal Crimes seldom got newbies. The unit was a plum preference for many detectives from other units. Someone with experience and juice would get transferred in. Maybe even someone as old as Frank.

A new dinosaur.

Dinosaurs, he reflected, didn't tend to get along well together. Too set in their individual ways. On the other hand, it would be easier than having to break in a green newcomer. Either way, it seemed like a lose-lose.

He was yanked from his unhappy reverie by one of the SID techs in a bright blue jumpsuit. "Detective, are you done with the body? Okay if we finish up processing?"

"Sure. Doesn't look like there's much to process. Were there any shells?"

"Negative on that. Probably shot with a revolver."

"Any other detritus around the body?"

"Nope. We've printed his clothes but frankly, there's likely not going to be anything. His pockets are empty. There are no defensive wounds, probably no chance of skin or hair from the assailant."

"Go for it," Frank said, waving a hand. "With my blessing."

There was nothing else he could do here tonight.

He headed back to the unit to see if he could find a contact number for Julius LaRoche. Perhaps there was a wife or even a family. He hated having to do it this way, late at night, but there was no alternative.

In general he didn't like the evening shift, and this was one reason why. Frank was at heart a leg man. He felt most comfortable running down leads and contacts in person. That was generally difficult after eleven o'clock at night.

Sitting at his desk computer, he found only one phone listing in the city for a Julius LaRoche, at the Institution Avenue office of Jellicoe and LaRoche, attorneys at law. Seeking a residence, and possibly a next of kin to notify, came up a blank. He looked at his watch: almost midnight. He'd have to return in the morning to talk to LaRoche's partner and anyone else in the building he could find.

His shift was over shortly. There was nothing else he could do right now. He walked over to the watch commander sergeant and informed him that he was clocking out and would be returning in the morning.

"You really love this job, don't you, Frank?" the sergeant said wryly.

TWO

"Julie's dead? Are you kidding?"

Carl Jellicoe was a tall, lean man with a prominent beak of a nose. He looked to be in his sixties, and not easy sixties at that. He sat back behind his desk, regarding Frank with shining dark eyes peering out from under scraggly white eyebrows, his mouth curled in a scowl. "The hell you say!"

"Yes sir. A robbery outside the building last night."

"So you just told me," Jellicoe said dismissively.

Frank stood before the desk looking down at the man, thinking that he reminded him of a character out of a Charles Dickens book he'd read in school. There were just the two of them in the room this morning.

"So if you don't mind if I sit down and ask you some questions about Mr. LaRoche?"

Frank reached for a chair without waiting for a reply. He already had his notebook in hand. Jellicoe impatiently waved him into the seat.

"I've got a dozen years on Julie, but I somehow always knew I'd out-live him."

"And why is that, sir?"

"Because Julie LaRoche is a schmuck, and always has been."

"Excuse me?"

"I presume you know the word, Detective…is it Vandecamp?"

"Vandegraf, sir. I'm just surprised to hear you say that. You and he were partners, were you not?"

"For eighteen years, yes. And I'm not sure we could stand each other for most of that time."

"That's highly unusual, wouldn't you say?"

"We stayed out of each other's way. To be honest, I don't know if either one of us could have found anyone else to get along with any better. Kind of like a marriage of convenience."

"Speaking of marriages: is Mr. LaRoche married—I mean, was he? I mean, is there a Mrs. LaRoche?"

"Divorced. Twice. Long ago. The exes might be around somewhere, who knows? He never spoke of them and I doubt he had any dealings with them. Julie was immensely more palatable viewed from a long distance."

"Family? Kids? Anyone?"

"One daughter from the first marriage. No idea where she might be. You might call her estranged."

"Close friends?"

"Clearly you didn't know him."

"Not the warm and fuzzy type, I take it."

The old man managed a pained smile. "I was probably his best friend and I hardly knew him and didn't really like him."

"And yet you worked together for almost twenty years?"

"Have you ever heard the concept of parallel play, Detective? We worked together pretty well because we knew to leave each other alone most of the time. He had his arena and I had mine."

Frank looked around the cramped office, filled with old file cabinets and heavy, distinctly unfashionable, wooden furniture. "What kind of law do you practice here, exactly?"

"When we started out we did a lot of personal injury but now it's mostly property law. Julie was more concerned with his own property holdings than in any clientele in recent years. I don't think he's had an actual client in a couple years now."

"Property holdings?"

"Julie liked to acquire property. He'd flip buildings, redevelop. He must have sold a few dozen buildings around the city. That's pretty much how he spent his time nowadays, buying and selling. It was like a giant board game, but with real money. Anything requiring *law*, like representation or, the Almighty forbid, actually going to court, generally fell to me."

"How's business been?"

"Abysmal, but on the bright side, it's getting worse every day. I'd retire but how can I give up living the dream?"

He could always try his hand at stand-up comedy, Frank thought.

"Just curious, Mr. Jellicoe, why *did* you say you thought you'd outlive Mr. LaRoche?"

"To be honest, I thought someone might show up and kill the bastard."

"Someone did, sir."

"Yes, but from what you tell me, it was a random act of violence, a holdup gone bad, right?"

"So it would seem."

"I always figured someone would bust in the door with a gun or knife or a flamethrower and just take him out. I honestly was a little concerned I might be collateral damage."

"You're saying he had enemies, then?"

"If he knew 'em, he hosed 'em, Detective."

"Nice guy, sounds like. Anybody he was specifically making unhappy at the moment?"

"Let's see. He recently negotiated a negligence settlement against a charitable religious order when he was injured on their property. For *that*, he would have walked inside a courtroom, had it been necessary, which it ultimately wasn't. Then there was the apartment house he converted to condos and evicted twenty-seven fixed-income tenants."

Frank paused, pencil in hand, mouth agape.

"And of course there's the pending purchase of the Bodega Building."

"Bodega Building?"

"That's what he's been calling it. It's a three-story building in a neighborhood that's becoming gentrified. He wanted to gut it and turn it into commercial space. There are only a few tenants upstairs but it presently houses a couple of mom-and-pop stores on the ground floor. There's a Cuban grocery and some kind of Central American restaurant that are well-established in the neighborhood. So he called it the Bodega Building. He was going to give them walking papers the moment the deed was in his hand, which would have been any time now. He seemed to have had some confrontations with at least one individual recently."

"Where is this building?"

"Over on San Mateo near Parker."

"Would you say these disagreements were pretty strong?"

Jellicoe shrugged. "I had nothing to do with any of Julie's goings-on. In fact, I made a point to avoid them whenever possible. I just heard about them, or overheard snippets if they happened to spill over to my office now and then. What's the difference? You just said he was killed in a robbery."

This, Frank asked himself, was the man's *partner*?

"Sometimes things aren't the way they look, Mr. Jellicoe. Everything is always worth looking into, just in case."

"Yes, well, he's been complaining about the intransigence of certain tenants. He said he was laying the groundwork to just throw them out the moment he owned the building. I swear he sneered in glee at the prospect."

Now Frank was feeling like he really had fallen into a Charles Dickens novel. Julius LaRoche, it would seem, was a true piece of work.

He sighed. "Did Mr. LaRoche have *any* redeeming characteristics, as long as we're on the topic? Tell me he was good to his mother, at least."

Jellicoe snorted a laugh. "Well, his mother was many years departed, but I'm sure when she was alive, he was totally beastly to her."

"If I could get his home address, that would be a help."

"Certainly. Why not? Not like you're going to invade his privacy now." Jellicoe recited an address which Frank jotted down.

"You have clerical staff here?"

"We've got a girl. She's fairly new. Recent college grad, I think. Works part time, mostly filing, taking calls, doing our administrative scut work. We've got a recurring staff turnover here. Not only is the pay terrible but the working conditions are execrable." He snorted again. "I suppose they'll get somewhat better now, though. I can't imagine I'm the easiest person to work for, but compared to Julie, I'm the offspring of Dale Carnegie and Saint Francis of Assisi."

"Did she do any of the work on any of Mr. LaRoche's activities?"

"It would make sense. If she did any work at all, which is dubious."

"When will she be in, or where can I reach her?"

Jellicoe looked at his watch. "She should be here now."

His desk phone suddenly buzzed. He picked it up, looking aggravated. "Yes? I mean, Jellicoe and La…oh, who is this…? Why aren't you here, Ms. Tarkenton? Well, hurry up then. No, thank you, I don't want anything."

He slammed the receiver down. "She's standing in line at the coffee joint downstairs. What time is it?" He pointedly looked at his wristwatch. "I'd complain about the quality of our help but it's the best we can actually get."

Frank rose from his seat. "I'm going to go down and intercept her to talk to her. Do you mind if I keep her from you for a few more minutes?"

"Why not. The office is going to hell in a handbasket anyway. Having to deal with Julie's detritus is just going to be the frosting on the cake around here." He waved his hands around. "Even in death, Julie's going to be a pain in the ass."

"She's in the coffee shop across the street? What's Ms. Tarkenton look like?"

"Dark hair, glasses, nondescript."

That should be a big help. He dropped one of his cards on the desk. "Please contact me if you have anything else that might be of help. I might be back, Mr. Jellicoe. Thanks for your time."

"I'll count the minutes, Detective."

Frank paused at the door. "I was just wondering. Are you familiar with Dickens?"

"Dickens. You mean Charles Dickens, the writer?"

"Uh-huh."

"Christmas Carol, Oliver Twist? Vaguely. When I was younger, I always liked the actor Alistair Sim as Scrooge. Why?"

"No reason. Just asking."

* * * *

"This is terrible news. Poor Mr. LaRoche. He was mugged? Right outside our building?"

Carl Jellicoe had described Marielle Tarkenton reasonably well after all. Frank might be a seasoned detective but he would have been challenged to describe her beyond her dark hair and glasses. She was about as average looking a person as he had seen: average height and weight, average voice, neutral eye color (they looked gray but he couldn't quite be sure).

What she was definitely, however, was nervous. She nervously gulped her coffee, nervously babbled, and nervously twitched at the table where they sat in the coffee bar while people bustled back and forth past them.

A painfully self-conscious twenty-something, he decided to himself. It wasn't the ideal place to talk but he preferred to do it outside of the office. This would have to do.

"I'm afraid so. I'm hoping you can help me out in finding the person who did this."

"Of course, of course, but…how can I help? What could I possibly know?"

"I'm hoping you can tell me something about Mr. LaRoche himself: who he associated with recently, what he was working on, if there was anybody he might have particularly alienated, that type of thing. And if you know anybody I could talk to who knew him well."

"Wow!" she exclaimed, eyes widening. "You think it wasn't a robbery then? You think someone disliked him enough to…?"

"Just looking at everything possible, Ms. Tarkenton. Maybe there's some connection that will help me find the killer."

"Wow!" she said again. "This is like a TV show! I don't know of any friends or family Mr. LaRoche had. He never had any personal visitors, you know?"

"There must be contact information for him at the office. Emergency contact, that sort of thing."

"No, that's the funny thing. I don't think he had anything like that on record."

"I understand he was involved in some transactions lately that were kind of hostile? A liability suit, some tenant evictions?"

"Well, yes. I've only been working there about three weeks, you understand. I couldn't tell you about anything before that. But recently, things like that, yes."

"Tell me about the lawsuit."

"Julius LaRoche versus the Little Sisters of Mercy Home for Women and Children. He stumbled on their pavement and in reaching to steady himself, slashed open his hand on a rusted metal bannister in front of the stoop of their building."

Frank was liking this guy more and more. "What was the outcome?"

"The insurance company settled with Mr. LaRoche. They usually do, in my understanding."

"For how much?"

Tarkenton hesitated for a moment. "$75,000. Oh, I guess I wasn't really supposed to divulge that. It was confidential. Well…he being deceased and you investigating his murder and all…"

Her fussing was getting on his nerves. "Seventy five…? Seriously?"

She nodded.

"Were there possibly any outspoken critics, shall we say, of this whole thing?"

"There was a small editorial in the paper about it, I remember. Very critical. Apparently Mr. LaRoche had a reputation for what they called 'nuisance lawsuits.' They referred to him as 'litigation happy'."

"You mean the *Blade-Courier*." It was the city's last remaining regular paper.

"Yes, that's right."

Great, thought Frank. The guy's sterling character had been public knowledge. There could be a list of people who had it in for him that could fill a small telephone book.

"How long ago was this settlement?"

"About two weeks. It was one of the first things he gave me to work on."

"I'll probably need to look at the background on that case."

"As long as it's okay with Mr. Jellicoe."

"It will be, I'll make sure of that. And the eviction cases?"

"You must mean the condo conversions at Webleyview. That was before I arrived but I've done a lot of the paperwork. Some of the prior tenants have been contentious."

"So the process has been less than friendly."

She stared at him blankly. "They're evictions. I guess those usually aren't happy occasions."

"Okay, but were any of the individuals particularly unhappy? Were there legal challenges, maybe personal exchanges with Mr. LaRoche?"

"Legal challenges, yes. A local attorney filed on behalf of several of the tenants."

"So the conversion is still in legal limbo?"

"Yes. It's generated a lot of paper, let me tell you."

"And personal exchanges? Did anybody, say, come to the office to confront Mr. LaRoche?"

"Just the reporter."

Frank stopped short and resisted the urge to plant his palm on his face. "Reporter?"

"Yeah. She works for some tabloid giveaway. One of her relatives was an evictee. She came up to interview Mr. LaRoche. He had no interest in it and they got kind of loud yelling at each other."

"What was this reporter's name, do you remember?"

Tarkenton bit her lip and rolled her eyes skyward. "I don't recall. You could look up her article that she wrote last week."

How much better was this going to get?

"Which paper?"

"I'm not sure. One of those free tabloids that come out on Thursday."

"Your office doesn't keep a file on published articles and editorials relating to your cases?"

She raised her hands as if experiencing a revelation. "Oh, of course. I think Mr. LaRoche was considering suing her. I have a file of the clippings back at the office."

"Speaking of which, I don't want to get you in trouble with Mr. Jellicoe for taking so long, so let me just ask you a couple more questions and let you get back to work. Tell me about the Bodega Building."

"That's the building he was about to buy on San Mateo. What about it?"

"His plan was to evict the shops that are currently there, was it not?"

"Yes. I heard him one day talking to a prospective architect for the project. It was going to be mixed use, condos on the top floor, high-end office suites below, and shops and an expensive restaurant on the ground floor."

"In that neighborhood? That's kind of a working class area."

"It's gentrifying rapidly. Mr. LaRoche was betting on the trends in the next few years."

Frank sighed. Was this guy for real? "He hadn't completed the transaction yet?"

"It was supposed to go into escrow this week. In fact, when I left yesterday, he was on the phone with the escrow office to try to get papers signed that day. He was impatient to get everything underway."

"What time was that?"

"Around two. I had to leave early for a dentist appointment. He had me call them a couple times earlier but as I was leaving, he was back on the phone with them again."

Employer and employee of the year, thought Frank to himself. "Any particular reason for his impatience?"

"I think he was trying to pre-empt a legal challenge of some sort by one of the tenants. The way he put it yesterday morning was that he was going to cut their legs out from under them."

"Out from under whom, exactly?"

"The Del Oso family. They operate the grocery store in the building."

"And were there any words between the Del Oso family and Mr. LaRoche?"

"Mr. Del Oso came to the office one day, with another, younger man. They had a polite but awkward conversation."

"You were present for it?"

"Not exactly. I was asked to bring in some files while they were talking, and I saw Mr. Del Oso when he left. As I said, the interaction was polite, no raised voices or anything. But the atmosphere was very chilly. He's a kind of intimidating person, quiet but big and very intense."

"Could you locate any of the documents pertaining to the purchase?"

"They must be in the office, unless Mr. LaRoche had taken them. I would think he was trying to get to the escrow office last night before they closed."

"He didn't have a briefcase with him when he was found. Let's take a chance on the office."

Frank closed his notebook and pushed his chair back. "I'll accompany you back and talk to Mr. Jellicoe about getting access to those files."

* * * *

Jellicoe had not truly counted the minutes before Frank's return and seemed not all that happy to see him enter with Tarkenton, but he grudgingly agreed to allow access to LaRoche's office and records.

Frank could have gotten a warrant for everything, but that would have meant returning for still another time, a contingency Jellicoe did not seem to find all that palatable. He seemed mostly upset that the indispensable Ms. Tarkenton's time would be devoted to helping Frank for the next half hour.

LaRoche's office was even more darkly oppressive than Jellicoe's, but it was reasonably tidy. Tarkenton quickly located the records he requested, as well as the file of newspaper clippings, and dutifully made copies for him, but could not locate any paperwork on the expected Bodega Building escrow. She found earlier correspondence on the pending purchase but nothing from the past week.

"Is it possible he had the papers with him when he was…uh, you know?" she asked Frank.

"If so, the assailant took them. He had nothing, certainly not a briefcase or a file of any kind. Even his pockets were empty."

"Well, they don't seem to be here. He had them on his desk yesterday."

"The escrow company he was dealing with—do you know their name?"

"Yes. It was Rovendale. I remember from typing up the papers." She gave him an address.

Frank perused a few more files and finally decided he had everything he needed for the moment. Tarkenton assembled the copies in a manila envelope and handed it to him.

"Thank you, Ms. Tarkenton, I appreciate your help."

"I hope you find whoever did this to Mr. LaRoche. What a terrible thing."

"One last question. Did he have a cell phone?"

"Yes, he did. He used it constantly. When he wasn't on the office line he was on his cell."

"So he would have had it with him when he left here last night, you'd think."

"I should think so."

Frank thanked her again and on his way out stuck his head into Jellicoe's office to say thanks and apologize for taking up his time. Jellicoe nodded silently, not even looking up from a file, clearly only wanting to see the last of Frank Vandegraf.

"If I need anything further, I'll give you a call," Frank said.

"If you really have to," Jellicoe murmured.

* * * *

He decided to drive to LaRoche's home. The address was in Sunnyview, the northernmost district of the city. The neighborhood was pleasant, upscale, and suburban. LaRoche's house was hardly opulent but looked comfortable, the front yard well-tended but with just a bit of seediness creeping in at the edges, as if the gardener or the landscaper hadn't come by in recent weeks.

Frank noted a car in the driveway: LaRoche's? If so, he apparently didn't drive to work. Nobody answered the bell and it looked dark and empty through the windows. Nobody answered the door of the neighbor to the left. When he rang the doorbell of the neighbor to the right, a tired-looking woman of about forty answered and looked at him quizzically until he identified himself.

"Mr. LaRoche? Has something happened to him? I hardly know him. We've been neighbors for years but he keeps to himself. Probably exchanged a dozen words over the years. One time he yelled at my kids for chasing a ball onto his front lawn."

Sounded like the right guy. "How long has he lived here?"

"I'd say he moved in here, oh, fifteen years ago. Had a wife at the time. She hasn't been around in many years now."

"Did you ever talk to her, or do you remember anything about her?"

"She was very nice. Her name was Violet, or something like that. Something floral. Rose, maybe."

"Any idea where she might have gone?"

"Or Lily. It might have been Lily. No, we never got very close, but she was always much more cordial than her husband. She would smile and say hello. He would just nod and grunt at us. Always seemed to be in a hurry."

"Any kids?"

"When they first moved in, there was a teenager who would come to visit. She stopped coming. I have no idea who she was."

"And the wife…?"

"Or it might have been Daisy."

"…about when did the wife leave the house?"

"Oh, it had to have been ten years ago now."

"So it's just been Mr. LaRoche since then?"

"As far as I know."

"I need to find his next of kin, or somebody to notify. Do you have any idea where I could look?"

"I'm sorry, Officer…"

"Detective, actually."

"Detective, I mean. I don't think anyone in this neighborhood could help you. I think he pretty much kept to himself, do you know? I never saw him socialize."

Another thought occurred to him. "Does he have a gardener or someone who comes by to tend the property?"

"There's a guy that comes and mows and blows. I don't know who he is. He doesn't come all that often anymore, maybe every three or four weeks. Usually on a Tuesday morning if I remember right."

The remainder of the conversation was equally non-productive. Frank thanked her and departed, giving the deserted avenue a look up and down before getting in his car. Nothing promising here.

The station was more or less on his way home so he decided to stop off there, drop off his pile of copies, maybe make another call or two then come back later for his shift that evening. It would be nice to be on the day shift next week.

It was already a busy Thursday morning in the unit: detectives and officers scurrying about and talking loudly, everybody multi-tasking to try to catch up on crazy workloads. The city was always generously dropping something new on the detectives' doorstep, and it was always a challenge to stay on top of it all.

He loved the oddness of the name of his unit, Personal Crimes. Some years back it had been called Special Crimes and before that Robbery-Homicide, but at some point a commission had decided Personal Crimes had a more meaningful ring to it, the sound of a true mission statement. They still dealt with basically the same types of felony offenses: murders, severe assaults, serious robberies.

The unit that handled burglaries and similar non-violent crimes had been re-named Property Crimes, which to his thinking was somewhat more lackluster. Frank had to wonder who would ever want to transfer to something called Property Crimes. It was probably where Athena Pardo was going to wind up.

Frank dumped the manila envelope on his desk and plopped into his chair, taking a deep breath as he switched on his computer.

Not that long ago, he would have pulled out a hefty telephone book and thumbed through it to find a number. Now even a Neanderthal like himself used his computer to look up a contact. He found Rovendale Escrow and picked up his desk phone to call. When a very harried-sounding man answered, Frank identified himself and said he was inquiring about Julius LaRoche.

"So what ever happened to that guy, anyway?" the escrow man replied, with a deep tone of impatience. "He bugged me over and over yesterday to push through a bunch of papers, then he bugged me to stay open late, and then he never showed up. And he's not answering his phone this morning! Now there's a cop calling me about him? What'd he do, shoot somebody?"

There seemed to be something about Julie LaRoche that just brought out the best in people.

"Actually, sir, somebody shot *him*. He's dead."

"Are you shitting me? When? What happened?"

"He seems to have been killed on his way over to your office last night."

"Oh shit! Tell me it had nothing to do with the protests over the building!"

"Protests over the building?"

"Yeah. The Bodega Building. The one he was buying. He was trying to ram through the sale, make it a done deal. That's why he kept prodding us night and day that we weren't moving the paperwork fast enough to his liking. This doesn't have to do with that, does it?"

"At this point it appears to have been a robbery gone bad, Mr...?"

"Roven. Ross Roven. Because that would be absolutely horrible publicity. So it had nothing to do with the Bodega Building?"

"The property on San Mateo he was trying to buy, you mean?"

"That's the one. That's not the real name of the building. I don't know that it's got a name. It's just what he called it, so we started calling it that. Not everyone there was happy about it. This has nothing to do with that, right?"

"At the moment, most likely not, Mr. Roven. But I'm looking into everything. I want to talk to you some more about this, but first of all I need to know if you can refer me to anyone who knew Mr. LaRoche. And then I'd like to know if you have copies of the documents he was supposed to sign last night?"

"Someone who knew him, no. Documents, sure. Had them all prepared and waiting for him. Too bad about what happened. So somebody just came up and shot him, like in a parking lot or something?"

"On the street, right in front of his building."

"And here I am railing on the man for not showing up. Kind of insensitive, isn't it? I've been told that, that I come off as insensitive."

"Well, under the circumstances, it's understandable. It sounds as if Mr. LaRoche could be a bit difficult."

"That's an understatement. First time I worked with him. And it would have been the last time. Oops, there I go again, huh?"

Frank navigated through Roven's digressions to ask further questions. It appeared that LaRoche should have had his own set of papers with him as well. If he did, they must have been taken by his attacker.

It took two more circuitous trips around the topic before Frank was satisfied that Roven knew of nobody close to LaRoche and had only dealt with him and his assistant. The seller of the property was a company called Bizel Financial.

There would be other questions but he needed to explore more pressing items at the moment. He thanked Roven and said he would shortly be in touch again and would like to be able to see the documents relating to the sale.

As he hung up, he shook his head. All of this may or may not be germane. For all he knew this was still a straight-up holdup gone bad.

He noticed two of the day shift detectives, Leon Simpkins and Art Dowdy, standing next to Dowdy's desk, talking. He strolled over to them, everybody exchanging nods as he approached.

"Frank, what's up? Aren't you on the other shift this week?"

"Yeah. I just caught a shooting and had to follow up this morning. I'm about to head home. I just wanted to ask about something."

They were a strikingly disparate pair. Simpkins was a tall, muscular, outgoing African-American with a ready smile; Dowdy was short, lean, ash-blond and dour. Both were in their thirties. Some on the unit jokingly referred to them as the Emcee and the Mortician. Frank thought of them as Mutt and Jeff, the old comic strip characters, but figured most of the younger guys would have no clue as to who they might be. Despite the jokes, he knew them both to be smart and aware. They looked at him expectantly. Dowdy drained the coffee cup he was holding.

"My vic got shot twice at close range in an apparent walk-up street robbery. You guys caught anything like that lately?"

Simpkins folded his arms in thought then shook his head. "Not really, no." He looked to Dowdy for corroboration. His partner just shook his head. "You're thinking it's a repeater?"

"Maybe somebody doing a string of quick swoops. He walked up to the guy on the street and just plugged him. Emptied his pockets but left a watch. Might have grabbed up a briefcase as well."

"Any witnesses?"

"One guy, not much help. Saw two guys bumping against each other and heard shots. He wasn't all that close. It was getting dark."

They both shook their heads again. "Not like anything we've caught of late."

"I'm just hoping against hope that there's a pattern of some kind. This has the potential to…"

Just then, Frank's phone began to buzz in his pocket. He fished it out, flipping it open.

"Frank's still got that relic," Dowdy said to his partner. Simpkins smiled back. They were two of several tech-savvy types on the unit that were his constant sparring partners. Frank just gave them a smirk and turned away.

"Vandegraf here."

"Detective, it's Marielle Tarkenton. Mr. Jellicoe asked me to give you a call."

"Yes, Ms. Tarkenton, what's up?"

"We might be able to help you find a next of kin. Mr. LaRoche left a will."

"A will?"

"Yes, and there's a copy on file at the office."

"That was good thinking, Ms. Tarkenton."

"Actually Mr. Jellicoe thought of it. He told me to look it up and call you before you decided to come see him again. He also specified I should pass that along as well."

"Salt of the earth, that man. Must be a joy to work for him."

There was a brief pause and the slightest sigh. Clearly she was within hearing range of her boss, or thought she might be. Then she said, very businesslike, "I'll tell him you said thank you. I looked it over and there's only one name mentioned in it."

"One name? He only remembered one person in his will?"

"He left everything to her. Her name is Sarah Hartnett and the address on the document is in Sycamore Creek."

Sycamore Creek was a town about twenty miles east of the city, an upscale locale where people who could afford to would flee when they tired of the big city. He hurried back to his desk and jotted down the specific address she gave him.

"What are the chances she's still there, do you think?"

"Well, he updated the will only last year, so I'd guess pretty good."

"And you have no other information on this Sarah Hartnett or even know who she is?"

"I'm afraid not. I asked Mr. Jellicoe and he'd never heard of her."

"I guess I'll have to go ask her myself then. Thanks for that. Please tell Mr. Jellicoe that I can't guarantee that he's seen the last of me, but his efforts are appreciated."

As luck would have it, when he checked online he found a Sarah Hartnett listed at the address. When he dialed the number it was picked up on the first ring. A voice both hoarse and nasal said, "Hello?"

"Hello, I'm looking for Sarah Hartnett?"

The woman on the other end sneezed. "And just who's this?"

"Police Detective Frank Vandegraf. Would this be Ms. Hartnett?"

She coughed. "Yes, this is she. What's this about?"

"Ms. Hartnett, I'm calling about Julius LaRoche. Do you know him?"

"Do I know him! What's up with Julie now?"

"Uh...Ms. Hartnett, I'm afraid something has happened. You're the only person I've been able to locate who might have some connection to him."

She coughed again and cleared her throat. "Something's happened? Did he give you my name or something? That would be a first."

"I'm afraid he's been killed."

"What? Are you kidding? Julie's dead?"

"Yes. He was killed last night."

"Wow." Another pause, this time with no coughing or sneezing. "I'm not sure how to react to that news, Detective."

"Had you seen him or talked with him recently?"

"No. Not in a long time."

"And how do you know Mr. LaRoche, exactly?"

"I'm his daughter."

Estranged daughter, as Frank learned from the rest of their conversation. When she asked, he went into greater detail about the circumstances of his death. She was surprised but didn't seem particularly upset. He learned she'd had no contact with her father since moving to Sycamore Creek a number of years earlier. The last she had spoken with him had been at his house.

"That was the house with his second wife. I was still living with my mother at the time. So you haven't been able to locate Dahlia then?"

"Dahlia?"

"The second Mrs. LaRoche, lucky woman. I understand she divorced him. Probably moved as far away from him as she could get." Hartnett coughed again. "Excuse me. I'm home from work with this cold or flu or whatever it is. Otherwise you wouldn't have reached me this morning. Excuse me again." She blew her nose. "So how did you find me, exactly?"

"You're mentioned in his will, Ms. Hartnett. In fact you're the only one in it."

That clearly took her aback. Another long pause.

"I'm in Julie's will?"

"Apparently he left everything to you."

"What the hell! Really? I can't believe it." She blew her nose again. For a moment Frank had regretted breaking this news to her on the phone rather than in person, but given her attitude and her communicably diseased state, he was glad it had worked out this way. "It's not like we were close, you know? I don't think we've even spoken in, like, six or seven years!"

"His law partner will be getting in touch with you about the will. I'm sorry for your loss."

"I really have to process this. This is crazy. I'm sorry, I must seem terrible to you, not breaking up over the news that my father's dead."

"Grief is a strange thing, Ms. Hartnett. Everybody reacts differently."

"I mean, I didn't hate him or anything. I just sort of wrote him off, do you know? Wow."

"Your mother was his first wife, is that correct?"

"Yes. She changed her name back to Hartnett and I did the same."

"Is it possible to talk with her?"

"Do you know the line from the classic old movie, 'I think you'll find the conversation somewhat one-sided'?"

"*Casablanca*. Conrad Veidt. So you're telling me…?"

"Yep, my mom passed away five years ago."

"I'm sorry."

"Thank you. She was pretty cool. She kinda got along with my father, even after he remarried. She was the one who encouraged me to keep contact with him and Dahlia."

"And you don't know what happened to Dahlia?"

"No idea. She was a very sweet lady. Very patient, very accepting. I don't know what she saw in Julie. She and I got along really well, all things considered. When I stopped visiting them, I missed her a lot more than I missed him."

"Why did you stop visiting them?"

"I was about sixteen. It was complicated. Some of it was issues with him. Some of it was just being sixteen, you know? Do you have kids, maybe teenaged kids?"

"No. But I have friends who do."

"It's not an easy age. I was probably a self-absorbed pain in the ass, and I wasn't very understanding. We were arguing constantly and I finally just got sick of it and stormed out one day and never went back. I felt bad because Dahlia seemed really upset by our fighting. My mom tried half-heartedly to get me to reconcile for a while. But by then she was starting to get sick. She was sick for a long time."

"I'm really sorry, Ms. Hartnett."

She sneezed again. It sounded as if she was wiping off the phone receiver. "It seems a long time ago, Detective…I'm sorry, what was your name again?"

"Vandegraf."

"Detective Vandegraf. I've made my peace over my father. He did the best he could. He just wasn't a great husband or father. I've made a life for myself here in Sycamore Creek. I've got a good job, friends, a fiancée. All that other stuff is like history out of a book."

"I'm still sorry to have brought you this news this way. I had no idea of your relationship. I won't bother you any further right now. Maybe we can talk later, and if I can be of any help, please feel free to contact me." He recited his office and cell phone numbers.

"One last question: do you think Dahlia would have taken back her original name after the divorce?"

"It makes sense. If it was anything like Julie's marriage to my mom, she would have wanted to get rid of his name as fast as she could. Her maiden name was Storm."

"Dahlia Storm. Thank you, Ms. Hartnett. Again, I'm sorry."

She started to laugh and it turned into a deep cough. Finally she said, "My sorries happened a while ago, I guess. Time will tell."

Frank shook his head as he hung up the phone. This guy left a wide swath of wreckage behind him. Was anybody going to miss him?

THREE

On his way in to the evening shift, Frank decided to drive by the so-called Bodega Building. There were still numerous people along the street and in the market and restaurant. Both looked to be very popular.

He started with the market, Mercado Del Oso. He elbowed his way through the narrow aisles to the register, and was directed to the back of the store, where the owner, Felipe Del Oso, was busy with a clipboard inventory of some sort. He was a bear of a man, over six feet tall, with dark curly hair and a thick dark beard. When Frank introduced himself and showed his badge, Del Oso put down his clipboard and flashed a huge grin.

"How can I help you, Detective? I'm Phil Del Oso, at your service." He had a deep, resonant voice.

"Have you got a couple minutes, Mr. Del Oso?"

"Sure, c'mon over here." He led Frank through a door into a storage area filled with crates of mangoes, bananas, and other fruit.

"Sorry, we've got an office but we got a late delivery of fish and SOME FOOL PUT IT IN THE OFFICE!" He shouted the last part with a laugh back into the store, at a young man lifting boxes, who grinned back and said loudly, "Hey, Pop, they had to go somewhere!"

"Anyway, plantains smell better. So here we are." He reached for a rag on top of one of the stacks and wiped his hands. "So what's up?"

"I wanted to talk to you about Julius LaRoche."

"The guy who's buying the building? Is he complaining about us or something?"

"Are you aware that Mr. LaRoche was killed last night?"

"Killed? No way!" Del Oso seemed genuinely surprised. "What happened?"

"It looks like a robbery. He was shot twice at close range."

The man's eyes opened wide. "Damn! The hell you say!"

"I understand he was about to buy this building and threatened to evict your market and the restaurant next door."

"Yeah, he was gonna throw *everybody* out. You say he was 'about to'… does that mean he …?"

"Yes, it would seem he was killed before he could complete the transaction. The sale never happened."

Del Oso sighed deeply. "I'm sorry it happened to him. But I have to admit, I've got what you'd call mixed feelings."

"I also understand you had some words with Mr. La Roche over the impending purchase recently, in his office?"

"Ah. So that's what this is about. We had a discussion, yes. My son and I went to his office to try to work out something. This market is everything I've got. My family is invested in this. We decided we'd try to present a counter-offer, buy the building ourselves. The seller told us LaRoche had first rights and we needed to talk to him."

"I assume Mr. LaRoche was not receptive to your overtures."

"No. No, he was not. His whole attitude was basically it was a done deal and for me to live with it."

"So you argued?"

"That's not my way, Detective." He smiled slightly through his thick beard. "You know when there are serious diplomatic dealings and they describe them as 'frank talks'? That was what we had. Neither of us raised our voice. Nobody threatened anybody or said anything intemperate. We spoke seriously but respectfully. I made my points and left."

"I don't think you were just going to leave it at that. What was your next move going to be?"

"We talked to a lawyer. We had a legal challenge in the works."

"So he was racing to get the sale done before your challenge could go through, it seems. He was in a hurry to jam the transaction through."

Del Oso shrugged. "Could be. I don't know. I was afraid he'd be moving fast, so we were trying to be just as fast. We were hoping to get a stay on it, build public opinion against it. Maybe even get the building declared a historical landmark. I was supposed to talk to a reporter this week from one of the locals. She's been working on stories about LaRoche."

Frank wondered if she might be the same reporter who had written about Julie's condo-conversion evictions. He made a note to follow up on that when he got the chance.

"You say your son accompanied you when you went to see LaRoche?"

"Yeah. Daniel's my second in command. Someday the *mercado* will be his… *if* we can keep it alive. I like to take him on my business calls, to wholesalers and such, so he can learn."

Del Oso stared intensely at Frank. "Are you thinking this really wasn't a robbery like you told me, that this was like payback or a message kind of thing?"

It was Frank's turn to shrug. "Right now I'm just trying to accumulate the facts, Mr. Del Oso."

"But you're thinking maybe I had something to do with it, right?" His bright smile was now gone, replaced by a cold glare.

"I've got no theories yet. It does seem a lot of people had it in for him."

"That wasn't a 'no' to my question, though."

"Chances are it's exactly what it seems, a holdup turned tragic. But when a guy's made as many enemies as he did, I have to investigate all the possibilities."

"You can ask around about me all you want, Detective. You'll find I'm a straight guy, not somebody who would do something like this."

Frank thought, but did not say, that in his experience everybody could have done something like this. That made his job a little harder and less pleasant, but there it was.

* * * *

The small, bustling restaurant was called *Rincon Guatemalteco*. The proprietor was a short, stocky man, who introduced himself as Oscar Argueta. He motioned Frank over to a tiny corner table and sat with him, looking attentive. They had to speak loudly over the tumult of the patrons. He was surprised to learn of the death of Julie LaRoche and shook his head sadly.

"I never knew the man. It's still sad to learn of anyone dying in this way. Did he have a family?"

"Not close. He was divorced. There's a surviving daughter."

"A shame. How may I help you in this matter?"

"It's my understanding that he was about to buy the building and planned to evict the tenants."

"Yes, there was word to that effect. It wouldn't have mattered to me. I hadn't mentioned this to anyone, but I planned to give my notice soon anyway. We found a larger location with an option to buy, and the rent was comparable. If anything, the sale might have worked for the best; I'm sure we could have negotiated out of the remaining months on our lease."

"What about the other tenants in this building? I mean besides Felipe Del Oso's market. The people upstairs."

"There're only a handful of apartments on those two upper floors, and they seem to be mostly vacant of late. I'm thinking the current owners were not renewing leases or re-renting. Perhaps they anticipated the sale of the building." Argueta frowned. "And as to what had been said to Felipe about his *mercado*, I don't have the slightest idea."

Frank decided this was a dead end and thanked Argueta for his time.

* * * *

Back at the station, Frank found manila envelopes on his desk: preliminary reports from the coroner and SID on the LaRoche case. It was still possible to get hard-copy results as well as to receive them by email, and while Frank was grudgingly coming around to reading them online, he still opted to receive printed reports he could hold in his hand.

They were brief and, as expected, offered nothing new: two bullets in the victim, .38 caliber, and the residue was consistent with both shots being fired into the chest at very close range. The bullets came from a revolver and no shells were found at the scene. No other evidence on the body or clothing. No defensive wounds or signs of a struggle. The slugs had been sent to ballistics to check for matches to other crimes. If he was very lucky there'd be a match to an actual gun, but he knew it was unlikely.

There were also transcripts of the uniformed officers' reports. They were likewise inconclusive. Nothing had turned up that could have been connected to the victim.

If this were indeed a straightforward anonymous robbery, Frank saw little chance of any further breaks. There were numerous robberies of opportunity in the city every week, assailant unknown to victim.

He had four other violent holdups on his desk right now and he was spinning his wheels on all of them. Every now and then, somebody died in the commission of such robberies. That was probably what had happened in this case. His only chance was if there was more to the murder—if it were actually personal—but the odds against that were large, even given the animosity that Julie seemed to inspire in every part of his life.

He started perusing the papers that Marielle Tarkenton had copied for him. He read through the unsigned *Blade-Courier* editorial, a brief, reasonably-restrained two paragraphs. It began by saying that the infamous Julius LaRoche had once again achieved an unspecified settlement in a liability suit against a convent of charitable nuns and went on to lament what it termed the "litigation-drunk" state of current society. Frank didn't see any specific potential in that, but it did reinforce Julie's infamy as the most hated man in the city.

He turned to the article on the Webleyview conversion, written by a reporter named Lorena Park for a tabloid called *The Urban Sentinel*. The article, entitled "Dumped On the Streets," ran several pages, punctuated by photographs of unhappy-looking people standing in front of the controversial edifice, and referred to LaRoche as LaRoach in several places.

It was passionate writing, Frank decided, but hardly objective. Park described several of the people who had lived for many years in the building before it had been bought and turned into Webleyview. Her elderly uncle and aunt, who had emigrated from Korea and now lived with her own parents, were among those she profiled, along with three people she claimed had become homeless afterward. One of them had passed away not long before the article had been written, and there was even a photograph of her gravesite.

Park had miraculously succeeded in actually portraying Julie LaRoche in an even more negative light. Frank could imagine what the conversation must have been like when Park visited the law offices, and could imagine the litigation that Julie was planning against her.

He figured it was worth a call to see if he could reach Lorena Park, even though it was getting late. He found the number for the *Urban Sentinel* and navigated a recorded directory through to her.

He was surprised when she picked up on the first ring.

"This is Lorena Park," she said in a clipped voice that announced she would brook no foolishness. This was a no-nonsense woman, Frank mused. He identified himself to her and explained he was calling because of Julius LaRoche.

"I heard this afternoon about the shooting. How can I help you, Detective Vandegraf?"

Someone who got his name right on the first try, he reflected. Good start.

"I see you wrote an article about him and I understand you were possibly following up on another one?"

"Correct on both counts. Are you thinking he was killed by someone he wronged? I was under the impression it was a robbery."

"It's looking like that, but I'm just checking into everything."

"Of course. It's not like he didn't have any enemies. You're probably getting that idea by now."

"He did seem to have a knack for making friends. How did you get interested in writing about him to begin with?"

"If you've read my article, you know when he bought Webleyview out from under all the tenants, that two of the people he displaced were my relatives. They're smart, wonderful people who came to this country and worked hard and did well. But they've gotten old and they're living on their pensions. When this eviction happened to them and my parents had to take them in, I was outraged and started looking into it. Most of the people being dislocated were elderly, minorities, people on fixed incomes, in general powerless and unable to fight back. It's not exactly an upper class neighborhood but it's been stable for decades, until the forces of destabilization started arriving. When I discovered what kind of a manipulative bully Julius LaRoche is—or I guess I should say 'was'—I knew I had to write about him."

"So you interviewed him for the article?"

"I tried. He put me off several times. Finally I went to his office and confronted him. That didn't go well. He never did offer any comment for the article. I went ahead and finished the piece and submitted it, mentioning that he had refused to be interviewed for the story."

"I can't imagine it was well received in his office. Any reaction?"

"A couple of angry calls to the paper threatening to sue. My publisher is used to that. He offered LaRoche the opportunity to write a letter of rebuttal which he would print. I don't think the offer was accepted."

"Conceivably he took offense to being called LaRoach, among other things."

Park laughed. "You think? The slimeball deserved it."

"Forgive me, but it doesn't exactly seem an objective approach to the story."

"It's called advocacy journalism, Detective. *The Sentinel* specializes in it."

"And you were pursuing a new story on the proposed purchase of the Bodega Building?"

"I hate that name. That's what LaRoche was calling it, not anybody else. Once again he was marginalizing the people in the building and the neighborhood. It was yet another attempt at destabilizing a vibrant and diverse community for his own profit. I especially hate what he had done to the Del Oso family, stealing the building out from under them like that."

"I'm not sure I know what you mean, stealing the building? I thought it had recently been defaulted and he was buying it from the current owners?"

"You mean Bizel Financial. I guess you don't know how they got hold of the building to begin with, then?"

"Educate me, Ms. Park."

"They specialize in refinancing mortgages. Let's just say they offer terms that might raise a few eyebrows. And if you look at their record, they have a suspiciously high rate of defaults and foreclosures."

"This kind of stuff still goes on, even after all the scandals?"

"The owner should have known better. It's a complicated story that I'm still digging into for the details. The point here is that he refinanced and lost the building. And I guess you don't know that the victimized owner was

Felipe Del Oso, huh?"

"Are you kidding me!"

"The things a reporter finds with her little shovel and spade, Detective."

"So who is this Bizel Financial? Any connection with LaRoche?"

"That's one of the things I was looking into. It's shady and complicated, and the scum often rises to the top of the pond altogether. But as of yet I've found nothing concrete."

Frank was furiously writing on a legal pad at his desk. His mind raced as he scribbled names and drew arrows and question marks to connect them.

Del Oso had not mentioned anything about being the prior owner of the building. Argueta, who must have known, had not brought it up either.

Nothing had been said about the possibility of Julie being in on the earlier foreclosure and sale.

Nothing pertaining to the transaction had been left at the office.

"This is fascinating stuff," Park continued. "But I'm not sure I'm seeing a connection to his death. I'm more thinking it was just his personal karma."

"Excuse me?"

"The guy just attracted hostility. It would make more sense to me that a random mugger approached him and he gave the guy too much grief."

"Not a conspiracy fan, then, I take it?"

"Oh, I love conspiracies. They're my bread-and-butter. But most of the time I'm disappointed when I go looking for them. It's usually the simplest solution, and that comes down to individual stupidity or venality rather than cabals."

"Occam's Razor," Frank offered.

"Yeah, sort of. Very good, Detective. You're a pretty sharp guy, you know?"

Frank rolled his eyes.

"For me," she continued, "the real story is the building and how it was procured. It's a treat when I can actually uncover some kind of deep collusion and this Bizel thing looks promising. I doubt it's connected to the murder, but your man LaRoche may or may not turn up involved in that. Keep an eye out for my story."

Frank found himself writing "Bizel Financial" on his legal pad and circling it over and over. It was tenuous, but so was everything else he had. He decided it couldn't hurt to call an investigator he knew in the Financial Crimes unit and ask if the name rang any bells. He caught him in the office and had a brief chat. Bizel was unfamiliar to the investigator but he promised to look into it and get back to Frank.

He continued to idly trace ink circles on the pad, around and around the word "Bizel."

Finally he realized that was exactly what his brain was doing: making circles over and over the same territory. He wadded up the sheet of legal paper and tossed it into his wastebasket.

Maybe tomorrow, Friday, something would present itself.

* * * *

"I'm starting to get the impression, Detective, that you are suspecting me of Mr. LaRoche's murder."

Felipe Del Oso had a broad smile on his face as he said that. They were sitting in the market's cramped office, looking at each other over the piles of invoices and other papers covering the cluttered desk. Del Oso had his legs stretched out to the side and was leaning back in his chair.

"I'm just curious as to why, last time we talked, you left out the simple fact that you used to be the owner of this building. That is kind of unusual."

"It just didn't come up, that's all. By the way, this room still smells of fish, doesn't it? I apologize for that. I'm going to give Danny a piece of my mind for letting them bring that stuff up here. Sea bass…great fish, we sell a ton of it, but it's definitely strong. I don't know what he was thinking."

"No matter, Mr. Del Oso. So, it's come up now. You owned the building and you…lost it?"

Del Oso's expression grew more serious now. His thick dark eyebrows knitted together low and he frowned through his beard. He sat forward and nodded. "I needed money in a hurry. Unfortunately I felt a certain urgency and took out a loan on my equity from someone I probably shouldn't have."

"So you're saying you couldn't go through a legitimate source."

Del Oso hesitated and nodded.

"Are you going to tell me why you needed the money, Mr. Del Oso?"

It was a long moment before he considered and made his decision. "My son got into some trouble. If he didn't pay certain people, there would have been unfortunate consequences."

"Your son Daniel, who works here?"

"No, no. *No.* Not Danny. My younger son. Jesse. You're not going to see him working here. Not at the moment, anyway. At the moment he's kind of what you'd call the black sheep of the family. He's also far away from here right now."

"What are we talking here? Gambling debt? Drugs?"

"Gambling. He was into them pretty deeply. By the time he came to me it was way out of hand. And with these guys, it grows by the day, if you get what I'm saying."

"What did he owe when he came to you?"

"It was over a hundred thousand. So I went to talk to them. They gave me three days to come up with the money or…well, things were going to happen to Jesse."

"So he tried to run?"

"He left town, yes. He was scared. But you don't run from these guys, Detective. You gotta know what I mean, right? You pay them. That's your only alternative." Del Oso buried his head in his hands on the desk. "I got problems with Jesse. He's the prodigal son, you now? But he's my son."

Frank nodded. "So you had to come up with a lot of money in a hurry."

"The only thing I had to put up to get that kind of money was the building. And it had to be fast."

"So you went to Bizel."

"Yeah. In fact they were, shall we say, suggested, as a source of quick revenue by the holders of Jesse's debt."

Del Oso looked up and cast a long meaningful gaze at Frank. He got the point.

"So you paid off Jesse's debt in full, got guarantees he'd be safe?"

"As long as he stayed away from them from now on. I told Jesse not to come back, to stay far away, just to be sure of that. And he hasn't come back."

"And the next thing you know, they're repossessing the building out from under you."

"We had this building for quite a while. When we came to this neighborhood, it was considered 'depressed.' Lots of new immigrants, especially from Latin America. Property was cheap. I saw the real promise in this neighborhood. It's vibrant, lots of energy, lots of good people. I believed in them and took a chance, buying the building, opening the *mercado*, leasing to the restaurant. It was paying off." He shook his head. "And then this all happened."

"How long ago was this, when they took over the building?"

"Maybe four months. But it didn't take long to see that so much was going to go down the drain. They were already driving away the tenants and emptying the building through attrition. Just like that."

"So you were trying to buy back the building. But how were you going to do that?"

"I had time to arrange some more legitimate loans. From private sources, who wouldn't look at the forfeiture. They were people I couldn't go to with my original problem, but this time I had to swallow my pride and explain the whole situation to them. Some of them came through for me. I could have swung it."

"But the deck was stacked against you, wasn't it?"

"Oh yeah. The fix was in. There was no way I was gonna get it back."

"When you went to talk to LaRoche...?"

"I think that *cabrón* had his hand in this. I think he was in bed with those *ladrónes* from the beginning." Del Oso glared at Frank. "So, now I guess,

Mr. Policeman, that you're really convinced I had something to do with the murder of that worthless weasel?"

* * * *

Friday evening was unusually quiet in the squad room, with only a handful of people around. It was almost funereal, compounding the heavy feeling on Frank as he sat at his desk, scratching out diagrams and notes on a legal pad. Some detectives preferred to lay everything out on a big white board in the conference room. He had become more comfortable with the intimacy of his legal pad.

In the center of the page he had written JULIE LAROCHE in large capitals, circled three times. Arrows radiated out to the peripheries of the paper, where he had jotted various other names and items. In one corner he had written BIZEL FINANCIAL and had drawn arrows (with question marks) to JULIE, to MISSING BRIEFCASE?, to GAMBLERS, to JESSE DEL OSO, and to FELIPE DEL OSO. The whole group took up a good quarter of his page.

Jesse Del Oso was apparently a bad apple to begin with, but had truly overextended himself into a trouble zone with the gamblers. Maybe they had deliberately maneuvered him into that zone in order to get their hands on the Del Oso property. It was an interesting digression that might perhaps interest the Organized Crime unit, but the only truly relevant factor was if it motivated Felipe Del Oso to kill LaRoche.

Could Julie LaRoche be directly involved in this? Frank couldn't yet see it that way.

Felipe had been in plain sight, with witnesses and employees, in the market that entire evening. He could have hired someone to murder LaRoche, but somehow that didn't feel right either.

His gut feeling was that Phil Del Oso was a straight-up guy. Straight-up guys had been known to commit crimes, even kill people. He'd have to keep exploring.

He could really stretch his imagination: Julie had been involved in the scheme; his co-conspirators had killed him and taken the documents to cover their tracks.

The potential connections and schemes seemed endless, and they mostly struck him as groundless fantasies. His experience and logic persisted that it was exactly what it seemed, a random robbery turned homicide.

He had to admit: he wanted this case to involve some kind of causal linearity, like a conspiracy or a crime of passion. Senseless crimes drove him crazy, not just because they were futile and unnecessary excursions ending in human tragedy, but because he wanted something logical and rational to explore and unwind. But the more he looked at it, the less that made sense.

He could fight it all he wanted but there it was.

He looked at the clock on the wall. One hour until his shift ended. He pulled out another legal pad, laid it next to the first, and dove back into his twisting diagrams.

FOUR

Frank hadn't made it to his desk Monday morning before being intercepted in front of Castillo's office and beckoned inside. The Lieutenant actually gestured for Frank to have a seat.

"Frank, did you make some inquiries with Financial Crimes about a company called Bizel?"

"Yeah, actually, I did."

"You're going to need to step back from that one. Leave it be."

"I don't understand."

"You couldn't have known, but you stepped into a hornet's nest. Bizel is apparently under deep investigation for money laundering or fraud or something, by a joint task force that includes the D.A.'s office and the FBI. Can't roil the waters or call attention to it."

"You gotta be kidding me, Lou!"

"Straight from the Captain. That, by the way is just between you and me. Nobody else hears about this."

Frank nodded and rubbed the back of his neck. "That came out of nowhere, but I shouldn't be surprised, I guess."

"I take it this has something to do with one of your current cases."

"Possibly. It's a long shot involving some background on the LaRoche murder. He was about to buy a building that might have been acquired by Bizel under dubious circumstances. "

Castillo grunted a short laugh. "Leave it to you to stumble onto something like that. But not overly germane to the murder, I take it?"

"I'd say it's a stretch. Interesting sidelight but I can't make a solid connection."

"Then consider it a dead end. You're going to have to work around it. How's that case coming along?"

"I've got a city of potential suspects. *Everybody* hated him. His own law partner couldn't stand him. It's not like he was a connected guy; he was just a litigious, mercenary SOB. The killing may well be exactly what it looks like, a random act of violence in the commission of a robbery. I just wanted to take a peek at some things on the periphery. There's more of a chance of solving it if it's not just a random attack."

Castillo nodded. "That's just like you, a thorough guy. I appreciate the due diligence, but don't get too caught up following red herrings. You know to follow the evidence and not get caught up in unsubstantiated theories."

"I know. And I'm not neglecting the rest of my caseload. I just want to get what I can on this one while it's still warm."

"And that's the other thing I called you in to tell you. You're getting a new partner."

Frank took a deep breath. This was faster than he had expected. He hadn't had the chance to prepare himself. "Lou, is this really necessary?"

"She comes highly recommended, Detective. It's time you stopped your solo act."

"She?"

"Yeah, our new detective's a woman. Have you got a problem with that?"

"The woman part, hell no. Come on, Lou. You know me. One of the best detectives we have in Personal Crimes is Jilly Garvey. A couple of the sharpest unis I know are women..."

Castillo nodded, a wry smile actually sprouting under his thick mustache. "Some of your best friends, you mean? Frank, you are digging yourself into a hole here, you know that? And I swear you're turning red, too, by the way."

"No, honestly, I mean it. I might never have closed that weird parking lot murder last year without that Officer Pardo doing all the extra footwork, and..."

"Now that's interesting," Castillo interjected, but Frank found himself continuing to babble.

"...it's just, you want me to babysit a brand new baby?"

"You're worried we're getting a dud. And the responsibility's going to fall on you. You're going to be wasting your precious time in training her."

"Well..."

"Frank, would it help if I told you that our new promotion is up from the uniforms and she's proven herself to be bright, resourceful, and highly effective?"

"A uni? Not a transfer from Property or somewhere? That's a surprise."

"Well, one of the things that influenced that decision was an absolutely glowing recommendation from one of our own detectives here."

Castillo stared at Frank and waited for the realization to dawn on him. "And who better to break her in than her patron saint?"

"Pardo?"

"That's right."

"Athena Pardo has been assigned to Personal Crimes?"

"She'll be here any time now. Think you can find her a desk out near you?"

Frank rose. "Sure."

He was halfway out the door when he almost collided with Athena Pardo. He nearly didn't recognize her with her hair down, wearing a blazer and slacks rather than a patrol officer's uniform, looking rather self-conscious. She held a cardboard box with some of her personal items. She gave him a startled smile.

"Detective Vandegraf."

"Detective Pardo," he replied. "Welcome aboard."

"Detective Pardo, come on in," said Castillo. "Frank's going to get you set up while we go over some things. Right, Frank?"

"Yeah. But of course," stammered Frank.

Frank commandeered a nearby empty desk and was able to haul it over so it faced his own. Then he rolled the accompanying chair over. He sat down and tried to follow his usual morning routine, jotting down notes and to-do items on his legal pad, but he found it difficult to concentrate.

Before very long, Castillo walked Athena over to his desk, said, "You're in good hands. Welcome to Personal Crimes," and disappeared.

Frank looked up at Athena. "Detective Vandegraf," she smiled. She was trying to be confident but he could detect an uncertain nervousness in her voice and manner.

"Detective Pardo," he smiled back. "I told you we'd be calling you that someday."

"Yes, sir, you did," she said, the hopeful smile still frozen on her face. She stood awkwardly, carton in her hands, waiting. Frank hated this uncomfortable ice-breaking nonsense. On a crime scene, detective and uniform, they would have been talking naturally and comfortably, but now the situation was different.

"Forget the 'sir' stuff. I'm Frank and you're Athena, okay? As the Lieutenant said, welcome to Personal Crimes." He pointed with the pen in his hand to the empty desk. "Stow your gear and let's get started."

* * * *

He gave her a quick tour around the unit, introducing her to various people, many of whom already knew her from the street. The reception was generally cordial but short. There was always some trepidation about a new detective but Pardo had a good reputation as a smart but righteous cop. That would help her over the first few weeks.

By the end of the morning, he had oriented her to the general routines of business. He regretted that his colleagues Jilly Garvey and Dan Lee were out on a case. He knew they'd be supportive: Jilly would no longer be the sole woman detective on the squad and Dan hadn't had his detective shield all that long either. Frank had to confess to himself that he felt a little dubious about being able to be a strong enough support for his new partner. He had never broken in a newbie. He wasn't sure if he'd go about it the right way. He'd find out soon enough.

They grabbed a quick lunch and then he concentrated on familiarizing her with the cases they'd be handling. As he had expected, she was a fast study. They sat at his desk while he gave her an overview of each of the cases and she nodded, asked the right questions, and made the right observations.

This might work out okay. Things were just going to go more slowly while she absorbed the system and procedures and they both learned to stay out of each other's way.

"Right now, I'm kind of in a wheel-spinning mode. I guess now it's *we* are." He picked up the stack of files and ceremoniously dropped them back on the desk with a thump.

"So you're mostly re-canvassing, following up with witnesses, that type of thing?"

"Exactly. I hate to do this to you in your first week, but we have to wade through some of this garbage and try to close some of these. It's a simple matter of re-asking questions, noting the answers, and hoping something new comes up. If we split these up they'll go twice as fast."

"No problem," said Athena, picking up one of the files and leafing through it. "Sounds like a good way to get my feet wet, in fact. How about this one?"

Frank shrugged. "They all gotta get done. Take your pick."

"So," Athena said as she perused the reports in the file, "this is the lunch counter operator that got mugged."

"Yeah, Garo's Cafe, over on Goff. Older guy runs the place. Business district, only open for breakfast and lunch until mid-afternoon. He was closing up when two guys entered and beat and robbed him. He was in the hospital for a few days with a concussion. When I finally got to talk to him he didn't remember much. Couldn't ID the assailants. They were masked. No other witnesses."

"I see he has a daughter who was there."

"She was lucky. She was back in the kitchen. She hid under a table until she heard them leave. She didn't see anything."

"And no other employees."

"He's got a kitchen guy who leaves early. Same for a couple of waitresses. His afternoons get slow so it's usually just him and the daughter for the last hour or so."

"Nobody on the street saw anything?"

"Nobody came forward. It's a business district: financial offices, banks, law offices and such. There wouldn't have been much foot traffic to speak of for another hour or so. The perps likely knew that when they picked their time and place."

Athena nodded, still reading. "No luck with canvasses, no cameras?"

"I had unis checking up and down and I was out there too. A couple of security cams were on but nothing to be found. These guys seem to have scoped out the venue pretty well."

"So maybe they're locals."

"Very possibly. They might even come in to eat there. No luck on that angle either."

"How's the victim doing?"

"He recovered, more or less. He's back at work."

"Okay, then." She packed up the file and slid it under her arm.

"I sort of expected you to follow up by phone."

"If you don't mind, I'd like to do this in person, to get a better handle on it."

Frank hesitated. He wasn't sure how he was supposed to handle this. "I'm thinking Castillo expects me to hang out with you the first day or two at least."

"Detective—I mean Frank—I appreciate that but it's not like I've never done follow-up interviews as a patrol officer, you know? This is a pretty routine case, isn't it? Let me at least try it once?"

Frank shrugged. "Okay, go for it. But don't take too long. In general the phone's the way to go on these. "

He picked up another file and hefted it as if it weighed a ton. "I'm going to start making the follow-up calls on this one. Same story. Too many cases going nowhere until we find something new."

Pardo smiled slightly. "You've got an extra pair of eyes and legs now."

"And they're appreciated. When you're done, head back here and we'll go over the LaRoche case together." He waved the file as if he had won the jackpot. "I definitely need a fresh viewpoint on that one."

* * * *

Garo Bedrosian hardly seemed thrilled at the prospect of the department's continuing interest in his case.

When Athena arrived around two thirty and showed her ID to the stocky and weary-looking man behind the counter, he finished pouring a cup of coffee for his lone customer and muttered, "So now they come back. And this time they send a girl."

She let the comment go. Nothing she hadn't heard before. "Detective Pardo, Mr. Bedrosian. Do you have a few minutes for me to ask you some more questions?"

Bedrosian grabbed a towel and began wiping down a stretch of the counter. "Two weeks and nothing. What do you expect to happen, talking to me now?"

"We've been trying, sir, but frankly, we just haven't had that much to go on. We thought maybe going over everything with you again, something might turn up we missed the first time."

Bedrosian stopped wiping and looked up at her with impossibly tired eyes. "We, you say. Who's this *we?*" He gestured at her. "I see you."

"You remember Detective Vandegraf. I'm his partner."

Bedrosian shrugged. "So now he's got a partner. A girl partner. Okay, partner, come on down here and ask me your questions."

He nodded his head to the end of the counter. It was a small narrow lunch room, a counter with a dozen seats and three small tables up against the window. As they walked to the end of the counter, the swinging door to the kitchen opened behind Bedrosian and a thin dark-haired young woman came out.

"Cecy, keep an eye on the customer, will you?" he said to her. "I need to talk to this policewoman here for a minute." The young woman nodded and headed towards the coffee and soft drink dispensers. The customer, shaking his head as she lifted the coffee pot, made a gesture to request the check.

"Detective, actually, sir," said Athena.

"Whatever. Whatever you like. Detective. So what can I tell you I didn't already? Doesn't sound as if you've had any of what you like to call progress, am I right?"

Athena sighed. "Maybe if we could just go over what happened one more time…" She pulled out her notebook and flipped it open.

Bedrosian also sighed, as if his patience were being taxed horribly. "I was closing up the place. I must not have locked the door completely. These two guys entered, pulled out guns."

"And that would have been…" she consulted the notebook. "Two weeks ago Tuesday. About three o'clock in the afternoon?"

"That's right. We do breakfast and lunch trade, mostly the banks and offices in the neighborhood. No dinner business here. Maybe some stragglers in early afternoon, late lunchers, people needing some coffee and sugar to get through the end of the day. I open at six and close at three."

"Who was here at closing time?"

"Just me and my daughter, Cecilia." He gestured over to her as she left the customer's check on the counter.

"I think I'd also like to talk with her as well."

"Why? She was in the back when it all happened."

"Still."

Bedrosian shrugged again. "Cecy, when you're done, please." He motioned for her to come join them.

"So you were saying," Athena resumed. "Just you and Cecilia and the two men came in."

"I was busy trying to get everything done so we could leave. Doing like five things at once."

"And where were you at that time?"

Bedrosian pointed to the cash register, where his daughter was ringing up the sale. "Right over there, by the register. I was about to empty the drawers and count the money before putting it in the bag for the night deposit. I had my back to the door. I figured I had locked it. I heard it open and turned around." He pointed to the door. "There they were. They had jackets and, like, ski masks over their heads? And they had guns out. Pointed right at me."

"What kind of guns, sir?"

"I don't know from guns. Pistols of some kind."

"Revolvers? Automatics?"

"I don't remember. They had guns. They looked plenty scary to me. My first thought was Cecy. I thought she had gone into the kitchen but I didn't want to look around and let on there was anyone else in the restaurant. But I got good, whattaya call it, peripheral vision. I could tell she wasn't out here, so I hoped she'd stay in the back."

"Their faces were covered, right? Could you see hands, eyes, anything?"

"The masks showed their eyes and their mouths. One guy maybe had like a beard or stubble or something. Don't remember the hands. Maybe they had gloves. A time like that, you don't think too straight."

"I understand. How about the eyes? Remember anything about them?"

Bedrosian thought for a moment and shook his head. "If I did see anything, you gotta realize, my memory isn't real good after what happened."

Athena nodded. "Just whatever you do remember, Mr. Bedrosian. Take your time. So they came in, then what? Did they close the door behind them?"

"They must have. I don't remember. Wait…yeah. The sound. Open and then shut."

"Was there anyone on the street going by?"

"I don't know. Probably not."

"Could there have been another guy that stayed outside, kept watch?"

"No idea. There coulda been an army out there for all I know."

"Okay. So…then what?"

"I just kinda froze there, taking it all in. The front guy yelled at me to be quiet, not to move or say anything unless they said to. Then he said to open the register. So I turned around and opened the register. One of them came around behind the counter and pushed me aside and started scooping up the bills out of the register. He asked if there was any more money. I said no, that was everything from the entire day. I was praying to myself that they didn't decide to search the back. But they didn't. They seemed nervous, in a hurry. The guy next to me gave me a look. It was scary. For a moment I thought he might shoot me."

"You looked into his eyes then?"

Bedrosian nodded slowly. "Yeah. Yeah. You know…I did see his eyes. I remember thinking they looked almost clear, like marbles. They were gray." He stopped for a moment. "I did see his eyes. I had forgotten."

"How about his voice, do you recall anything about it?"

"He kind of growled. I thought maybe he was purposely trying to sound gruff. Like he wanted to be scary. He was."

"Mr. Bedrosian, you said he scooped up the money. What did he put it in?"

"I don't remember. Maybe he had a bag. Or stuffed it in his pockets. I just can't remember."

"Then what?"

"He told me to turn around, to stop looking at him. The other guy said something to him about hurrying up, they had to get out. The first guy hit me across the back of my head. Hard. He hit me more than once. That's all I remember. Next thing I knew, Cecy was looking down at me, looking really worried, saying the paramedics were coming. It was all confused. Nothing made much sense for a while until I found myself in the hospital."

"You were in the emergency room with a concussion and internal head bleeding."

Bedrosian nodded "Yeah. It all kinda ran together for a few days. It still does, now and then." He kept shaking his head, looking down at his hands on the counter.

The customer had departed. Cecilia closed and locked the door and walked over to join them. Bedrosian smiled and placed a hand on his daughter's shoulder. "Thank heaven she's here. It's taking me a long time to get right again."

She looked at Athena expectantly, with large dark eyes full of concern. Things had not gotten right again here. Maybe they never would.

"Ms. Bedrosian, your father says you were in the back of the café the whole time the robbery was going on. Is that right?"

She nodded, casting an eye at her father. "Uh-huh. It's my job to straighten up whatever's left in the kitchen at day's end."

"Did you hear the robbers enter?"

"I heard the door open and slam shut. My first thought was, we hadn't locked the door and there was a customer. Then I heard the voices."

"You could hear what they were saying?"

"Oh yeah. They were shouting and angry. I got scared and hid under the sink back there."

"You must have been worried about your father out there."

Bedrosian interrupted. "She did exactly the right thing. There's nothing she could have done by coming out with us. I was praying she'd do just what she did, hide back there."

"Forgive me, Mr. Bedrosian. I wasn't suggesting otherwise. But …" she turned back to Cecilia. "You must have thought about doing something. Did you do anything before you went to hide under the sink?"

Cecilia looked very perturbed. She shook her head. "No. No, I just… ran and hid."

Athena noticed that Cecilia was not looking her in the eye anymore.

"You didn't look out the window of the kitchen door, or through the hand-through window over there?"

"No. No. I was too scared. I just hid."

"And you could hear at least one of their voices?"

"Yes. I heard them both, yelling. It was really scary."

"Do you remember anything about their voices, what they sounded like?"

"They were deep. Harsh."

"What do you remember after that?"

"I heard them yelling at my Dad. Then there were some other noises, they yelled some more, and I heard the door slam again. I waited under there for a long time. I was afraid one of them might still be out there, waiting to see if anyone else was there. I wanted to go check on my Dad but I was so scared…" She looked as if she might cry. "Finally I knew I had to take a chance. I went out slowly and looked around, I found my Dad lying on the floor behind the counter." She pointed towards the register. "Over there."

Athena simply nodded and waited. After a long moment Cecilia resumed. "I ran over and checked to see if he was okay. He wasn't conscious. So I went to the phone and called 911."

"And then you just waited with him?"

"I didn't know what else to do. I don't know how to do that CPR stuff but he was breathing, he just wasn't conscious. I sat with him and kept talking to him. He would make noises and stir now and then. I kept telling him to hang on, help was coming."

Athena stood up. "Let's take a walk around, you can show me where you were when everything happened, okay?" She walked to the register, followed by both of them. "And the only thing they took was the money out of here, correct?"

"As far as I know," said Bedrosian. "Nothing else to take, really."

"And how much did they get?"

"It was our busiest day of the week. I had left the cash from the previous day in there as well. There had to be close to a couple thousand dollars."

"Is it usual for you to leave money overnight?"

Bedrosian looked sheepish. "Yeah. I'd been getting kind of lax. Just easier to bag it up every couple days and take it to the bank deposit. The neighborhood's good. I've never worried. I guess I learned my lesson the hard way."

Athena carefully examined up and down the counter and the rest of the lunchroom. "Can I see the kitchen?"

It was a small but tidy back area: metal prep table, grill, refrigerator, and sink. Not much room to navigate around. There were storage cabinets under the table and grill and a small dark crawl space beneath the sink. "You hid under there?" Athena asked, pointing. Cecilia nodded. She still couldn't look at Athena directly.

There was something, Athena decided.

She took a long look around, running her hand over some of the surfaces, judging spaces and distances. She walked to the pass-through window where a cook could hand out orders to be picked up. The Bedrosians simply watched and waited, looking impatient.

"You were in the hospital for how long, sir?" she finally asked.

"Eight days. Cecy and the crew kept the place open. It wasn't easy." He looked at his daughter with a proud smile. "She was here every day, early to late. We would have gone under if not for her."

"You must have been worried about her after what happened."

"I was kinda not very responsive for a few days or I would have told her no. But she insisted on keeping our doors open. She's a brave girl."

Cecilia looked embarrassed. "I made sure Curtis was here with me. He's a pretty big guy. And Rosie and Yolie. We all pitched in."

"So I finally come to and find out that they've been keeping the place going. What a family, this place."

"It seems you came back to work pretty quickly yourself. Was that wise?"

Cecilia looked at her father with extreme concern. He waved his hands in dismissal. "I was needed. I'm not a hundred percent, but I'm okay."

"You must have been hesitant to return. That was a traumatic incident. It's not unusual for a victim of a violent robbery to feel apprehensive for some time afterward."

"I've been in fights, worse than that. My big concern was for my daughter and my people. But they all keep telling me they're not afraid."

"Have you considered hiring a security guard?"

"Young lady, this could have happened anywhere to anyone. I've been here for twenty years and this is the first time such a thing has occurred. I'm not going to let it spook me. And besides, we can't afford a security guard. Especially after losing so much. I've got responsibilities to pay the people

I've got already."

Athena nodded. "I think that ought to do it." She turned to the door that led out of the kitchen. Bedrosian took the hint and led them out to the front.

Her business cards had not yet arrived, but she didn't want to have to explain that her detective shield was brand new, so she had come prepared. In the pocket of her blazer were several blank cards upon which she had written her cell number, and she now handed one to each of them. She asked them to call her if they could provide any further information whatsoever and tried to reassure them that she and her partner were energetically following the case.

Bedrosian nodded wearily through it all, clearly not buying any of it.

As Athena put her hand on the doorknob, she paused. "Mr. Bedrosian, how do you lock this door?"

"What do you mean?"

"The night of the robbery, can you just run me through exactly what you did to lock up, what might have been different about that night?"

Bedrosian didn't respond at first until Athena coaxed him further, asking him, with a self-effacing smile, to humor her. He sighed and walked to the door and started to grab the knob and the lock mechanism above the knob. Then he stopped, and his expression went blank. He simply stood there, looking down at his hands for a long moment.

"Mr. Bedrosian?"

"I don't remember," he said quietly. "What I always do is to turn these locks and..." He went silent for several beats. Then he shook his head, looking confused. "I don't remember. It's a blank."

"It's okay. Head injuries often affect short term memory, especially from the time of the trauma. It's not important. I was just wondering. Thanks again. We'll be in touch to keep you up to date on the progress."

"Progress," scoffed Bedrosian. "Sure. Thank you, Officer."

"It's Detective, actually." She forced herself to smile. She turned to look at Cecilia. This time Cecilia was staring at her with an odd expression on her face.

She sensed there was something here. She had to figure out a way to talk to the daughter alone. That wasn't going to happen with her father hovering protectively over her.

She smiled at Bedrosian. "Hey, as long as I'm here, I keep hearing about someplace around here that sells knockoffs of designer bags and accessories really inexpensively. I thought I might check it out while I'm in the neighborhood. Would you know the place?"

He shook his head. "No I don't know anything about that kind of stuff, sorry."

"I know the place you mean," Cecilia said. "I can show you where it is."

She walked to the door.

"That'd be great. Thanks." Athena opened the door and left, followed by Cecilia. "And thank you again, Mr. Bedrosian, for your time."

They stood on the sidewalk in front of the cafe and Cecilia pointed down the street. "The next block down, see the building with the blue awnings? Their offices are one flight upstairs. It's called Latest Look Imports. No signs downstairs. You sort of have to know that it's there. I hear they've got bags that look just like the real thing at about a third of the price."

Athena looked at Cecilia. The girl had that same expression on her face. "If you don't mind my saying, you look like you need to talk to somebody. It might help to talk to me."

Now she looked as if she might break out in tears. Athena waited. The words came slowly. "I think it's my fault, what happened. You can't tell him."

"What is it you think you did?"

Cecilia waited a long time, considering if she should—could—continue and what to say. "My father wasn't the one who locked the door that night. He doesn't remember, probably because of the head injury. It was me. I locked up that night. I must have not turned the lock all the way. It was still open when they came."

"You're saying you left the door open?"

"I must have. It was an accident. You can't tell him. He can't know!" Her eyes grew wide and her lips set tightly, but she didn't cry.

"And you don't remember seeing anybody on the street outside when you were closing up?"

Cecilia shook her head. "No, nobody. I'm scared to death he'll find out. It was my fault he got put in the hospital. He could have..."

Athena nodded. It didn't have to be said. Sometimes they died.

She looked back through the window of the restaurant, where Bedrosian stood watching them, hands on hips, waiting for his daughter to return. "You've got my card. Give me a call if you want to talk some more, okay?"

As Cecilia turned to the entrance, Athena said, "And I'd suggest you might want to stay away from Latest Look, okay? What they're doing there is illegal."

In fact, she happened to know but wasn't about to say, it was on the Department's radar for a number of reasons, and was ripe for an official visit any day now.

FIVE

"So like I said, I don't have anything new to help you, Detective, but I appreciate your calling to assure me that absolutely no progress has been made in finding my attacker or my valuables."

Victoria Jasmine's voice on the other end of the line was throaty and brusque.

"It's not true that there's been no progress, Ms. Jasmine. These things take time, especially if it was a random crime of opportunity. I had hoped he might have had some connection to you, maybe he had encountered you somewhere, something however small you might have remembered in the meantime…"

"As I just finished telling you, I'm sorry, I can't help you. I was walking to my car and the bastard pushed me into an alley against a wall, told me not to make a sound, cut my purse strap and ran off with it. That's it." There was a deep irritated sigh. "Except that ever since, I feel like he's going to come back and I can't get comfortable anywhere. I'm looking over my shoulder constantly…"

Frank listened patiently. It was the third time she had run through the exact same litany. Despite her sarcasm, it was clear that the crime had traumatized her deeply. He was frustrated but could only imagine how much worse she was feeling it.

"…yadda, yadda, yadda. Now is this the part where you tell me you're definitely going to find the guy?"

"I'm not giving up, Ms. Jasmine."

That was the best he could give her. He was always tempted to assure them he would definitely find their assailant. He knew it was a lie. He wanted to once again remind her she had done the right thing following the mugger's orders, that she was fortunate to have survived the attack, that sometimes the victims like her didn't make it. He had already told her that many times.

"Yeah, so you say. Let me know if anything breaks, as you guys say."

"I'll keep you apprised. Don't hesitate to call if you come up with anything, however inconsequential you think it might be."

Wearily, he hung up and consulted his open notebook for the next telephone number to dial.

Athena noticed that Frank, hunched over his desk, didn't look very happy as she approached. He was just hanging up his phone and looked up to nod to her.

"How'd your follow-up go?"

She pulled over a chair and sat across from him. "Interesting."

Frank's eyebrows shot up. "Let me hear, partner." He stopped and shook his head.

"What's wrong, Frank?"

"Sorry. I just haven't said that in a long time. I'll get used to it. So fill me in."

Frank listened as Athena recounted the interview. He had to admit to being impressed. There might be something to the idea of another pair of eyes and ears on a case.

"I've got a feeling there's more to it than what she's telling me," she concluded.

"You think she knows something? You think she's involved in it?"

"I don't know if I'd go that far. But she's got something we need to know, that's all I'm thinking."

"Sounds to me like you've got good instincts, Athena. I'd trust them."

"Hopefully I—we—can have the opportunity to talk to her outside of the shop. I don't know that it would do much good but it'd be worth the try."

Frank nodded. "If that's your gut, we should go for it. You should go for it. She seems to be willing to open up to you. She didn't seem all that receptive to me at the time. Maybe I remind her of her dad."

"How'd you do on that other case?"

"Same old, same old. As I'm sure the others will also turn out. How about we talk about the LaRoche murder?"

"Sure. What's our next move there?"

"You were on the ground with the unis that night. Maybe there's something I haven't heard. Fill me in on that."

"Not much to tell. We covered the area for a few blocks around in case any of the victim's belongings had been dropped. We looked for wallet, briefcase, loose IDs, anything. Nothing found in the trash cans, gutters, or alleys. We scoured for witnesses who might have seen the perp pass them, talked to bus drivers, cab drivers. No luck. I'm sure you saw the reports."

"I did."

"Only two pawnshop type businesses in the immediate area. That was a long shot considering his watch and ring hadn't been taken, but maybe there was something else of value he had with him that hadn't been accounted for. No luck."

"We've got no way of knowing what he might have been carrying. No idea how much money he might have had in his wallet, or what else. I ran a search and could only find two credit cards in his name, one of which was also his ATM card. He hadn't run credit in months and only used the ATM now and then. So far, neither card has shown any activity since the robbery. He might have had a briefcase or a courier bag of some kind; he was apparently bringing documents to the escrow office. But nobody has been able to confirm anything."

"A smart robber would try those cards immediately, before the word got out. Sounds as if he wanted cash…or hoped for something else of value. Maybe he figured, just an easy mark coming out of that building late."

"Why not just rob him? Why kill him?"

"Maybe something went bad? Maybe the guy was overly nervous. Maybe he was jacked up on something. Maybe LaRoche resisted…just made the wrong move or said the wrong thing. It happens all the time, doesn't it? His death could have been totally unnecessary."

"Yeah," Frank replied slowly.

"What?"

"I just can't shake the alternative scenarios, that it was one of the dozens who held a grudge against him."

"Okay…I could be wrong. It just feels like a random crime to me. But I'll trust your experience. So where do we go from here?"

* * * *

Daniel Del Oso was a younger image of his father: dark haired and big-framed, though less stocky and with a stubblier beard. He was in the alley at the store's dumpster, tossing a few empty crates that still reeked of fish, when he heard the voice behind him.

"I sure hope you didn't put those in the office this time."

He turned to the two people a few steps away and laughed. "You're the cop who was here the other day, right? Pop's still giving me grief about that."

"That's me. This is my partner, Detective Pardo."

Daniel nodded at Athena and wiped his hands on his jeans. "He's inside if you need to talk to him. You can come in the back door with me."

"Actually we were hoping to talk to you, Daniel, if you've got a minute?"

"Sure, a minute. Then he's gonna ream me out if I don't get back to work."

"Your dad works hard, and I guess he expects everyone else to do the same, right?"

"You got that right. He's a good man." He stared at them pointedly. "A damn good man."

Frank nodded. "Daniel, I know he couldn't have committed the crime we're investigating. He was working here last Wednesday night."

"That's right. He's always here."

"But here's the thing, Daniel…" Frank remembered an old television mystery show that his former wife had loved, featuring a police detective who was far craftier than the bumbling character he gave the impression of being. He would often pause at a crucial moment while interrogating a suspect and suddenly say, "But there's this one thing I don't understand, maybe you can help me…"

He couldn't help feeling he was taking a page from that character right now. Daniel waited for Frank to finish his sentence.

"Here's the thing…I was wondering where *you* were on Wednesday evening, because nobody seems to be able to confirm that you were working here with him."

Daniel looked bewildered. He raised his hands, palms up. "What do you mean? No, I wasn't working last Wednesday. I took the night off."

"So…you were, where? At home? With friends? This is just routine stuff, to get you out of any conceivable doubt if somebody comes along and asks about you, you know? You must have been with somebody who can vouch for your whereabouts, right?"

"Actually, no. I was…oh hell, I was with a woman."

"Okay. Your girlfriend? What's her name? Can we just talk to her? Just to, you know, dot the I's and all that?"

"Uh, no. Honestly, I don't know her name. Not her real name. She's, well…this is really embarrassing." He shot a glance at Athena and back to Frank. "Look, you can't tell my father, okay?"

Frank nodded in understanding and clapped a hand on the young man's shoulder. He hoped it was a fatherly gesture, or at least a conspiratorial one. "Yeah. I can see this is kind of a bad situation." He looked at Athena. "Would you excuse us for just a second?" He led Daniel a dozen steps down the alley.

Athena, taken by surprise, shot him a sharp look and stood with her arms folded as they walked away.

"Daniel, I still have to do my job," said Frank in a low voice. "So you were with a…temporary companion, let's say. Just tell me who she is or where I can find her and this will be the last we speak of this, okay?"

"I don't know her name. She called herself Candy. Or Mandy or something like that. She's a dancer at one of those clubs along that strip a few blocks from here?"

"The district they call the Prime, you mean? Which place?"

"I don't remember. I had been drinking."

"Daniel, you're not helping me here. Is this something you do often?"

"Never. Honest. I was just a little crazy that night. Most of my friends work at the market or were busy. I don't have a girlfriend right now, know what I'm saying? I get lonely. And okay, horny. I wandered into this joint, had a few drinks, and this sweet girl offered some *special* dances, one on one in the back room? It just…seemed like a good idea at the time."

It was kind of amusing. Daniel was a big guy but he was acting like a guileless teenager.

"So you're telling me the only person who can vouch for where you were on Wednesday is a mysterious exotic dancer named Candy or Mandy, at any one of a number of sleazy joints. Daniel, how can I help you if you make it so hard?"

"I'm sorry. It's the best I can do."

"Can you at least describe her for me?"

"Dark hair. And, well, nicely built." He cupped his hands in front of his chest and thrust them forward dramatically. "That's all I remember." Daniel stepped away from Frank, looking very uncomfortable. "I gotta get back in now."

Frank walked towards the mouth of the alley, joining Athena partway.

"I can't believe you did that."

"Sorry. The kid's obviously been raised old school. He was embarrassed to talk about getting a lap dance and a happy ending in front of you."

Athena rolled her eyes, but chewed that over for a moment as they walked. Then she nodded. "You're right. Just like Cecilia Bedrosian wouldn't have talked to you. This is about getting them to open up, playing to each other's strengths, right?"

Frank laughed. "Louie, I think this is the beginning of a beautiful friendship."

Athena stared at him. "Who the blue blazes is Louie?"

"Claude Rains in *Casablanca*. Oh, never mind. You are young, aren't you? I'm going to have to introduce you to a classic film or two one of these days."

* * * *

None of the four clubs along the block nicknamed the Prime were yet open for business, but there were managers or staff on the premises. In all, there were four women using the name Candy, Brandy, Mandy and Randi that had been dancing the previous Wednesday. All of them were said to have "darkish" hair and presumably all of them were "nicely built." None of them were currently available.

Every single employee expressed shocked outrage at the very suggestion that any kind of inappropriate, much less illegal, services might be solicited at their establishment. Nobody could officially remember a patron meeting Daniel Del Oso's specific description. The entire neighborhood was one huge stonewall to them. They basically got nowhere.

On the walk back to their car, Frank muttered, "It's not going to be worth coming back for this. Nobody's going to remember anything for us."

"Are you really interested in Daniel Del Oso for this?"

"It's a *possibility*. I don't think Felipe was behind it—not directly, at any rate."

"But you like the Del Oso clan in general? You seem to be pushing this."

"I don't know, Athena. It's just something I need to clear up or I'm not going to feel comfortable."

"Maybe Del Oso senior gets his son to do the dirty work, is that what you're thinking?"

"What I'm thinking is this is a wild goose chase. Daniel was never here and never with a girl named Candy or Sandy or whoever. He knew this would be too obscure to confirm or deny and that we'd just be wasting our time."

"Meaning he was involved in this in some way?"

Frank raised his eyebrows as he opened the car door. "It would seem to indicate he's involved in *something* he'd rather we didn't find out."

SIX

Frank arrived early Tuesday, resolved to catch up on some of the loose ends of the LaRoche case that still nagged at him. The first thing he decided to do was to track down Dahlia Storm, Julie's second wife.

He booted up his computer and began by tracing divorce records. He was proud of himself, only taking less than ten minutes to locate the documentation he needed. Dahlia and Julie had indeed finalized their divorce almost ten years ago. The records actually gave a new address for Dahlia since she had already moved out and adopted her maiden name once again.

Did they still call it a "maiden" name, Frank wondered, or would he offend someone by using that term today? He had no idea. No matter; if his arms were longer, he would have patted himself on the back. He was rolling now. He ran several more searches, each time gleaning some new piece of information. He found a Dahlia Storm listed in the staff directory of Last Hope, a non-profit legal aid agency that specialized in indigents and seemingly hopeless cases..

How perfect, Frank mused. A reaction to Julie, perhaps?

He dialed the agency's number from their website. Despite the early hour, a receptionist picked up almost immediately. Frank identified himself and explained he was trying to locate Dahlia Storm.

"Oh dear," said the woman on the other end of the line. "Can you hold for just a moment please?"

He was only on hold about twenty seconds before a deep-voiced man picked up and said, "I understand you're asking about Dahlia Storm?"

"Yes, that's correct. This is Detective Vandegraf from the Personal Crimes unit. I found her name on your agency directory. Is she still working there?"

There was a short pause. "We do need to update that directory. I'm afraid Ms. Storm has left us."

"You mean she moved on to another job? Do you have any information of where she might…"

"No, no, detective, I mean she *left* us. She is literally no longer with us. I'm sorry to have to be the one to tell you this. About seven months ago, she suffered a seizure at work. She was rushed to the hospital and they performed emergency surgery."

Frank took a deep breath and waited for the punch line.

"There were complications. Dahlia unfortunately died on the table."

Dahlia's death was a true dead end. She had listed no next of kin and had left everything in her will to Last Hope.

Tuesday morning, Athena could see, did not seem to be going well. Frank seemed clearly agitated as he scribbled on his legal pad at his desk. Since arriving for work, she'd felt like she needed to avoid him. But now, a half hour later, she decided to approach him. He didn't look up.

She noted a short printout report on his desk, in large type, that stated that the slugs found in Julius LaRoche did not yield a match to any known weapon. There were several wadded-up sheets of legal paper strewn around the desk.

"I think we need to go back and give Daniel another shot," he muttered, still staring at his desk.

"If that's what you want," she said quietly.

Frank finally looked up.

"What?"

"What do you mean, what?"

"What's on your mind, is what I mean?"

"Not my place. If you want to talk to Daniel again, let's go."

"Wait a minute, what's this nonsense, 'not your place'? If you've got something on your mind, you tell me. That's how this works."

For a moment Athena considered what to say before Frank continued.

"It sounds as if I've been rubbing you the wrong way. I'm probably difficult that way. But I really want this to work. They could have assigned you to a goldbrick like Morrison, or I could have ended up with someone who doesn't know what they're doing. It's just that I haven't had a partner in a long time…"

"I know. You keep telling me that."

Frank shook his head. The background noise of the unit filled in the awkward silence for several heartbeats.

"You're right, My bad. Pull up a chair, Athena, and tell me what you think we should be doing."

She rolled her own chair over and plopped herself down, crossing her arms. "I know it's important to be thorough. But it seems you're determined that this not be a random holdup by a stranger. Yet you see those all the time, don't you?"

"And we've got a handful of them on our desks right now." Frank gestured in frustration at the pile of manila folders on one corner of his desk. "I hate constantly trying to reassure vics when they know as well as I do that we're probably not going to find their attackers. And in this case, the victim died. If it's random, there's likely not going to be any evidence. I've seen it happen before. What else can we do but grasp at straws that might turn out to be evidence?"

"Are you following the evidence?" she said. "Or are you trying to make it fit?"

"There's still a gaping hole in the Del Oso side of things. It bothers me."

"In general is your gut telling you the Del Osos murdered LaRoche?"

"Honestly, I'm not sure that my gut is telling me anything different from what my head is telling me, that Julie got killed in a random crime of opportunity. But my heart is telling me not to give up just yet."

"Okay then. Let's go talk to Daniel again. But then maybe we need to start considering another avenue."

"And just what do you suggest?"

"You said if it's random, there's likely not to be any salient evidence. Maybe there is, but it's not where you've looked. Maybe we need to start expanding and innovating. Looking in new ways."

Her phone began to buzz in her pocket. She pulled it out, looked at the number and answered. "This is Pardo."

Less than a minute later, she ended the call and re-pocketed the phone. "This ought to be interesting. That was Cecilia Bedrosian. She wants to meet with me right now in the park." After a moment she added, "I guess I mean us."

"No, you were right the first time. You've established some kind of trust with her. You go take it. I'll go pay that call on Daniel. Give me a buzz and let me know what transpires."

"Aren't you supposed to be my parent and guardian?"

"Oh hell, if you don't tell Castillo, I won't."

Athena nodded and stood up.

"Hey, Athena."

She had turned partway around and looked back at him.

"Be patient with me. Rome wasn't built in a day."

She laughed.

"First time I think I ever saw you laugh. When we're back, you can start telling me your ideas about looking in new ways. And from now on, no elephants in the room, okay?"

"Okay…partner."

As she walked away, Frank thought: was he ever going to get used to that word again?

* * * *

Frank made a point of walking directly up to Daniel, who was giving instructions to a stock clerk. When he finished and the clerk bustled off, he looked expectantly at Frank.

"Is your father in the office, Daniel?"

"Actually, he's out back talking to a supplier. What's up?"

"I'm afraid I'm taking him in."

"You're arresting him? Are you crazy?"

"I'm not exactly arresting him, just bringing him in for questioning. He's what we would call a 'person of interest' in this case."

"Aw, come on! What's the matter with you? You gotta know he had nothing to do with that fool's death! He was here all that night! Why are you harassing him like this? You're gonna kill the store as surely as all this other stuff will!"

"There's this nagging problem, Daniel. He was here, but you weren't."

"I already told you where I was!"

"And we both know that's total nonsense."

The two men glared at each other. It began to draw the attention of customers farther down the aisles. That made Daniel nervous.

"Okay…come on up to the office. I'll tell you where I really was."

In the cramped little office, Frank couldn't help noticing that the fish smell had still not abated, despite the obvious use of some kind of floral deodorizer. Now it just smelled like sickly-sweet flowery fish. Daniel closed the door behind him and leaned against a wall. Frank stood and waited.

"It was my brother."

"Jesse? He came back to town?"

"I asked him to. We met at a bar over by the waterfront."

"Go on."

Daniel braced one arm over the other across his chest, looking defiant. "My pop had nothing to do with this. It was all my idea."

"What was all your idea?"

"Getting rid of LaRoche."

* * * *

Sunset Park was its formal name but nobody in the city ever called it that. It was simply the Park, a four-block respite from urban sprawl, with rolling hills and wooden benches. The day was cool and overcast, with rain in the air, so there were very few people on the walkways or benches.

Athena found the bench they had agreed upon, nestled under the protection of several high flowering bushes, and sat down to wait. Soon she saw the familiar figure of Cecilia Bedrosian approaching, head down, hands in the pockets of her leather jacket. She sat down next to Athena without looking up or offering any kind of greeting. They both stared around the park, at the gray clouds in the sky, anywhere but at each other.

Finally Cecilia broke the silence.

"My dad thinks I'm running some errands, so I haven't got very long."

"So why are we here, Cecilia?"

The girl bit her lip and took a deep breath. "It was all my fault."

"You told me that the other day. You didn't lock the door all the way."

"I think I know who one of the robbers was."

"You said you didn't know them, that you were in the back and didn't see them."

"But I still think I know."

"Okay. Who is he?"

"His name is Tommy. He's kind of a boyfriend. I should say *was*. I haven't heard from him since then and I don't want anything to do with him."

"Maybe you better back up a little bit here. How did this start?"

"I was seeing him on the sly. My dad is so old fashioned…he doesn't want me hanging out with certain kinds of people. He wants me to spend all my time at the store and in the house."

"And you had other ideas."

Cecilia nodded. "I know he needs my help. It's just him and me. But I want a life too."

"So you met this Tommy, and you've been sneaking out to be with him?"

"Yeah. I thought he liked me and cared about me. He just seemed so cool, a little dangerous."

It was Athena's turn to nod. "The 'bad boy' thing."

"I guess. But at the same time he was so sweet. I guess I was flattered that he liked me and paid so much attention to me. Most handsome guys talk about themselves a lot. With Tommy the conversation always seemed to center on me."

"So you're not seeing him anymore?"

Cecilia shook her head violently. "No. No, I'm not."

"You think that Tommy robbed the café?"

"When I was hiding in the kitchen, I could hear his voice. It was muffled, under the hood or whatever he was wearing. But I could tell. And I remembered he had been asking all those questions, and I realized I had told him all about the restaurant and when everybody left and when we closed and all that."

"How about the second man? Do you know who he was?"

"No. His voice wasn't familiar. The second guy was the one who hurt my dad. He sounded pretty scary."

"This Tommy—what's his last name?"

"He told me Karras. Now I'm not sure he ever told me the truth, what his real name might be."

"You told me before that you didn't see anybody, that there was nobody on the street when you went to lock up."

"There wasn't. I didn't see anybody until they came into the café."

Athena thought for a moment. The damp air was heavy and still.

"So you were afraid to say anything about this until now?"

Cecilia nodded.

"My father would kill me if he knew I was sneaking out to see Tommy. And that other detective?"

"Detective Vandegraf."

"Yeah. I'm sure he's a good guy and all, but…he just reminds me of my dad, very old-fashioned, you know?"

Athena smiled despite herself. "He can be. But he's a very good man."

"But I knew I couldn't tell him this. You just struck me as, I don't know, nicer, more understanding? Younger?"

"Whatever the reason, it's good that you're coming forward now. You haven't seen or talked to Tommy since the robbery?"

"No. I think he was just playing me. Just a stupid little girl. He's probably laughing about me now."

"If you had to, could you get in touch with him? Do you know where to find him?"

Cecilia shrugged. "Maybe the place I used to meet him, where he hung out."

"Did you ever meet any of Tommy's friends before this?"

"One or two, just really briefly, like they'd be with him when he came to meet me and they'd leave. I couldn't tell you anything about them." Cecilia heaved a huge sigh and sunk her head between her shoulders. "I don't believe what I've done."

"So you're pretty sure that the guys you met, none of them were this second robber, then? And the first robber was definitely Tommy?"

"I'm pretty sure, yeah."

"You're doing the right thing, Cecy. Can I call you that?"

"Sure. Everybody calls me that. Am I in a lot more trouble now?"

"Not if you're telling me the whole truth."

"I am. This time I am."

"Maybe we can find these guys and make this whole thing a little better."

Something bothered Athena: Cecy still could not look at her while they talked.

* * * *

"So you're telling me," Frank asked Daniel, "that you and Jesse got rid of Julie LaRoche?"

"No. Jesse wanted no part of it. He didn't even want to come back home. He only did it because I insisted pretty strongly. He heard me out and told me no."

"What exactly did you tell him you wanted him to do?"

"Jesse's what our pop calls the *oveja negra*, the black sheep of the family. He's kind of infamous, almost a legend. I wouldn't have the slightest clue how to go about getting rid of someone. I figured he knew people."

"So what happened?"

"He actually laughed at me. His innocent big brother. He said he'd never killed anybody and he wasn't going to start. I told him he must have friends. He got real serious with me then, gave me this intense look. He said, 'I don't ever want to hear you say stupid stuff like that again, *hermano*.' Then he gave me a short lecture about the mistakes he had made in his own life. He didn't see himself as anybody to look up to, to emulate."

"And then what?"

"Then we got kinda drunk together. We were there 'til pretty late. Finally he got up, said nobody was going to be seeing him for a long time, that it wasn't safe for him here anymore and he was gonna make a new life somewhere far away. He told me I couldn't tell anyone that he had come back to town. If I had to account for myself, I should just say I was with a dancer he knew named Candy. We hugged and he left. That was the last I saw of him."

"How late did you leave there?"

"I don't know. I don't hold my liquor all that well. Maybe eleven."

"Anybody else in the bar that saw you two there?"

"Just the bartender. An older lady, like fifty."

Frank winced. He was somewhat beyond that milestone himself. "And where's this waterfront bar with the grande dame behind the bar? Do you remember the name?"

"I think it's the Ancient Mariner."

Frank shook his head. "Perfect."

* * * *

The bartender at the Ancient Mariner was named Luella Fanning. The "older lady" was likable and reasonably attractive, with full auburn hair and a roguish gleam in her eyes. She didn't look all that old to Frank.

She was in fact the proprietor, having purchased the joint after a notorious shooting had occurred and her longtime employer had decided it was an opportune moment to return to his native New Orleans. She never liked his choice of ambience and had renovated and renamed the place in hopes of attracting a larger clientele. It apparently hadn't worked, but she seemed stoical about it.

Frank sipped a glass of club soda and politely bantered with her before getting to the point. "Do you happen to remember your customers from last Wednesday night?"

"There we go. And here I hoped you'd come here because you'd heard of my vaunted charms, Detective. I remember almost every night here. One's not all that different from the next."

"Do you recall two guys who might have come in here that night?"

"Sure. Two big tall Cuban guys."

"How'd you know they were Cuban?"

"They were speaking in Cuban Spanish. I've spent some time in the Caribbean."

"Could you hear what they were saying?"

"In general, no. First commandment of bartending, mind thy own business. But I caught a few words, let's say. They were nice enough guys, looked like they might be related. One had kind of a rough exterior, scars and all that. The other guy seemed pretty young and sweet."

"Sounds like they made an impression on you."

Luella rolled her eyes. "When they're your only customers, they tend to do that."

"How late would you say they were here?"

"Maybe close to midnight. They put quite a few back. The tough one was drinking rum and coke. The younger one drank beer."

"Actually, if they're the guys I think, he's the older one."

"Maybe in years. Not in life."

"What was the tenor of their conversation like?"

"Listen to you, the 'tenor'! We don't get many men of letters here in this establishment! You mean like the drift?"

Frank slapped his hand on the back of his neck and sighed. "Yes, like the drift."

"They started out real hushed and serious, a little *contentious* almost. After a while the subject changed, they relaxed, and they just seemed to be shooting the bull, you know? You might say it began more *somber* and became more *congenial* with the passage of time."

"Well, fancy that, a woman of letters in the establishment as well. What are the odds?"

"You just never know, Detective. Anything else I can help you with?"

"I think we're good." Frank reached into his pocket and pulled out a couple of bills to leave on the counter.

"Your seltzer's on the house. Always happy to assist the city's finest."

"And that's appreciated, madame, but I insist." He left the bills and stood up from the stool.

She beamed a smile at him. "Come on back when you're off duty. Maybe I'll start karaoke on Friday nights."

Frank's phone began to buzz in his pocket. "Not a big karaoke fan. I tend to shatter the glasses. Excuse me."

The waterfront street wasn't exactly busy. He flipped open his phone as he walked the thirty or so steps from the bar to his car. "What's up, Athena?"

"Frank, I think we might have a break in the Bedrosian robbery. Are you coming back to the unit soon, or can we meet up somewhere?"

"Heading back right now, in fact. See you there."

* * * *

"I'm hoping this Tommy Karras figures Cecy's too scared to say anything and that he'll still be hanging around." They were sitting in the unit conference room, serious expressions over weathered mugs of hot coffee.

Frank nodded as he absorbed her story.

"If we can pick him up maybe he'll give up his pal."

"This likely isn't his first job. Maybe we can make him for some other holdups."

"Let's find the guy first. We can't even be totally sure he's good for the café yet."

"There's still something that bothers me about that girl. Her story isn't quite right."

"So far you've done great by giving her free rein. If there's more to her story, it may come out in time. Let's concentrate on this Karras character." He raised his eyebrows. "So she's sending us to a *bowling alley*? Really? She met him bowling?"

"She says she meet him at a dance club. He would seem to have some serious moves, according to her."

"And not just on the dance floor, I'll bet. So how does the bowling alley fit in?"

"He works there, or so she thinks. She would meet him there now and then, when she got off work and could sneak away. He didn't talk about himself all that much either. She wasn't all that clear on her Prince Charming. He's a mystery man. She isn't even sure at this point that he gave her his real name."

"Lovely. What do girls see in a guy like this?"

"I'm not the person you should be asking." Athena smiled. "I was a good girl growing up. Hey, don't smirk, I was."

"Oh, I believe it. You're still a straight arrow."

"But I was definitely more aware than a lot of kids. Cecilia's very sheltered. Her father's pretty old-fashioned. I think this Tommy was sort of forbidden fruit. But besides that, from what she tells me, he showed a lot of interest in her. He didn't talk about himself, he talked about her. She must have found that very flattering."

"So I assume this guy is astoundingly handsome, awesomely captivating, and swept her off her feet. A regular Cary Grant. In a bowling alley."

Athena shrugged. "She's a kid. She told me he's very handsome and described him. Maybe we can find him over at the lanes."

"I guess our plan is set then. Shall we?" Frank rose from his seat and downed the last of his coffee.

"And by the way, before you ask, yes, I do know who Cary Grant was. I'm not that young."

"You know, Pardo, you've only been on the job here a couple of days and you're already getting snarkier. I think that's a good sign that you're loosening up. I must be rubbing off on you."

"I didn't know old guys knew what 'snarky' meant," she stage-whispered as she followed him out of the conference room. Frank actually laughed.

The Gold Dust Bowl was situated in the basement of a building that also housed a pool hall and a rundown gym. The bowling alley had seen better days and had a kind of burnished patina to it—at least, Frank decided, that was how the proprietors would have spun it. The walls and floors were dark brown and orange, as much from tobacco and grime as from any kind of paint or wood varnish. There were twelve lanes and eight were occupied with bowlers.

It struck him as the kind of place where street guys hung out, maybe some lower echelon crime figures. Despite being in need of a facelift, the alley looked popular. It was a good under-the-radar kind of gathering joint.

After they both did a quick scan of the lanes, Frank stood by the door and let Athena walk to the counter and ask for Tommy. She had swapped her blazer for a stylish leather jacket from her car and looked somewhat less like a cop than he did. Maybe she wouldn't spook the guy. There was a short conversation, then the woman behind the counter disappeared through a door and an older man came out. He exchanged more words with Athena and pointed to his left to the end of the lanes. They both nodded, and she walked back to the doorway and Frank.

"His name's Tommy but it's not Karras. It's Lukacz. He works over in the bar."

"Better get over there. That guy's going to tell him that a lady's asking for him. Maybe he'll be interested."

Tommy Lukacz was clearing a small table when she walked in. She recognized him immediately: he looked to be in his late twenties, lean with long black hair. He watched her approach as he placed some glasses on a round tray. Then, standing up straight, he smiled at her, as if he was trying to figure out who she might be.

"You're Tommy, right?" she said with a smile.

He hesitated and then said, "Yeah. And you are…?"

"Detective Pardo. I'm here to ask you a few questions."

The attitude abruptly changed. "Detective? I don't understand. Look, I'm really busy right now, and I can get in trouble if I stop to talk, you know? So…" He was already turning to head for the door, leaving the tray of glasses on the table.

There was a larger, older man filling the narrow doorway. Tommy stopped, impatiently, to let him in so he could get by him. But Frank Vandegraf wasn't in any hurry to get out of the way.

"Stick around, Tommy. We need to talk," Frank said with a smile.

SEVEN

"I'm still not sure how you think I can help you," the young man said as he sat in the interview room, idly rotating his can of soda in both hands. "Like I said, I don't know anything about any holdup in the café."

He stared at Frank and Athena across the scratched paint of the aging table.

"And you never got to talk to Cecilia about it because you stopped talking to her right after it happened," Frank said.

"Uh, yeah. That's right."

"You two had been seeing a lot of each other up until then, hadn't you?" Athena said. They watched as Tommy's head swiveled back and forth, looking at one and then the other.

"I wouldn't say a lot. We'd get together now and then."

"So why did you stop? Why then?"

Tommy shrugged. "No reason. I guess she lost interest in me."

"It doesn't sound as if you were all that interested in her either." For some reason Frank found himself irritated by his smug smile and attitude.

"She's a very sweet kid. Kinda young and sheltered."

"You did seem pretty interested in her for a while, though," Frank said, leaning forward. "Even if she was young and sheltered, as you put it. What happened to change your mind exactly?"

Tommy hesitated. "Nothing. Nothing at all. It was never that big of a deal. What, did she tell you something different?"

"We're more interested in what *you* tell us, Tommy," said Athena. "You have to see it from our viewpoint. You used to meet her all the time, go dancing, go to the movies, things like that? And all of a sudden, her father's restaurant gets robbed and now you won't have anything to do with her. You see how that looks to us?"

"Wait a minute, are you saying you think I had something to do with that? Am I a, whattaya call it, a suspect here?"

Frank raised his hands and smiled slightly. "Let's not get ahead of ourselves, Tommy. We're not accusing you of anything here. We're just asking for your help. You're what we would call a 'person of interest'."

"A 'person of interest'. You mean like someone who knows stuff they can tell you?"

"Yes, sort of. You haven't been arrested or anything, right? We appreciate you came with us voluntarily and want to help us out."

Tommy nodded. It wasn't clear to Frank how many lights were on behind his eyes and how much he actually understood of what was going on here.

"It did kind of surprise me when you tried to get away from me in the bowling alley, though," Athena added. "Like you had something to hide. You don't have anything to hide though, right?"

"Oh no, right, nothing. I wasn't trying to get away, I was just a little confused, was all. I sometimes get in trouble at work because stuff isn't getting done and they find me talking to someone, you know?"

"So tell us a little more about your relationship with Cecilia. How long ago did you meet her?"

"Let's see. She was with friends at a dance club. Insanity."

"What was insane about it?" asked Frank.

"No, I mean that's the name of the club. *Insanity*."

"Ah. Okay. And when was this?"

"Maybe a couple months ago, like that."

"And how did you two meet?"

"One of her friends knew one of my friends and we were all introduced. I danced with her and then we arranged to meet up again after that night."

"So, what, you would go pick her up and take her out?"

"Uh-uh. She said her old man was pretty strict. She kinda had to sneak out to see me. She'd call me and tell me she could get out and we'd meet at the Gold Dust. A couple times I met her over at the Cineplex and we'd see a movie."

"It all sounds awfully clandestine," said Frank. "So you didn't consort much in public."

"Consort? Naw. We went dancing a couple times. Went out to eat now and then. Mostly just hung out. Sometimes she'd come by while I was working. I had to pretend I wasn't."

Sterling employee, Frank mused. What a catch this guy would be for any fair young damsel.

"Did Cecilia tell you much about herself, her family?"

"She told me a few things. I know her old man kept her on a tight leash and that she was bored with working at the restaurant. I guess he's pretty old school."

"What did you tell her about yourself?" asked Athena, watching him carefully.

"The usual stuff. She seemed more interested in talking about herself."

"Did you tell her your real name?"

Tommy hesitated. "What do you mean?"

"I mean, didn't you tell her your name was Karras? It seems your name is Lukacz, isn't it?"

It began to dawn on the young man that they knew more than they had been letting on. "Uh, yeah," he drawled slowly. "I figured, she looked Greek, so she might feel more comfortable hanging out with me if she thought I was, too…"

Both detectives exhaled audibly. Frank ran a hand over his thinning forehead. He tried to imagine a perspective from which this dumb hunk of meat would seem charming and captivating, as Cecilia had apparently found him to be.

"Actually," interjected Athena, "she's *not* Greek. But I happen to be half Greek, and you don't seem Greek to me whatsoever."

"Uh," grunted Tommy, a perplexed expression on his face. "Well, whatever."

"Just curious, does that ever work? When you tell a girl you're a Greek named Karras, I mean. Or whatever names you try with them?"

The perplexed expression turned to a dumb grin, a feeble attempt at cute. It got no reaction so he just shrugged.

"You said you weren't all that interested in her, but you seem to have gone to some trouble to try to make a good impression."

"It was just a thing, you know?"

"No," Athena said, folding her arms, scowling. "I don't know. What is that supposed to mean?"

"Supposing we told you," said Frank, "That someone saw you the afternoon of the robbery and was able to identify you in the café?"

"What? Wait a minute!" Tommy looked back and forth at the two stone-faced detectives, who just stared back at him.

"We might just have enough, in fact, to promote you from 'person of interest' to suspect, Tommy. What do you think about that?"

"There's no way!"

"So help us out," said Athena. "The holdup took place two weeks ago today, around three o'clock. Can you tell us where you were then? All you have to do is show us you were somewhere else, where people saw you, and you're off the hook."

"I must have been at work! I was working, like I do most Tuesdays!"

"So if we go talk to the manager or the owner, they'll tell us you were there all afternoon, right?"

Tommy Lukacz hesitated. "I'd, uh, rather you didn't do that. Um…I'm in a lot of hot water at work now as it is."

"What I'm hearing," said Frank, "is that nobody's going to be able to vouch for your whereabouts two weeks ago. Am I right?"

"I think I want to go now. I don't want to talk to you anymore."

"Oh, come on, Tommy. Do I need to read you your rights and place you under arrest?" Frank made a large production of pushing back the metal chair with a loud rasp across the floor, and lifting himself to an upright position. Glaring down at Tommy, he suddenly looked awfully big and very annoyed.

The last of the young man's fading bravado dissolved. All at once, he looked like a frightened kid.

"Wait," he said. "It wasn't my fault. The way things went. It wasn't my fault."

Frank sat back down and waited.

It took a long time and a fair amount of effort to keep Tommy Lukacz on track. The expression "herding cats" occurred to Frank as he and Athena struggled to keep the scatterbrained suspect on point.

"But it wasn't me, it was him, the other guy."

"The other guy. You keep saying the other guy," said Athena. "Who is this other guy?"

"Brando. The other guy."

"So who's this Brando and how do you know him?"

"He's one of the guys that comes by the alley all the time. There're a lot of players hanging out there."

"By 'players'," Frank said, "you mean wise guy types?"

"Yeah, and wannabe wise guys, the kind of guys who are looking to get into the game, you know? If you know who to talk to, it can be like job interviews."

"So this Brando, is he a player, as you call them, or is he a wannabe?"

"He strikes me as a pretty serious dude. He's not major league yet, but he's done some heavy stuff, if you know what I mean?"

"And you were interested in doing some heavy stuff with him?" Athena asked.

"Well, there's just not much going on for me right now, you know?"

Frank really wanted to ask him to stop the "you knows" but they had finally gotten him on something resembling a linear track and he didn't want to derail it, so he said nothing.

"I had a few conversations with him, just small talk, and I was kinda impressed. He seemed to know his way around. I thought he would be a good person to know."

"So, what, you two decided to pull a job together?"

Tommy rested his head in his hand. "I guess I was trying to impress him and I started talking big. Next thing I know he says to me, 'Are you gonna put your money where your mouth is?' and I felt like I had to come up with something. All I could think of was the café where this girl had been telling me she worked. Brando seemed interested at that. He told me I should, whattaya call it, cultivate her, ask her a lot of questions, find out about the place. So I did. I started asking to see her and got her to talk about herself and her family and the restaurant. She said there were days when her father left the money in the register for a few days before banking it. And she said that at the end of the day, there was just her and her father. Brando said that's when we should hit the place."

He looked up back and forth at the two detectives. "It was just supposed to be walk in, show the guns, scare them, take the money. Nobody would recognize us, nobody would get hurt."

"But it didn't go that way," said Frank.

"This guy…I had no idea. He's a crazy dude. Scary-crazy. We got to the register and pulled out these bags and filled them with the money and I figured that was it. But he wasn't happy with how much was in the register. He started yelling there must be more. Then he just started hitting the old man. I mean, like beating on the guy, he was really angry. I was afraid he was going to kill him. Then he yelled at me to get out of there fast, so we ran out."

"How did you get to the café?"

"We drove and parked around the corner. We pulled on the masks as we walked to the café. When we left, we just kept them on until we got to the car. I didn't think anybody saw us. Brando said even if somebody did, odds were they wouldn't want to get involved."

"Whose car was it?"

"Brando swiped it, I'm pretty sure. Then he wiped it and left it somewhere."

"Where'd you go after the robbery?"

"Some empty garage or something that belongs to a friend of his. We split up the money in the two bags. He was still ticked off that it wasn't anywhere near what I had said it was gonna be. He told me to find my way home from there and he took off."

"You didn't try to go hide or anything? You weren't worried that Cecilia might have recognized you or that somebody saw you?"

Tommy got lost in what passed for thought. "Brando said I had nothing to worry about. I should just act normal, show up for work as usual, not do anything different. She wouldn't tell anyone. Nobody was going to say anything. They were too scared to look carefully at us and we had the masks."

"How about the guns?" asked Frank. "Where'd they come from?"

"Brando brought them. I don't know guns. Couldn't tell you what they were. They were automatics, I guess meant to look big and scary. He brought the ski masks, even gave me a pair of gloves so we wouldn't leave prints on anything."

"Quite a teacher, huh?" asked Frank.

"This guy Brando," said Athena. "What's his real name?"

Tommy shrugged. "I dunno. Everybody calls him Brando. Not many people use their real names that hang around at the alley, you know?"

"Including you, right?"

"Well, I work there, so they know my name."

"So what does Brando look like?"

"Big guy. I'd say over six feet. Shaves his head. Keeps his beard stubbly."

"What color are his eyes, do you know?"

"Man, he's got scary eyes. Wolf eyes. Like clear marbles."

"But what color would you say?"

"Kinda gray, I guess."

"Has he been back to the alleys since the robbery?"

Tommy shook his head. "Haven't seen him."

"Do you have a way to get in touch with him?"

Tommy shook his head again. "We always just met at the alleys."

"What about the money?"

"It was only around six or seven hundred for each of us. I kinda spent it."

"And you've been avoiding Cecilia since then, right?"

"I didn't want her involved in this. I felt terrible about what happened to her old man. I figured I should stay away from her. If she came looking for me I'd tell her to get lost. But she never came back. That's a good thing, right?"

The two detectives sat with stony glares. He looked back and forth at them, getting no reaction from either.

"I've never done anything like this before. I swear. And she had nothing to do with it either. It was Brando, the other guy. You gotta believe me. I've never been in trouble like this before."

"Help us find this guy Brando," Frank said evenly, "and you'll help yourself as well."

By the time the interview was over, they had convinced Tommy to make a written statement and contacted the prosecutor's office to send over an assistant DA to negotiate a plea deal. They both felt exhausted.

Guys like Tommy Lukacz just did that to you.

They plotted their next move in the elevator back to their unit.

"If we can find this Brando character," Frank said, "we might have a good case with Tommy turning on him. The trick is to find him."

Athena nodded. "What if I reach out to some of the uniforms I know? He doesn't sound familiar to me but maybe our gray-eyed perp is known on the street somewhere."

"Why not? Nothing to lose."

"There are still things that bother me about Cecilia. It's a remarkable coincidence that those guys showed up the very night she forgot to lock the door. Something's missing from the story."

Frank nodded. "I think you're going to do okay here. You strike me as someone who won't let go of something until you're sure you've got everything in place."

"Sort of like you. You're still not willing to accept Julie LaRoche's death was a random act, are you?"

"Nope. In fact I think I'm going to make a few more calls as soon as I'm back at my desk."

* * * *

She picked up in the same don't-waste-my-time way. "This is Lorena Park."

"Ms. Park, Detective Vandegraf here. I assume you remember me from our last conversation?"

"Of course, Detective. Are you the one that's obstructing my story?"

"Obstructing your story? What are you talking about?"

"The Bodega Building, as you called it. Why is there an effort to scare me off?"

Frank took a deep breath. "I've got nothing to do with that. Someone contacted you about your story? Who was it?"

"Someone who identified themselves as a Special Agent with the FBI. Aren't they all special though? Well, it might make my job harder, but it's not going to stop me. They even expected me to turn over my notes. That is not going to happen."

"Ms. Park, you might not believe me, but we're on the same side here. I've been frozen out of that area as well. In fact I was hoping you might be my only resource right now."

"What's so important about that building anyway? Apparently my instincts were pretty good about Bizel Financial."

"What else do you know about it?"

"First one to give up what they know loses, Detective. So what do you know?"

"Nothing that you don't. Guaranteed. My only interest is how Julius LaRoche fit into this."

"I can't help you much there. I've found nothing to indicate that he was anything other than the buyer they lined up. He was unprincipled enough to jump at the chance and not ask questions."

"The other tenants—besides the market and the restaurant. They seem to have cleared everyone out. They didn't renew leases and didn't bring in new tenants."

"Makes the building easy to turn over for a profit," said Park. "That's all any of these people cared about. Screw the tenants."

"You don't see anything in this that could have gotten Julie killed?"

"Bizel itself seems to be trying to stay pretty clean of mob tactics. They're a white-collar crime outfit. I'm not saying it's totally out of the question, but it's incongruous for them to kill someone in such an obvious way."

"For an investigative reporter, you seem to be pretty tentative, Ms. Park."

"Detective, in some ways your job and mine are similar. We can't get caught up in what we'd like to have happened. We have to follow the hard evidence. As much as I'd love a juicy murder conspiracy, I just don't see it."

* * * *

After hanging up, Frank opened the folder and pulled out the newspaper clippings. He re-read Lorena Park's impassioned article on the Webleyview evictions and stared at the photographs. The Sentinel's article pulled no punches in setting up Julie LaRoche as the classic villain who threw indigents, children and oldsters into the streets. All that was missing was a picture of Julie twirling a long handlebar mustache as he cackled.

There were photos of several of the people who had been displaced, including Lorena Park's relatives. The article even included a photo of the gravestone of the evicted woman who had died, Camilla Wardell Valdespino. Her full name and birth and death dates were prominently engraved onto the stone. She had been sixty-one when she died. He peered intently at the photos and the article re-reading it over and over. There was something…

"Hey! Frank! Frank!"

He looked up. Athena was hanging up her desk phone, staring at him across the space between their desks.

"I've put the word out on this Brando guy. Let's see what comes back."

"Good." He stared back down at the clippings. "There's something else here. How many bus routes do you think there are that run along Institution Boulevard?"

"Not many. Three, maybe. Why, what do you have in mind?"

Leon Simpkins happened to be walking by and found himself in the crosstalk between Frank and Athena. "Whoa. Excuse me for interrupting."

"No problem, Detective Simpkins."

"Call me Leon. And you're Athena, right? How do you like the unit so far? Is this guy doing right by you?"

"Interesting place," Athena replied. "And Frank's great."

"Give him time," Simpkins grinned.

"Hey, Leon," Frank said, "do you happen to know the Gold Dust Bowl, in the basement under the Pool Cue and some kind of gym?"

"Do I know it? Unfortunately, yeah. Art and I have spent some time down there. A lot of dumbbells." That was his pet term for the lazier, less clever locals who nonetheless aspired to become underworld kingpins. They were often gym rats or pool hustlers.

"Any chance you'd know anything about a guy called Brando? Big guy, shaved head, stubbly beard?"

"That could be a handful of guys."

"He's supposed to have these gray, piercing eyes, kind of scary, like a wolf."

"Now that sounds like…what's his name?" He turned to call to his partner across the room. *Hey, Art! C'mere, wouldya?*"

Art Dowdy threaded his way between desks and around other personnel, the usual doleful scowl on his face.

"Athena, you remember the Mortician," Frank said. Dowdy nodded to Athena and she nodded back.

"I'd prefer you called me Art," he said seriously.

"Art, do you remember that big guy with the gray eyes we questioned a few weeks back over at the Pool Cue?" asked Simpkins.

"Bronstein," Dowdy said. "No. Bromberg. That guy?"

"That's the one! Bromberg! You remember his first name?"

"How could I forget it? Hildebrandt!"

"Come again?" said Frank.

"That's right," smiled Simpkins. "That was his name."

"Ever hear him called Brando?" asked Frank.

"We heard him called a lot of names, mostly behind his back. A lot of guys avoid him. Mean mother, that one. He kinda scares them."

"So what did you have him for?"

"There were a couple of robberies nearby, and we developed a theory that whoever was pulling the jobs might be basing their operations there. Like I said, lots of would-be tough guys hang out in the pool hall or the bowling alley. Bromberg was one of the guys who looked good to us."

Dowdy looked even more downcast. "Couldn't find enough to bring anybody in. But we still liked him for a couple of those jobs."

"What kind of jobs?"

"A tavern a few blocks away, and a liquor store. Both had similar MOs. They came in late at night, faces masked, flashing big guns that looked more for fright, seemed to know the places and their routines, got the proprietor to open the register. In both cases there was only one person in the place and both of them got knocked around before the perps left."

"Two-man jobs, both of them?"

"That's right."

"Why'd you like this Bromberg for them?"

"Of all the guys hanging out there, he best fit the description of the bigger guy."

Frank and Athena exchanged glances. "Any idea how we might find this guy?"

"He gave us an address," said Simpkins. "Maybe he's stupid enough to actually be there."

As luck would have it, he was. Two uniforms brought him in without a fight.

* * * *

"You're serious?" Bromberg sat at the interview table across from Athena and Frank, leaning back in his chair, stretching out his long legs, a cocky smile on his face. "Again with the holdups? You guys keep bringing me in about these holdups. Can't you find the real bad guys, you gotta keep bothering me?"

"We've got your buddy Tommy," said Frank calmly, scratching the side of his nose. "He's got the fear of God in him, let me tell you."

Bromberg snorted. "Bowling alley Tommy? That little wimp? He's no buddy of mine. He's got a great imagination, that one. Wants to be a hot shot gangster."

He cast a narrow-eyed gaze back and forth at them. "The little rat is talking? I'm not saying I did anything, mind you. But he's saying I did?"

"Maybe you'd better tell us your side of the story," Athena said, "seeing as how he's telling us his. And you don't seem to come off too well in his version."

"We've also got a witness who got a very good look at those very unusual eyes of yours, even with the ski mask," added Frank.

Clearly Bromberg's confidence suddenly took a small bump. He had figured that Tommy was too scared to say anything to anyone, and that the Bedrosians were too scared and confused to step up to make an identification.

Guys like this, thought Frank, were convinced they had everybody frightened. They figured they could carry on their criminal lives with impunity. They didn't have to hide or keep a low profile. Up until now he had been right.

"Maybe I should ask for my lawyer," Bromberg said, sitting up.

"Sure," said Frank. They both stood up. "He or she will very likely advise you to cop a plea in exchange for giving up the rest of your buddies."

"The rest of my buddies? What's that supposed to mean?"

"Oh, we're not done with you, Brando. There are two other detectives out there who are very, very frustrated about some other similar robberies. There are going to be enough charges to keep you locked up for a long, long time. Unless you start thinking about a deal."

They read him his rights and handcuffed him, then knocked on the door for an officer to take him to a holding cell.

"Do you think the Bedrosians will come in and ID him?" asked Frank as they waited at the elevator.

Athena nodded. "I think so. Mr. Bedrosian for sure. I'm interested in how Cecilia is going to react to all of this."

"Good work on this one. You're off to a good start."

Athena, trying to maintain a professional demeanor, was clearly pleased and couldn't resist a smile. "Thanks. Now what about the LaRoche case? You said you got something new?"

"I think so. If I'm right, we just need to do a little bit of homework. Are you up for that?"

"Of course. What are we doing?"

"Bus schedules," said Frank.

EIGHT

"I appreciate your coming in like this to help us, Mr. Wardell," Frank said cheerily as he opened the door to the interview room and gestured for Cameron Wardell to enter.

"I'm only too happy to help, Detective, but I really don't know how I can. There's just nothing I haven't told you already."

Athena was adjusting a video monitor and placing a remote control on the table. She turned and extended her hand with a smile.

"You may remember Detective Pardo," said Frank.

"No, I can't say as we've met, have we?" said Wardell, mystified, taking her hand.

"Sure we have," she said. "I was in uniform last time."

"Ah…yeah…you were the patrolman…I mean, patrolwoman…patrol person…?"

"Patrol officer, right. Thanks for helping us out here. Have a seat. Sorry the room's not all that comfortable."

Wardell looked around the room as Frank closed the door. "Didn't you say you wanted me to try to ID somebody for you? Where are they?"

"Actually, they're on the video we're going to show you, okay?"

"Sure," Wardell said, his mystified look deepening. He and Frank sat down. Athena remained standing, picked up the remote and aimed it at the monitor, bringing a video to life.

"It turns out the buses have security cameras," said Frank. "We were able to pull scenes from this one. Watch, now."

"But there were no buses going by when the guy was killed," Wardell said.

"Just watch, okay?"

The camera's angle was over the shoulder of the bus driver towards the front door. The video was slightly grainy and the color was washed out, but they could clearly see as the bus came to a halt, the door opened, and two people climbed aboard the bus. Athena froze the action.

"There," said Frank. "Do you see that person still standing in the kiosk at the stop?"

"What about him?"

"Isn't that you, Mr. Wardell?"

"Uh…it could be, maybe. Hard to tell."

"There's not much color in this footage but you can see that strong orange color of your jacket. That looks exactly like what you were wearing that night, doesn't it?"

"If you say so, sure. There were a couple of buses that went by while I was waiting."

"Do you remember people at your stop, then, getting on that bus?"

"Yeah, now that you mention it. Sure."

Athena started the action again. The bus door closed, leaving Wardell in the kiosk, and pulled away.

"You were still waiting for your bus at that point then?"

"Uh-huh."

"The number ten, was that right?"

"Yes. The number ten was my bus. It doesn't come very often that time of the evening." Wardell looked at them both expectantly. "I'm confused. Why are you showing me this? Where's the person you want me to try to identify?"

"Mr. Wardell, we're confused too right now. Maybe you can help us out here. You see, that *was* the number ten bus."

"It couldn't have been!" Wardell exclaimed.

"I suppose you didn't happen to notice the date and time register in the lower corner of the video. There. That was the number ten bus…it came by that stop at six fourteen P.M."

Athena stopped the video again. "A good forty-five minutes before you saw Mr. LaRoche killed and called it in, you were already at that bus stop. Why was that?"

"There must be some mistake," Wardell stammered.

In the short awkward silence that followed, Frank opened a manila folder in front of him and extracted a large photo. He turned it so Wardell could see it. "By the way, our condolences, Mr. Wardell, on the recent death of your mother. That is your mother's grave, isn't it?"

He looked numbly at the image. "Yes. Yes it is. Thank you. What does that have to do with anything?"

"This is where we were hoping you could help us," said Frank, leaning in towards the young man. "An awful lot of people *could* have been suspected of killing Julius LaRoche. He was disliked, even hated, by many people because he did some pretty terrible things. One of those things was to evict a woman from her home, a woman who then slipped into indigence and died. By a strange coincidence, the only witness to LaRoche's murder was the son of that woman. And stranger still, that witness had been standing at that very place for probably an hour or more."

Frank and Athena now both leaned closer in to Wardell, who was looking at them with wide eyes. "Come on. Once we figured out what we were looking for, we found…well, enough to hold you and to charge you."

"You'd be amazed," added Athena, "the places there are security cameras that will place you on that corner for such a long time."

"You were the one who fingered LaRoche," Frank said. "Maybe you wore that orange jacket specifically so the killer would see you?"

"I'm guessing you phoned him to alert him," Athena added. "You had to wait a long time for your intended victim to come out."

Frank looked at Athena. "He probably cleared his phone history afterward, too. That'd be the smart thing."

"But perhaps it didn't occur to him, we could get his phone records from the phone company," Athena replied.

They both turned to Wardell.

"You wouldn't object that we checked your cell phone records, would you, Mr. Wardell?"

The young man stared, mouth partway open.

"Cameron," said Frank earnestly, "you're in this pretty deep. I don't see any way you're getting out of this."

"And frankly," added Athena, "you're our only connection to the guy who pulled the trigger, and if we don't find him…well, there's just you, and you can imagine how that's going to go."

Frank nodded thoughtfully. "There's a lot of publicity on this case. And

Athena and I are feeling pressure from above, let me tell you. That's how things work around here. The DA really wants someone to go down for this and he's going to make sure he gets *someone*. And right now, you're what we've got to give him."

He reached out and laid a hand on Wardell's shoulder. "The best you can hope for is to make it easier for yourself and cooperate."

Athena also leaned in still closer to Wardell. "Cameron, you know what I'm sensing here? You're not the kind of guy who contracts a murder. You know that and it's been eating away at you ever since you set it up, am I right? You're way out of your element. Part of you is scared shitless of this killer and his world—is he going to come back and take you out, just to be safe? You don't know, do you? The greater part of you, though, must be haunted with plain guilt."

Wardell looked up at her. She met his gaze. "Most people who commit this kind of crime, they're neither smart enough nor decent enough to care. Then we see people like you, who make terrible mistakes and *are* smart and decent enough at heart to recognize it. It eats at them big time. Take it from me, you're never going to be free of the demons until you come completely clean."

It seemed to hit a nerve. Frank was impressed at Athena's tactic. Wardell kept staring at Athena, but there was something different in his eyes now.

It was a slow process. It took them another hour to get Cameron Wardell to piece together the improbable story.

Warren and Camilla Wardell had not been a good match for one another. By the time their son Cameron was a teenager, their fights had become increasingly bitter and their incompatibility clear. He was too young to comprehend many of the issues between them, and perhaps he had the tendency to see things in very black-and-white terms. In any case he found himself siding with his father and when the split finally came, he chose to leave with him. Camilla ultimately agreed. They moved out of state and had no communication with her thereafter. The divorce was accomplished long-distance through attorneys.

It took some years before Cameron began to see the dark side of his father, who began to drink heavily and relinquish his responsibilities, finding it harder to keep a job. They moved into a series of progressively seedier apartments. One day, on a drunken bender, Warren Wardell got into his car and never made it home. Cameron was twenty-three.

He had to grow up in a hurry. He scraped together what little resources were left and gave his father a cheap burial. Warren's legacy consisted of a stack of cardboard boxes and a small closet of old clothes. In the process of disposing of everything, Cameron read letters that his father had kept. It shed a new light on his parents' relationship.

There was no reason for him to stay, so he decided to leave that world behind him and return to the city of his childhood, to try to find his mother, reconnect with her...tell her he was sorry. He had no idea where to start but he found a cheap apartment and a job in a restaurant that actually paid decently. He had always had an affinity for computers so he found extension courses with the aim of a career in code, web design and development.

He discovered that Camilla Wardell had remarried and that her second marriage had not been any more successful than her first. No sooner had Paul Valdespino departed than she received the notice that her apartment building had been purchased and she was being evicted. Perhaps that was the final straw in her tenuous ability to cope with reality, but acquaintances of hers would later tell Cameron that she had taken to wandering the streets and had one day been found dead. Her death had occurred only weeks before he had arrived to look for her.

Paul Valdespino had come forth to pay for a funeral service and a headstone. He wasn't hard to find. Cameron did not particularly like the man but they had something in common: an overwhelming sense of guilt. They talked and when they parted, Valdespino tucked an envelope into Cameron's pocket. It contained five thousand dollars in cash. Valdespino walked away and they had not spoken since.

Cameron found the newspaper articles about the Webleyview evictions and conversions. There was one name mentioned repeatedly of the man who was painted as the villain in the case: Julius LaRoche. He was so despicable that the writer of the article even referred to him repeatedly as La Roach.

Cameron had an envelope full of unreported money and a seething sense of frustration and guilt. He formed a plan of vengeance. It was totally deranged but in his state of mind, it made sense. The villain—the cockroach—would pay.

"How did you find this guy, this assassin?" asked Frank.

Wardell raised his eyebrows and made a gesture with his hands.

"The Dark Web," he said. "Of course."

"What in hell is the Dark Web?" asked Frank.

"It's the inaccessible part of the internet," Athena said. "It's not indexed by search engines and such. The Dark Web's the site of a lot of illicit, untraceable activity."

Frank looked baffled. "If it's inaccessible, how do you get to it?"

"You have to know how," said Wardell. "You need special software, configurations, authorizations, stuff like that."

Athena seemed to know what she was talking about here, which was good since Frank felt even more like a caveman than usual.

"And how did you know how to navigate your way around it?" she asked.

"I learned about it from the people in my classes. Then it was just a matter of trial and error to find what I was looking for."

"And you were looking for a professional killer?"

Wardell nodded. "As I got deeper into the Dark Web, I started thinking maybe I should find someone a little less scary. There are international syndicate kinds of guys, expensive, serious. To be honest, they were terrifying. There were other sites with people advertising that they would administer beatings, put people in the hospital. I thought one of those might be safer to negotiate with. They were like…friendlier."

"Friendlier," repeated Frank, dumbfounded.

"How exactly does this work?" asked Athena. "How do you contact the person? How do you pay them? How can you be sure it's not a scam on their part?"

"The sites where they advertise link you to a private chat room where you can work it out. You pay in bitcoin and arrange the details."

"Bitcoin?" asked Frank.

"It's a digital payment medium," said Athena. "And when you pay, it's gone, no trail. So you set up an online bank account?"

"Yeah, that's easy."

"…and took a chance that this guy wasn't going to just take your money and run?"

Wardell shrugged. "I took a chance. I gambled that someone advertising a lower level of crime might be less likely to rip me off."

The detectives looked at one another. This was definitely an infant way out of his comfort zone.

"I scouted around and found a guy who advertised various acts of violence. He'd show up and deliver a beating. He had different levels of harm and kind of a price list. He limited the area in which he worked to about a five hundred mile radius, and I was in it. For fifteen hundred dollars or so, he'd put someone in the hospital; I sent him an inquiry, would he be willing to go all the way and for how much? He said sure. We agreed on a price of three thousand and set a date."

Frank shook his head. What kind of brave new world was he living i

"Did you meet with this guy?"

"No. That was an important point, we never saw each other. We r general arrangements and he gave me a number to call. I gave him the and the place, told him to dress like a gang member and make it look mugging. I told him to wait nearby, described what I'd be wearing an I'd give him a call when the target showed up."

"You didn't expect to wait as long as you did."

"No, but I figured that was an advantage, since the street kep emptier."

"So you went shopping for a professional killer, with no idea what this guy looked like, or if he'd even show up," said Athena. "Pretty stupid. A lot of things could have happened to you, starting with him simply scamming you out of your money, and going downhill from there. The Dark Net is no place to be messing around."

"I know, I know. But it was the only way I could figure to do it. I don't exactly hang around with criminals."

The detectives exchanged a look. That was pretty clear. He looked totally over his head right now, and he seemed to be developing a severe twitch.

"What's his name?" asked Frank. He was repelled but fascinated by the sordid novelty of the whole tale.

"I only knew him by his screen name. Black Flag."

"He's got a flair for cheap dramatics. So you had a number to call him when you saw LaRoche. Probably a cheap burner that he got rid of right afterward, but we're going to look for it anyway. You told him to rob Julie, then kill him?"

"Yeah. I told him to take his money, wallet, anything he had. He could keep any money or valuables but he should get rid of anything incriminating. I told him to burn everything." Wardell shuddered. "I knew what was coming but I wasn't ready. When I heard the gun go off...it was like it wasn't real. It was awful."

"And can we assume you haven't had any contact with Mr. Black Flag ever since?"

Wardell shook his head. "Nope. Got no idea where he went or who he was. After that I really didn't want to talk to him ever again."

"Cameron, you realize this is the one card you've got to play. There's got to be some way you can contact this guy and bring him back here."

"I don't know," Wardell said. Suddenly, the gravity of the situation ned to be hitting home. He reminded Frank of a character he had seen in aissance painting of the Last Judgment...a sinner being borne to hell.

nk pondered for a minute. "I assume he's still advertising on that

n?   s so."

       he be willing to come back and take out somebody else for

ade
time
like a   u mean?"
d said
       —or someone saying they were you—had another job for

       ,"

t getting   iking."

       catch on. He stared, uncomprehending. Frank
       a deep breath. "That's how we bring this guy

back."

* * * *

"I'm finding it hard to believe all of this," Frank mused, the two of them again at his desk. "A dark secret internet with drug dealers and killers for hire."

"It gets much worse," said Athena. "Much worse. Sick, perverse stuff. It's a perilous place, a good place for most people to stay away from."

"Sounds like it's got its share of idiots and fools as well."

"None of this would have happened if the guy *had* just taken his bitcoin and never showed up."

"If only," sighed Frank. "I guess we didn't luck out. Especially Julie."

"The payment was totally untraceable and there was no evidence of the transaction. He would have gotten away with this if you hadn't made the connection."

Frank nodded. "Right now Wardell's pretty scared. We might still not have that strong a case against him and he might start figuring that out sooner or later. We have to hope this works."

"Frank, I have a feeling. We're getting this guy."

* * * *

Cortado Lane was appropriately named. Its name was Spanish for "cut off" and it was indeed a short, dead end street, a forgotten area of mostly abandoned old houses and small brownstones, with outdated lighting fixtures that the city likely hoped it would never have to replace. What spare lighting did exist was blotted by thick overgrown trees. The figure standing in the deep shadow of an alleyway, watching a house across the street, decided this was very much to his liking.

He once again went over the email instructions he had memorized earlier:

Address is 9678 Cortado. He returns home every night at nine, like clockwork. No streetlights in front of the house. Street usually very empty.

He would wait for his subject to appear, cross the street and push him into the space between the buildings, and begin his work.

The message had been simple and not overly specific. *Don't kill him. Anything else OK.*

The dark figure's real name was Edgar. He had no idea what the name of his intended victim was, and didn't care. He had a description of his objective and he was just happy that he had gotten another paying job.

He was a little disappointed to not get another opportunity to make a kill; the last one had been particularly enjoyable, a step up. But in general he enjoyed his work. He decided he had finally found his calling; he liked to hurt people. The day he had been shown that hidden corner of the internet had been a turning point in his life. He never had to travel more than a few hours from his home and was making a nice living, tax-free, untraceable.

He looked at his watch. Five minutes to nine. He heard footsteps up the dark sidewalk. A dark hunched-over figure, hard-soled shoes scraping on the pavement.

He took a quick look up and down the street, satisfied that there were only the two of them—him and his prey. A true predator, Edgar snapped into total concentration mode.

Edgar wore soft-soled athletic shoes that made no noise as he moved among the shadows and crossed the street. He fell in about ten steps behind the ambling figure, closing the gap between them. He timed it perfectly. He was within arm's length of the hunched-over man just as they reached the slender space between two buildings. He reached out to grab the victim's shoulders, ready to shove him into the dark narrow abyss. He was so intently concentrating on his target that he failed to notice several other dark shapes emerging from nearby shadows of buildings and trees and converging upon him.

Suddenly the hunched-over man was noticeably taller. He had spun around and shoved the barrel of a police service automatic right into Edgar's face. Several pairs of hands grabbed him at once and he found himself being wrestled easily to the ground.

"Well, what have we here?" asked Frank, holstering his weapon and peering down at the dark struggling figure being held to the pavement by three of his colleagues.

* * * *

All of the unit's interview rooms were dingy but the one they jokingly called the Fortress was the grimmest of the lot. Dirty green paint was peeling off the walls and a couple of the lights didn't always work very well. It was also the most secure, with thick metal doors, heavy locks, constant video, and heavy metal tables with steel rings for cuffs or shackles.

Edgar Boyle looked right at home, leaning on one elbow, his other wrist handcuffed to the table, pitch-dark eyes blazing with hot hate from beneath thick dark eyebrows. He was a large hairy man, ample tattoos displayed beneath a white muscle shirt. Short-cropped dark hair and a goatee amplified his scowl.

"Quite a record you've got here, Edgar," Frank said absently as he stood in a corner of the room, flipping through a file. "Juvie at twelve. Stints in a couple of prisons. Assault, battery. They know you in Reno, Bakersfield, Phoenix…" he trailed off and looked at the silent man. "Looks to me like you've never been very good at this stuff. You're a violent criminal but not a very good one."

Boyle refused to say anything. Athena, standing in another corner, arms folded, suddenly let loose a string of what sounded like Spanish. It got a reaction. He turned to her and spat, "Don't talk your fucking school Spanish to me, bitch. I know English just fine."

"Just wanted to see if you knew how to speak in *any* language," Athena said. "And by the way, it's not school Spanish. I grew up speaking it in my home. I figured since your record says you once fled to Mexico and got extradited, you were probably fluent."

"Reality check, Edgar," continued Frank, "or should I call you Mr. Black Flag? You probably thought you had stumbled onto a good thing here, with this Dark Net gig, but it looks as if you're not all that good at this either. We found your car. We found your laptop in it...and a whole string of messages. Nothing was even password protected. You might as well have left us a trail of cookie crumbs. I'm not all that tech-savvy, but compared to you I'm Bill Gates. This is supposed to be a super-secret black-ops kind of internet, and here even I could follow the trail from your computer! We contacted the police in your home town and there are Federal cyber-crime agents that couldn't wait to get warrants and run to your home. There are probably half a dozen law enforcement agencies crawling all over your digs as we speak."

"You're basically screwed," said Athena. She smiled nastily. "I can say that in five languages if you'd like."

"It would probably be a good idea at this point to request a lawyer," Frank said. "We've already read you your rights and unless you have anything else you'd like to tell us, I think we're done here."

Edgar glowered back and forth at them and in a gruff low voice he uttered a string of the foulest, coarsest epithets Frank had heard in a long time. He thought he had heard every conceivable degrading intimate act described and suggested, but Edgar managed to come up with some creative new ones. It actually took him aback but when he shot a look at Athena, she was simply flashing a small tight smile.

She said, "Thanks for the input, Mr. Boyle. I guess we finally got through to you. Frank, I agree, we're done here."

* * * *

Garo Bedrosian was indeed surprised and delighted to hear that there were suspects in custody for the robbery of his cafe. When he and his daughter showed up for the line-up, Frank and Athena greeted them and explained the identification procedure. Bedrosian would stand behind a one-way glass and several people would each step forward where he could look at them carefully.

"Cecilia, " asked Frank, "you're sure you didn't see or hear anything that night?"

Cecilia shook her head. "I came to support my Dad, but really, I don't know what I can do to help you."

"Okay, then we're going to ask you to sit out here." He pointed to a wooden bench along the corridor wall.

"I'll stay with you," said Athena. "Come on." She led her to the bench. As the two men walked down the hall Cecilia plopped herself down on the hard bench and hung her head morosely.

"Have you spoken to your father yet about that night?" asked Athena.

Cecila shook her head. "I can't. I just can't."

"You know, that day you told me about it, I can't imagine that was very easy."

"I felt I could talk to you. You're the only woman who's talked to me. In the police, I mean."

"Cecy, I think you felt guilty—so guilty that you needed to get something out. But I think there's still more than what you told me. I keep wondering how Tommy and his partner happened to show up right after you forgot to lock the door."

Cecilia did not look up. "That's what happened. Just like I told you."

"You're, what, nineteen?"

"Twenty."

"Okay. You're like any other normal twenty-year-old girl. You feel stuck with your father and you want to go live your own life and have excitement. So you sneak out to dance clubs with your friends, things like that. Tommy is older and he's handsome and charming. He's got that dangerous thing going on too, doesn't he? He turned your head. I'll be honest with you: I think being charming to young women is maybe the *only* thing he's good at, but he is clearly pretty good at it. I think he talked you into helping him out, leaving the door open that night. He might have told you he needed the money to spend on you, to take you somewhere or buy you something. Or maybe he just made you feel like you wanted to be part of his dangerous life."

"Nobody was supposed to get hurt," whispered Cecilia, still not looking up.

"So you did tell him you'd leave the door unlocked that night?"

Cecilia froze momentarily. "No. No, it happened just like I said. I made a mistake."

Athena sighed and gently placed a hand on Cecilia's shoulder. "Believe it or not, Tommy was in kind of the same position. He was trying to impress an older, more dangerous guy. But he feels like a scared, embarrassed kid right now, just like you probably do. He rolled on the older guy. Tommy's not much of a stand-up guy when you come down to it. But there's one place he is being a stand-up guy. He refuses to implicate you in any of this."

Athena bent down to be closer to the girl and spoke softly, urgently. "These are guys who made choices about the kind of lives they lead. You still have choices. That guilt is going to eat away at you, because you're a decent person at heart. You're going to need to take responsibility for your actions, sooner or later."

"I didn't do anything," Cecilia said. It came out as a sob. A tear rolled down her cheek. "I forgot to lock the door. I forgot." Her voice trailed off as she repeated it over and over. It was as if she was trying to drown out not just Athena but other voices within herself.

"Your father still thinks he's the one who forgot, right?"

Cecilia nodded.

Athena decided she would leave it there. It was ultimately up to Cecilia.

The two sat in glum, heavy silence, neither saying a word until Frank and Garo returned to them.

NINE

The morning shift would not begin for another half hour, but Frank found Athena already sitting in the cafeteria. It was really not much more than a coffee bar with a refrigerator case of day-old pastries, salads and sandwiches, but someone had seen a need to dignify it with a name like "cafeteria." He got himself a mug of coffee and joined her at the old Formica table.

"You look downcast," Athena said. "How'd the meeting go with Castillo?"

"First of all, he already spoke earlier this morning with the Assistant District Attorney. She's declining to go after Cecilia Bedrosian. She's as overworked as the rest of us and has to pick her battles. She says there's nothing there to get a conviction."

"That's all the prosecutor's office cares about, right?"

"Did you really want the kid to go to jail?"

She sighed. "No. Cecilia's going to have to deal with her father and her own demons. I hope this has scared her and I hope she comes to terms with it."

"Tommy and Brando bailed on each other. She's cutting deals with them both. Brando bragged he could do the time, but the next thing you know, he's throwing his other partners in crime under the bus as fast as he can to try to reduce his sentence. Some hard guy. Anyway, it looks like Simpkins and Dowdy will be able to clear a couple of their own cases as well."

"Honor among thieves."

"Gotta love it. On the other hand, Tommy hasn't said a word about Cecilia. He's got his own weird code of chivalry, I guess."

"Cameron Wardell has been charged too, I take it?"

"He cut a deal. So did his crackpot assassin, though that won't really be of much help to him. There are about four federal agencies looking into his activities as well as a few locals. He apparently negotiated assaults for hire, and possibly murders, across a few state lines. What a deranged lunatic. Glad he'll be off the streets."

Athena stared at her coffee mug. "Wardell's just a kid. Where does someone like him get the idea to sponsor a murder for hire?"

"Search me. I keep hearing that millennials are crazy. His deal isn't going to keep him out of a stretch in prison, you can be sure of that."

"And what about the Bizel thing?"

"The Lou tells me the Feds swooped down on the whole place last night. Sweeping indictments against everyone. Racketeering, money laundering, extortion. His contact in the Department didn't mention anything about La-Roche. I'm thinking he didn't have anything to do with any of that. He was just an opportune buyer who smelled out a bargain and didn't care that it wasn't totally legit. Lenora Park called that one right."

"Her inflammatory story was partly responsible for motivating Wardell in the first place. I wonder how she's going to feel about that."

"Maybe it'll her stop and think. Maybe she'll temper her reportage. Maybe not. It remains to be seen."

"What's going to happen to the building, to the Del Osos?"

"Castillo seems to think that in the end Felipe will be able to get the building back. It'll be a long process but for now he'll be able to keep the *mercado* there." Frank paused. "I guess that's about it. He asked me how you're doing and I told him you're doing fine. You did some great work your first week, you know that? "

"I don't know how great it was. To be honest, this job and *this place* are kind of overwhelming."

"Your first day on the job, you went out to do a routine re-interview on a case I figured was a dead end. You cleared it. That's impressive. I would never have gotten there. Maybe I've just gotten too cynical about this stuff."

"I lucked out. The daughter was willing to talk to me. On the other hand, I was ready to toss in the towel on LaRoche. My instincts told me that it had to be a random robbery gone bad, and that we should pursue it that way. You knew better. You wouldn't let go and you found the key…and an obscure one, at that. They've always told me you're a good detective. I should have trusted you more."

"I'm thinking we might make a good team, Pardo. You can learn from the dinosaur and maybe the dinosaur can learn from you. If you can put up with me."

Frank's smile was weary but genuine.

Athena, still staring into her mug of coffee, managed a weak smile in return. A pineapple Danish pastry sat on a paper plate, untouched.

"Is it always like this?"

"What do you mean?"

"We did good this week, right?"

"We did outstanding this week."

"So why doesn't it feel good?"

"Athena, it's not like you haven't been on the streets for a few years already. What do you expect it to feel like?"

"I know. But being in uniform is different. You see a lot of stuff that's hard to process, but there are also times when you feel you've done some good. I know it's only my first week here, but...aside from clearing the cases, there doesn't seem an upside yet."

"Sometimes it feels better than others. Often, clearing the case is pretty much all you can hope for. In the end it's what we do. We try to do it well and make everyone count. It's not a warm fuzzy job we've chosen."

Frank reached into his shirt pocket and pulled out a folded envelope. he opened it and handed it to Athena.

"Maybe this'll help."

The envelope was addressed to DETECTIVE VANDERGROFF at the unit.

"Nobody ever gets the name right. I'm used to it."

She unfolded the note paper inside and read the short letter.

Dear Detective Vandergroff,

I saw in the news that you found the people who killed my father. Thank you for your hard work. Not many people liked my father. He didn't exactly go out of his way to make anybody like him. He was a complicated man and I'm only now coming to grips with my own feelings about him. It would have made sense to me that nobody would have cared who killed him.

I thought he never cared about me and wanted nothing to do with me. It turns out he thought enough of me to leave me all he owned. That, and the fact that you must have gone to great trouble to find the truth behind his death, has led me to re-evaluate my father and my own family history. I think it's going to be a long process but I've taken the first step. And for that I thank you.

Sincerely,

Sarah Hartnett (LaRoche)

Athena handed the letter back. "Well, somebody found closure. Do we ever find it here?"

"Now and then. Like those new-age types like to say: it's a journey, not a destination."

Frank made a wry face. He pointed to the Danish. "So…are you gonna eat that?"

She broke it in half and handed him a piece.

Frank stuffed the whole thing into his mouth and chewed it rapidly. "Better than usual." He rose from his seat. "Once more into the breach?"

"Sure. And by the way, I know that's Shakespeare."

"And by the way, do you really speak five languages?"

She finished the last bite of her piece of the Danish. "More or less. Some better than others."

He nodded, impressed. "Pretty good for a rookie kid. Still, maybe there're things I can teach you. Keep an open mind, okay?"

She nodded, a little grimly, and stood up, gathering her refuse and sweeping up the crumbs. "I think there's a lot I can learn from you, Detective. Make no mistake about that."

"Oh yeah, and while I think of it…there's something I can learn from you too." Frank reached into his pocket and held out a brand new smart phone. "No more Stone Age flip phone. But I'm already boggled. I think I'm going to need some help getting up to speed on this…and the Information Age in general."

"You want my help, huh? Looking forward to it."

Maybe, Frank mused, this really would work out.

THE END

ABOUT THE AUTHOR

Tony Gleeson, an inveterate fan of jazz and classic mysteries, is a writer, illustrator and graphic designer. He has now published nine mysteries in the Personal Crimes series. He lives with his wife Anne and their cats, Django and Mingus, in Los Angeles, California.